PLAGUE WITHIN

THE ALTERED EXPERIENCE BOOK II

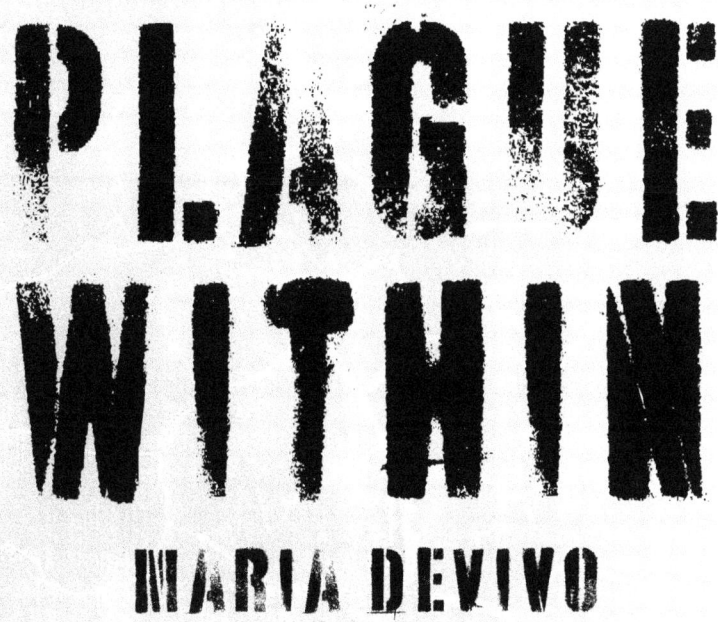

PLAGUE WITHIN

MARIA DEVIVO

4 Horsemen Publications, Inc

4 Horsemen
Publications, Inc.

Published By: 4 Horsemen Publications, Inc.

4 Horsemen Publications, Inc.
PO Box 417
Sylva, NC 28779
4horsemenpublications.com
info@4horsemenpublications.com

Cover Illustration by CD Corrigan
Typesetting by Autumn Skye

Library of Congress Control Number: 2024944609

Paperback ISBN-13: 979-8-8232-0637-2
Hardcover ISBN-13: 979-8-8232-0638-9
Audiobook ISBN-13: 979-8-8232-0640-2
Ebook ISBN-13: 979-8-8232-0639-6

DEDICATION

For Joe—This crazy ride, this crazy life... I am so glad that you're my partner in crime. Wouldn't have it any other way, wouldn't want it any other way. You are my rock.

For Joel—Your inspiration and constant motivation kept me going through this whole process. Actually, through the whole process of life. The man on the side of the road in the dirt. Our constant talks of bigger and better. There IS a bigger and better. The heart has four chambers. I owe you so much, and love you so fiercely. #shouldastoppedat2.

For Morgan—it's always for you, and always will be for you.

CONTENTS

1

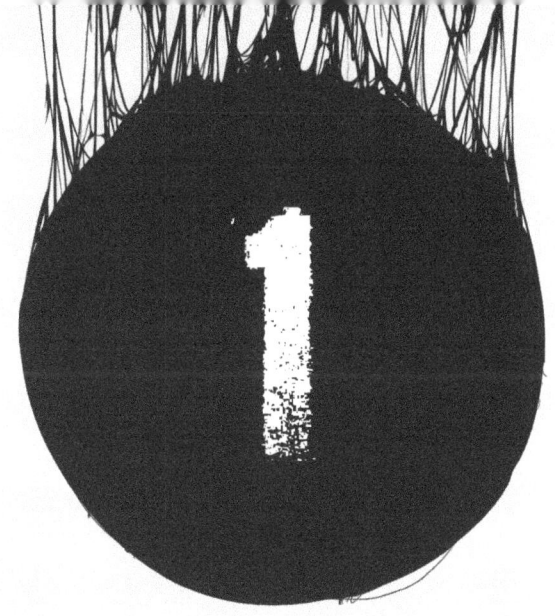

THE WORLD SHAKES. VIOLENT AND JARRING. I'M JOLTED from my sleep. Disoriented. Hazy. Shaking. I'm not shaking on the inside, though. There's an outside force that is literally moving the floor beneath me—as if the walls of my apartment are going to split open from bottom to top and slide open like some kind of Japanese fan butterflying out to reveal the rot and ruin of the city it overlooks. Machine sounds blare in my ears, penetrating the deepest recesses of my brain. Mechanical hums and drums and clawing and lifting and breaking and tearing all at once, all in sync. It fills me with a hint of familiarity—sounds that drone out any natural world senses, leaving me to feel as if I'm trapped underwater. Muffled. Filled.

Altered.

The windowpanes rattle with every movement of the monster outside. I anticipate they will burst open—shards of glass flying through the room, slicing into my eyes and ears, relieving me of the dreaded underwater sound. The black-out curtains don't do their job very well, as hints of sunlight manage to peek their way in. I tighten my eyelids shut as the world shakes harder—a low rumble that increases intensity with every passing second. Vibrations that will soon overtake the structure of this building, and when those windows finally do break, a sucking gush of air will fill the room in a giant wave, like a vacuum-sealed can of something opening. *Then* the shards can come and pierce me.

But it doesn't happen. Not going to happen. The world has been shaking for quite some time, and still, I'm here. No hell-sucking earthquake, no wall-splitting catastrophe, no super-sonic flying shards of glass. Just construction going on outside my apartment bedroom—the sounds of the continuous rebuilding of a world that suffered the almost unimaginable. I rub my eyes and unintentionally let out a groan. I guess that must be an indication of the day I'm going to have.

The evil red-light numbers on my alarm clock scream 7:30 a.m. at me, but my night shift doesn't begin until 5:00 p.m. I've had about two hours of dreamless sleep, but I'm up now, and there's no way I'm going to be able to get back to the quiet abyss of slumber.

Someone on the construction crew yells about pushing a button and holding a line. Someone else screams back and then something crashes hard to the pavement. That's code to me that the world is not ending again.

I could only be so lucky.

Amber stirs beside me in the bed. Her warm breath gently exhales against my arm sending goosebumps throughout my body. The shaking and construction going on outside doesn't bother her like it does me. Even though her senses are as heightened as mine, she could sleep through anything—a fact I learned rather quickly.

See, when we were released from the Re-Assimilation Center two years ago, Dr. Holston didn't just let us fend for ourselves. He eventually set up a 'privately owned' organization he called *Alt Home,* and it became a meeting place for all the Altered to come and talk, hang out, and in a way, be monitored—and not just the Altered who were staying at the Re-Assimilation Center. Apparently, there were more. Many more. During the mass inoculation with the purple smoke, they were able to cure a lot more than they were able to house at the Re-Assimilation Centers. Only a handful—30 to be exact—was selected for the program, but the rest? They were left to their own devices. Holston had always felt guilty about this, and Alt Home was a place for all the Altered, even those left behind, to get the care and assistance they needed.

When we met at one of the first gatherings of Alt Home, Amber and I clicked right away. I think a lot had to do with the fact that I was number 24 at the Re-Assimilation Center, and she was number 25, and we were both kinda in our right minds. We both had a weird kind of apathy towards the whole situation. We didn't get all worked up when we were turned down for jobs (like how 20 got when some guy from a furniture store cursed at him and kicked him out of his office), and we didn't get all crazy mad when the news people had some unflattering things to report about us (like how 28 got when the AAC—the Anti-Altered Coalition—got some bills passed in Congress regarding our 'new race'). Amber and I just went about our day to day, trying to adjust as best as possible, not letting all the nit-picky topics affect us.

And, of course, there's no denying her beauty. I'd be a liar if I said I wasn't attracted to her the moment I laid eyes on her.

But that was almost two years ago. She lies next to me in my bed now, but I'm not sure how close I am to her. Yes, she complements me. Yes, I'm still attracted to her curly black hair and crystal blue eyes, her cute pixie-doll nose, full lips, and bright smile. Yes, we have common ground. However, I can't put my finger on the recent feeling of distance. Do we love each other? That's something I wrestle with all the time. What is love? Are we even capable of love? Do we have the capacity to love? To receive love?

Bottom line is this—I don't understand girls. The only experience I've had being around them was with my mother, my sister, and the girl I once ate, so that's hardly any 'real-world' experience. I think I love Amber. All signs point to it. All feelings point to it. There's just this weird, undefined space in my heart, so I guess I'll leave it at that.

Lately though, I get this sense that she's drifting away from me—fumbling into her own mind, in a way. Like, she's putting up some kind of wall between us, right in the middle of this bed. A wall that will undoubtedly split open from bottom to top and spread out wide. I'm not sure if she knows I know. She's a great pretender if I've ever met one.

She tosses her arm across my chest. This is her normal position right before waking up. I've watched her, studied her in the early moments of dawn, so that I know her habits like they were my own. I brush her hair from her cheek. Strands of black are glued to the corner of her mouth with morning drool. My fingertips smooth over the raised bump of her scar just under her right eye. She bears the mark. *Our* mark. Our reminder to the world that we are different, we are changed, we are Altered.

She smiles at me. Dreamily. Still half asleep. I often wonder what she dreams about. I ask, but she never tells. All I know is she wakes up to me every morning with a smile. She says it's her secret, the only one she has left, and I suppose I have to respect that. There are no secrets among us Altered. Amber and I have our unspoken moments of laughter and pain. We share delicate moments of regret and fear. She's the only one who truly knows me, truly knows *my* secrets. And maybe that's why I feel she is pulling away...

"You're awake?" she asks me in her groggy morning voice.

I nod.

She stretches her arms above her head and yawns. "Silly," she scolds. "Whatever am I going to do with you, Griffin King?"

I give her a side smirk. "I don't know, Amber Fields."

She lightly slaps my shoulder. Lovingly. "You let the construction bother you too much. You know you don't have to be up until..."

"I know, I know," I finish for her. "I can't help it."

She lets out a small huff. "Super-sense Griffin is what I call you!"

She's teasing. But she's not. It's no secret my senses have changed. It's no secret I can hear things and see things and feel things differently, intensely, like I've never heard or felt or tasted in my life before. She's teasing, but she's not, because I know she can feel it, too. I know now she's awake, away from her clandestine dream-world, she too can feel the vibrations in the apartment like earthquakes in Norway.

"Why are you up?" I ask. "It's Saturday. You're off. You should sleep in."

"No, no, no," she says, reaching for the remote on the nightstand on her side of the bed. "You know I can sense when you're up. So, when you're up, I'm up." She snuggles back to me and presses the button on the remote. I throw my arm around her shoulder, smooth her hair back again, and kiss her forehead. Our Saturday routine.

A news program blooms to life on the television screen. In the upper-right hand corner, the graphic in the box reads: "Re-outbreak Declared Hoax." It quickly fades away, but it was there long enough for both of us to read it. There's a weird, awkward silence between us for a moment. Amber powers off the TV and throws the remote to the edge of the bed. Her legs wind up around my waist and she nuzzles her face on my chest. She doesn't say anything, but for some reason I get the feeling the graphic bothered her. Me? Nah. Nothing I haven't seen before. There's always talk of re-outbreaks, newly infected, new strains, blah blah blah... nothing ever comes of it. And if it did, then so what? Who cares? We lived through it before, right? And then it hits me... two years of bottling her emotions inside is maybe starting to get to her. Maybe she isn't as indifferent as I am. Maybe Amber is starting to emotionally crack like those concrete walls. Bottom up. Butterfly fan out. Reveal the truth and lies. Maybe my heightened senses knew all along, and that's why she feels so removed.

She slides out from underneath my arm and onto her side of the bed. "Do you want breakfast?" she asks.

An odd question. How am I to respond? Ham and eggs? Fingers and toes? She asks because the question is a normal one. One that normal people ask on Saturday mornings. One that normal people have answers to. She knows damn well I'm not hungry, nor do I eat breakfast, but I guess she has to ask to fill some sort of void within her. It makes me sad to think she can't be content with the way things are. That she feels a need to go back to her old life.

"Not hungry," I say.

She stands up, backlit by the ever-increasing sunlight through the black-out drapes. Bending down to pick up her silk robe from the floor, her spine juts out like a bony highway pressed against thin flesh. "Ah," she moans, "not your time of the month, I suppose."

"Har har," I reply and roll my eyes. But she's right, yet again. Since I was Altered, I don't eat very much. None of us do. I guess it's just one of those things. We don't have hunger the same way the non-Altered have hunger. I could go a few days at a time with so much as a glass of juice and a piece of toast in my system. Yet, ever so often, I get a ravenous hunger and my appetite swells to full force. Amber, too. We'll go on eating extravaganzas where we consume anything and everything in sight until we're completely sated. Dr. Holston says it's not good for us to do that—starve, starve, starve then shock our systems with food overload—but I can't help it. *We* can't help it.

Just as Amber is about to leave the bedroom, the doorbell rings. She looks at me with a suspiciously raised eyebrow and I shrug my shoulders. I don't move from the bed, making it obvious I'm not getting up to get the door. She folds her hands over her chest and huffs, "I guess *I'll* go see who it is."

I exhale loudly, rubbing my hands over my face.

I hear it all, because I can hear everything. Amber opens the door, and I can see in my mind's eye her lips curl upward into a childlike smile. The deep, male voice booms her name in a jovial tone. I hear her hands clap together around the visitor's neck; her lips kiss his cheek with a daughterly *smack*.

It's Holston.

I get up, put on my sweatpants and t-shirt, and head out to the living room to see him.

"Dr. Holston, I presume," I joke as I walk in.

His eyes light up when he sees me—a shimmer and a glimmer in the chocolate brown darkness. I wish I could have the same reaction towards him, because when I catch a good glimpse, Dr. Holston is looking worse for the wear. I must have given my thoughts concrete substance by my facial expression because Amber quickly ushers the Doc over to the couch. He hobbles over as she takes his briefcase and sets it down beside him. She opens her eyes wide at me as if to say, "stop it!"

"Sit down, Doctor," she says in a cheerful tone. "I was just about to make Griffin and me some breakfast. Can I get you something?"

He waves his hand in the air, "No dear, I'm fine, I'm fine."

She pouts and puts her hand on her hip like a defiant nine-year-old. Like my sister Sydney used to do all the time. "C'mon, Doc," she goads, "let me get you something so I can ensure you'll stay for more than ten minutes."

She's good. Like a chameleon, changing her color to fit the mood of the crowd. She can be anything she wants to anyone around her, and right now she's playing the part of the dutiful daughter doting on her estranged dad. It's the same chameleon skin that adjusted and changed so nicely to match my dispirited disposition two years ago. Holston can't resist her childlike innocence and nods his head in agreement. "Coffee, dear. Cream and sugar, please."

Amber smiles wide, satisfied. "Coming right up!" And she turns on her heels and heads for the kitchen.

"Oh, she's a keeper, that one!" he says as he feebly adjusts himself on the couch.

I sit down across from him on the rocking chair. "Yeah, she's something else," I say, but my attention is on his strained motions.

"Stop staring, son. You're going to give me a complex," he says.

He noticed.

"Hey, just giving it back," I recover. "All those times you stared at me something awful, like I was some kind of monster, ya know?"

He pauses. "Is that what you thought *I* thought? That I saw you as a monster?"

I don't hesitate with my answer, "Well, yeah. Of course."

He leans forward and places his hands on my knees. There's a faraway look in his eyes, like he's happily reflecting on some profound past memory. "No. Never. I never thought you were a monster. None of you. Especially you. You were more like a newborn baby fawn wobbling its way into the world. Delicate and fresh. There was a newness to you. Not monstrous, but magnificent. Awe-inspiring, and..." He coughs violently. His whole body jolts forward.

I put my hand on his shoulder as he calms down. "You okay?" I ask with great concern.

With his eyes closed, he nods, and mumbles a "yeah."

"Yeah? You sure?"

He nods again. He's lying, I know, but I'll let him tell me on his terms. I don't wish to pry any further if he's not offering. Besides, it's been a while since he's come around. Over the course of two years, Holston's visits have greatly diminished. He used to call daily and come over once a week, then he would call a few times a week and visit once a month, then he'd call once a month but not visit. He checked in on us, but we knew he was busy. Doctor stuff, Alt Home—we knew he had to keep tabs on everything and everyone, and we knew he wasn't getting any younger. But this? Now?

"So, what do we owe this pleasure and surprise?" I ask, trying to lighten the mood.

"Oh, this and that," he answers.

"How's Alt Home?"

"Fine. Fine, for now," he answers with a slow nod. "How's everything over at the center?"

He means the Brandon Medical Center, the medical office where I work the night shift as a janitor. "Yeah. Everything's fine. Just wish I had better hours, but it is what it is, right?"

"Right," he says, and his voice drops lower. He turns to his briefcase and pops the locks open. Papers spill out and he rummages through the chaos and retrieves a manila envelope. "Here." He hands it to me.

My face contorts. "What's this? Another one of your magic files?"

He smiles and rubs his hands together. "Something like that. Truth of the matter is, I need your help, Griffin. I'm not long for this world." He pauses. "Pancreatic cancer."

Well, no surprise there. The smell of sickness radiated off him when he walked through the door.

"I'm so..." I begin.

"It's okay," he interrupts. "Of all the things I've seen, come into contact with, created, I would have expected a far more dramatic and interesting exit." He laughs, but his laughter soon turns to a coughing fit. He continues when it passes. "I need you."

Amber walks in and hands the coffee mug to Holston. He smiles at her and barely mutters a "thank you."

Her heightened senses pick up on the obvious solemnity in the room and she looks at me. "What's up? What's going on?"

I motion my head in Holston's direction. "Doctor isn't doing so well, Amber. How long did they say you have?"

"Wait, what?" she practically yells.

"Sit down, dear," Holston says, forcing a smile. "Six months, if that."

"Six months?" she repeats. "As in—you have six months to live?" She's visibly upset, and Holston shifts again on the couch.

"Amber, sit down," I say and pat the fat arm of the rocking chair. She obeys and props herself next to me, both hands on her cheeks. Tears swell in her eyes, making the crystal blue color of them look almost metallic.

"It's okay," Holston says trying to coax her. "I've made peace with it."

Amber sniffs and her hands race to meet the descending tears. She swats them away as if they were annoying flies dancing around her face. "What do you need us to do? You know we'll both help you in any way we can."

Holston looks at Amber, smiles, then focuses his attention back on me. "The folder contains a chunk of my life's work. I need you to guard it, protect it, don't ever let it get into the wrong hands. I set you up at the Brandon Medical Center for a reason. That nightshift you complained about is going to be advantageous to the cause." He leans forward and puts a hand back on my knee. "Griffin, when I'm gone, I need you to be my eyes and ears. I need you to watch over them, protect them, for they are all my children. I'm going to need you to take care of the Altered."

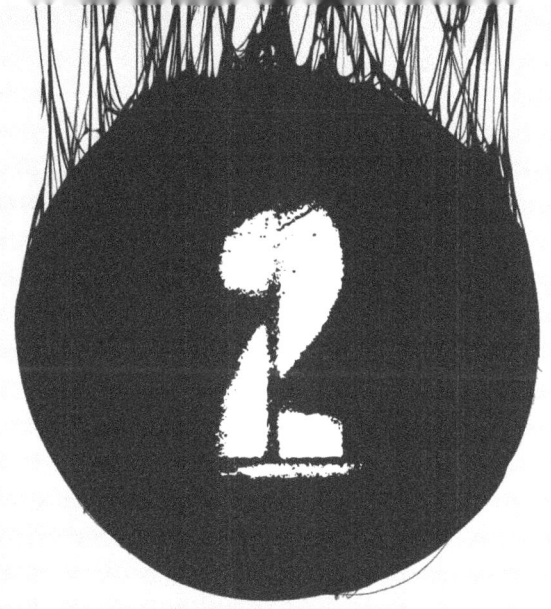

2

EVERYTHING IN THE ROOM SEEMS TO STOP FOR A moment and does this dancey, swirly-like motion. I'm sound enough to know the room isn't actually spinning, but it certainly does feel like it. It's like how most of my nightmares start out as I descend into slumber. Since I left the Re-Assimilation Center, my nights are filled with either dreamless sleeps or vivid nightmares.

Wait. I don't know if I can even call them nightmares. Aren't nightmares supposed to scare you? Aren't nightmares supposed to be ultra-manifestations of your wicked inner-most thoughts and fears? If, by definition, that is what a nightmare is, then I guess what I have are just my memories—tucked away so deeply during the day, only to replay themselves at night—over and over and over and over...

Darkness creeps into my peripheral vision, and all I'm focused on is Holston's wrinkled mouth moving up and down. Logic tells me there are words coming out of it, simply by the human movements they are making. Actually, I hear the words he is saying, but numbness has crept into my body and isn't allowing my brain to fully process the information. Sounds are just pinpricks in my ears, and I study his face—the way it moves, the way his glasses sit perfectly perched on his wrinkled cheeks, the way the deep craters in his forehead crinkle up every time he raises his eyebrows, the way he compulsively blinks his eyes. It all looks familiar. His movements and motions barrel down into my subconscious, and I descend into a daytime dream, a daytime memory...

I hunted.

And I was good at it.

In the beginning, there was instinct and logic—two distinct emotions at war within my body and brain. My instincts knew that dining on insects and animals was not sufficient enough to satisfy my growing hunger, but the logical side of me knew the alternative would have far worse ramifications. The infected blood that ran in my veins craved human flesh, yet my human mind, or whatever humanity I was able to hold on to, knew that was wrong.

People don't eat people. People don't eat people. People don't eat people.

But I caved. Eventually, the instinct took full control, and the Infected me took off running. The *zombie* me was in the driver's seat.

God, I hate that word. *Zombie*. Sounds like some silly B-rated movie monster that can be shot in the head and put down. What else can you call it, though? What did I do? I killed people. How did I do it? I ate them until they died. Who's known for doing that? Zombies.

There. I guess I answered my own stupid question.

Anyway, my hunting skills were phenomenal. I was stealthy when I needed to be, and I was extremely strong. Most of the infected people who I saw ambling in the streets had absolutely no self-control. They appeared to be mindless. Not me. I was disciplined, and aware. I had a significant amount of self-control when I needed to, and even though my vision got cloudier each day, I knew when to run, when to walk, when to lie in wait, when to *stalk*. Yes, I was good at hunting, but I was even better at stalking.

I had been following a small group of people. Time was a blur, so it could have been for a few hours, or a few days—I had no way to tell. All I knew was that their scent was glorious, and my mouth watered every time the wind blew their aroma in my direction—a middle aged man, a middle-aged woman, two teenaged boys, an elderly gentleman. I'm not sure what it was about them particularly, but they had a fresh smell to them like a summer salad filled with raspberries and mandarin oranges. I figured they hadn't been traveling long. Maybe their home had been overrun with infected people—*zombies*—and they had just made their way out onto the backroads and wooded area.

Whatever the case, one of the teenage boys kept looking over his shoulder nervously and tugged at a bulge in his pocket, and although I kept a safe distance behind, I knew it wouldn't be long before he spotted me.

Crouch. Duck. Sneak. Stalk. Repeat.

The fire in my stomach heated up. Just watching them fueled my hunger. They stopped, they continued, they talked in low voices, they walked, they stopped again, they said "water," and "perimeter," and "fire," and "be right back," and...

Be right back.

The man left. The woman left. My heart pounded faster, and my brain tried to calculate my next move. *Where were they going? Why were they splitting up? Have I lost my chance at my meal?* The boy left. The other boy left. I seethed with anger. Fired up with pure rage and emptiness and the underwater sounds filled my head and the cloudy veil fell over my brain and the pulsating agony behind my distorted eyes and the old man sat alone with his back against the tree.

His hair was like a white ice-ball against my nose when I collided with him. He barely had time to scream as I clamped my teeth down onto his ear. I jerked my head back in a violent snap and the blood sputtered out into my eyes like a thick garden hose forcing water out from a few tiny holes. I shook my head back and forth to clear my vision, ready to dive my teeth into his face for round two. His wrinkly mouth gaped open. Sound came out of it, but all I heard was the pulsating *whoosh* sound from my own ears. His eyes were wild, like two green marbles rolling around his head, yet they weren't focused on me.

Why aren't they focused on me? Why is he looking behind *me?*

The click of the boy's safety latch sprung me into action. I dove to the side, ear still in mouth, and tumbled in the crunchy grass. A bullet whizzed by me, grazing my calf. I popped myself up and ran deep into the wooded area, zigzagging like a wild alligator whipping its tail back and forth with herky-jerky motions. Another bullet fired, and I prayed the boy had sense enough to put the old man down before the infection took root in his body.

I blink my eyes in time with the snapping fingers in front of my face.

"Griffin? Griffin? You with us?" Amber says with two final snaps.

I narrow my eyes at her, and she steps back. Is she kidding me? If I wanted to, I could tear her fingers one by one from her hand! "Yeah, yeah," I mumble.

"Are *you* okay?" Holston asks.

I blink my eyes again, trying to erase the episode from my memory, but every time my eyes open and close, Holston's wrinkled mouth isn't Holston's, it's the old man's, but it's Holston's, but it's the old man's, but it's Holston's...

"Fine, fine. Just trying to wrap my head around everything, ya know?"

Holston exhales, and his breath reeks of sickness. "I know it's a big undertaking, but I trust you. I know you can do this."

"What do you need me to do, exactly?"

"Like I said, I need you to be my eyes and ears when I'm gone. In the file I gave you you'll find all the information for every Altered who was in a Re-Assimilation Center. Names. Last known whereabouts. That sort of thing. As a patient of a former government program, you know you are all required to have blood work done every three months for the next three years."

"Who could forget?" Amber chimes in sarcastically.

I put my arm around her waist in hopes of calming her down. "So, my job at the medical center? My hours? Let me guess..."

"They are no coincidence, Griffin. All the medical records are sent and filed there. The Altered from the New York, California, and Texas Re-Assimilation Centers also filter through there, and because of your graveyard hours, you would have easy access to all of it. I need you to monitor the files. Examine the blood work. Be able to spot any inconsistencies or anomalies."

He's slick, this Dr. Holston. That's why he's the best, I suppose—a true visionary. He's always thinking ahead, always five or six steps ahead of the curve. If it weren't for him, I don't know what state the world would be in now.

"How do I know what to look for? I'm not a doctor."

"Don't worry about that now. I'll lay it all out for you in good time."

"But the others? The Ferals?" Amber pipes in.

Ferals. The other Altered people who were left to fend for themselves. The others who never went to the Re-Assimilation Centers. The others who wandered aimlessly, trying to survive. Lost, alone, and afraid. The others who were left with remnants of a plague within them and no one to explain what was going on...

Holston reaches for his coffee on the end table next to the couch and takes a long sip. "What about them?" he says matter-of-factly.

"Well, do you need me to monitor them, too? I don't even see how that would be possible if..."

"No," he answers. "You can't. There are too many of them. We only had so much room. We only had so many resources. We could only take a handful of specimens back to the Centers, and it was my decision to take the first ones who survived the initial gassings."

Amber's tongue makes an obnoxious clicking sound. "Specimens?" she huffs.

Holston tilts his head forward slightly and looks up over his circular glasses. The dark circles under his tired eyes look elongated. "You know what I mean," he answers, exasperated.

This isn't new to me. When the infected were gassed, it paralyzed or killed anyone in its path. CDC men threw smoke bombs into the streets where masses of infected had populated and descended from large helicopters while special forces set up a perimeter on the ground. Infected people who didn't die from the initial gassing were given the serum. I remember all too well—the stench of rot all around me, bodies disintegrating at my feet, and pulses like pure electricity surging throughout my body after they injected me with the cure. The crews had to work quickly—there were only so many spots to save in the helicopters and ambulances, and they had a strict time frame of 'get-in and get-out.' The first of the infected to respond to the serum were taken to the Re-Assimilation Centers, the others—the Ferals—were left like abandoned dogs in the streets.

I open the envelope, take out the thick folder, and start flipping through the pages. My hands get slick with the sheen of anxiety. The Florida Center, the Texas Center, the California Center, the New York Center. Almost 100 in total. "How am I supposed to contact every one of them?"

"Just call them. Check in. Lie if you have to. Say you're from my office and are doing the routine checkup, but don't say you're one of them because you might not get a warm reaction. Many are moving forward with their lives, and just want to put the past behind them. Many are resentful of the limitations the government, and society, have put on them. Many are in permanent treatment facilities, and you'll have to talk to their caretakers. Many are deceased. It's been two years, Griffin. Two years can do a lot to people. Especially your people."

My people.

Amber exhales and wiggles her body from my grasp.

"The two of you know how cruel people can be," he continues. "How... *unforgiving* a place the world is."

Amber and I nod simultaneously. Yes. Unforgiving says it best. I flip the pages some more to the Florida section. Numbers now have names; identities I never knew existed. Next to 2's information is a big red stamp that reads "Deceased," and I can't help but remember the little tune I learned at the Center regarding the ever-so-manipulative Dr. Graves—*"he'll kill you like he killed 2."*

I stop reminiscing and stop flipping. "Um, 31?" I ask. "Why are there 31 people in the Florida section?"

Amber's back straightens up as Holston removes his glasses. He places them in his lap and takes a deep breath. "Crystal McKenna. She was Number 7. Do you remember her?"

Remember? How could I forget? 7. She was the buddy of 16. She was the girl who was completely off her rocker, mumbled and moaned, and looked like there was a basketball under her shirt. 16 said they experimented on her, but he was such a twitchy dude that it was hard to take him seriously. I do know that she disappeared at some point during my stay at the Center. Vanished. Gone. Poof. Without a trace.

"Yes," I say quietly.

"Well, she has a child now. Her son, Troy, is almost two years old."

Amber fidgets something awful. Her left leg is crossed over her right, but her foot is bouncing fiercely up and down. "A baby? How can she have a baby? We were told... we were all told the infection left us sterile!" she practically screams. This topic has clearly struck a sensitive nerve. "You said the Altered can't have babies!"

Holston rubs his eyes. He looks sad. Sad for her. Most little girls play with baby dolls and go on thinking that one day, just one day, they'll grow up to be real mommies. He gazes at Amber sympathetically. No. *Empathetically*. There's an underlying pain in his gaze, like he gets it, he knows how she feels. He's connecting with her on a level I could never understand.

Amber wants children? That thought had never occurred to me, but I guess it should have. She's a healthy, 19-year-old, former human being, who maybe one day in the future would like to settle down with a good ole husband and raise a bunch of snot-nosed kids. And I remember Holston has no family either, and he looks at her like he doesn't have the heart to repeat the unrepeatable, like he understands how she feels, like he *knows*.

"She was pregnant when she was infected, pregnant when she was cured with the second iteration of the antidote," he says to her, and she lowers her head. "We've been monitoring her son as well. His blood is... *interesting*. I've been working with his blood to synthesize a newer, stronger vaccine. One that would put to rest all this talk of antibodies and reinfections."

Amber jumps up from the arm of the rocking chair. "Re-infection? Are you serious?" she squeals. The terror in her voice makes me raise an eyebrow. This display of fear is unlike her. "We just saw something on the news about..."

"Not to worry, my dear," Holston says with his magic-touch voice. "Of course, there are kooky people out there, and there are always going to be scares and hoaxes. Some people get a thrill out of causing chaos. My job is not to deal in the fantastic, though. I have seen what can happen." He folds his hands together and extends his arms forward, stretching and crunching his fingers and knuckles at the same time in a dominant and self-serving kind of way. "I know what can happen. Hell, I pretty much predicted the apocalypse almost 20 years ago! My job is to be prepared. And with this unforeseen death sentence looming over me, it's even more pertinent now that I get all my proverbial ducks in a row."

"B... but," she stammers.

Holston raises his hand to silence her. "You can't be re-infected," he says nonchalantly. "If there ever was another outbreak, those things could kill you, but they couldn't re-infect you. You've had the virus, you've had the vaccine. You're essentially immune."

I had pretty much figured that out, but Holston referred to the infected as *things,* and once again I see the vision of the crazy mad scientist, Doctor Frankenstein, sitting before me. Only after the antidote are we considered his children. Only then are we viewed as cherished kin. I wonder how he feels about the Others—the other Altered who were left alone and out of his care. Does he cherish them, too?

The thought of infected people populating the world again makes me shudder. For the brief time period I spent hiding out in my old house with my mother, sister, and Toby, was a time period I do not wish to revisit. What if it came down to the Infected and the Altered? The last two races of people left. Who will be the last race standing? The flesh-hungry Infected, or the unable-to-reproduce-Altered? Either way, non-humanity is doomed.

"Why me?" I ask bluntly, because to be honest, I'm done with the talky-talk.

"Excuse me?" he asks, eyebrows raised.

"Why me? Why do you want me to be the keeper of your secrets?"

"Because I trust you," he says, but it sounds rehearsed, as if he just pressed play on a tape-recorded message.

"And..." I probe.

"You're one of the least suspecting people, Griffin. No one would even think that I would entrust my life's work into the hands of an Altered."

Amber picks up Holston's coffee cup and whisks away into the kitchen. She's annoyed. Hurt. Confused. I know because she's usually silent when something is really bothering her. She has a penchant for literally walking away from a bad situation.

"What aren't you telling me? If you want me to do this for you, you're going to have to be honest."

Holston takes a deep, labored breath. His chest puffs up a little. "I acquired some documents," he begins quietly.

"Stole?" I correct.

He nods. "My old partner, the one who worked with me on the original U-Virus..."

"You told me about him. The one who let that dog go back to his owner when you thought it should have been euthanized and studied."

"Yes. Him. Dr. Trager. He caught wind that I was sick and is making a play to continue my work, but I know there's something else going on. I don't trust him, Griffin, and as long as I'm alive, I can stop him, but once I'm gone I'm sure he'll make a strong case as to why he should have access to my files and why he's the perfect one to continue on. I can't let that happen. I don't trust him, and..." he repeats and pauses. His eyes peer up from his glasses and he tries hard to stifle another cough. "And I have reason to believe that he would completely compromise everything I've worked so hard for."

"You have Trager's documents, don't you," I say matter-of-factly.

Holston closes his eyes and nods again. "I was able to get a hold of a flash drive. Both his and mine are in the envelope as well. Please, Griffin. Please give this dying man one last piece of mind. Please tell me that you won't let my files get to Trager, and that you'll watch over the Altered, especially young Troy. Alt Home has enough funding to last about a year after I'm gone, but no longer than that. All Centers will shut down, but I'm going to need you to keep my house, so to speak, in order."

Do I have a choice? Is there even a question in the matter? How can I deny this man after he gave me a second chance at life, or whatever it is you want to call what I'm experiencing right now? His lips press together in anticipation. The wrinkles around them weigh heavy on the skin, dragging the corners of his mouth down into an eerie sad clown face. This time, the old man face staring at me is dying from some natural cause, not from some physical wound that I inflicted. I feel a strong need to make it up to that old man. Redeem myself in some weird way.

These papers, these documents, they're *us*. They're *me*. The Altered. The culmination of who I am, and who I've become. This is my origin story. My true Now. My birthright, in a sense.

I breathe in deep, and exhale noisily. "Alright," I say. "Tell me what I gotta do."

3

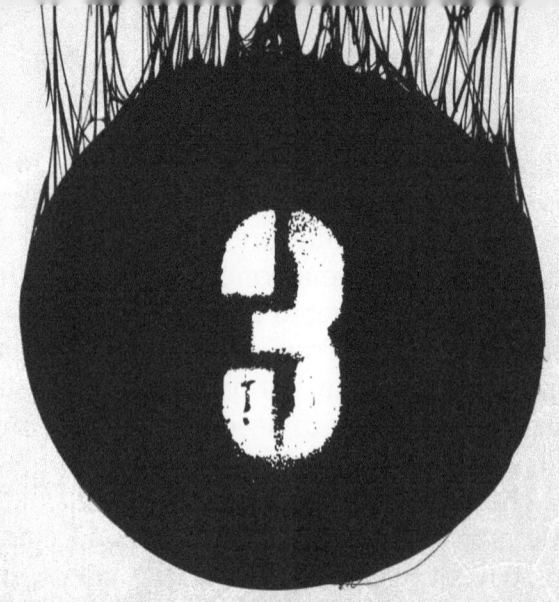

HOLSTON STAYED FOR MOST OF THE DAY INSTRUCTING me on how to read the blood samples, how to sneak in and out of the blood lab, that kind of stuff. I took a lot of notes and tried my best to organize the papers in the file into some fashion that would make sense to me. At around noon, Holston's eyelids started to get droopy, so I told him to sprawl out on the couch to take a nap. The second his head hit the cushion, he began snoring. I needed to rest, too, so I pulled the lever on the rocking chair, kicked back the recliner, and closed my eyes. I never did fall into a full-blown sleep, partially because there was so much information for me to digest, and partially because Amber had the TV on in the bedroom at a fairly high volume.

By the time Holston woke up, it was four o'clock. I needed to get myself in gear for work, and he said he was going to go straight home for some dinner and a restful evening. He slept for nearly four hours on my couch, and he wanted a *restful evening*? The cancer must really be taking its toll on his feeble body, but from the hearty handshake he gave me before he left, it was hard to tell exactly what was going on with the good doctor. He told me to kiss Amber goodbye and that he'd be in touch again soon.

When I got to the Brandon Medical Center, I staked out a route just as Holston had instructed. Make a right at the nurses' station, down the hall, left at the receptionists' desk. I hid in the shadows and watched as the doctors and nurses and other personnel came and went, calculating their break times, making mental notes of their structured routines. All the while, I was unassuming—like a villain in disguise walking through a shopping center carrying a shotgun in a box of fake roses. I was just the lowly Altered janitor boy mopping up the floors like I always do. They had no idea that I was listening to their conversations and plotting out my next move. I have to admit, the covert operation that I had embroiled myself in was exhilarating!

On my dinner break at around eight o'clock, I decided to take a shot at "checking in" with someone from a Re-Assimilation Center. California time is three hours earlier from Florida time, so I figured I would start there. I got Holston's file out of my work locker, went to the office they let the staff use as a break room, and called the first living Altered on the California list. I had no idea what to expect, but one thing I did know for sure—the caller ID on the receiving end would identify the call as coming from the Brandon Medical Center, and that would somehow make my inquiry legit.

The call I made was to the caretaker of Barbra Hartung. She was Patient #104. Holston had explained to me that each Re-Assimilation patient was given a three-digit number. The first number in the series indicates which region the Altered person was treated: 0 for Florida, 1 for California, 2 for New York, 3 for Texas. The last number indicates the vaccine number—the numbered batch, or as Holston called it, iteration, the patient was given. I'm #024. Amber is #025. We're so close in our vaccine level, we're practically related, which is kinda strange but kinda not.

So, this Barbra Hartung lady is Patient 4 from the California Re-Assimilation Center. *4*. Meaning she got the first dose of the vaccine, and as history has proven, the first dose of *anything* is never a good thing. When I called the rehab center she's in, I spoke to Sarah Something-or-Other—the woman who takes care of Barbra around the clock. I asked all the key questions that Holston prepped me for, took down the appropriate notes. I tried to deepen my voice and changed my name, but in hindsight, I don't think that was necessary. By the end of the conversation, I realized I was speaking in my normal cadence anyway. "Hi, my name is Jack King from Dr. Holston's office at the Brandon Medical Center. Just doing a routine checkup. How's Miss Hartung doing? Sleeping well? Eating? What's her physical activity like? Emotional state? Is she responsive?"

Responsive.

That was a key word that Holston told me to say when referring to patients 1-8, because most weren't. Responsive.

"Yes, she's doing fine. Sleeps most of the day. Eats very little, which Dr. Holston said was typical. We get her in physical therapy a few times a week, but mostly she's confined to the chair. Emotionally, no real change. Mumbles a lot. Lots of outbursts. We still have to give her a daily sedative, so there's no change there. Responsive? Very little."

"Thank you for your time, ma'am. Don't forget Miss Hartung's next blood analysis is due next month."

"I won't. Thank you, Mr. King."

When I hung up the phone, I felt a little sad. This poor woman, Barbra Hartung #104, probably lost everything and everyone she ever loved, was infected with some God-awful disease, did God-awful things, only to be left to rot away in some wheelchair doped up on sedatives for the rest of her life. It's pretty pathetic, actually.

After I spoke with the caretaker, I tried calling Amber's phone. I knew she was bothered and upset, and I figured I'd play the part of the good boyfriend, but the calls went straight to her voicemail, and I figured she was royally pissed off at me.

It's now 2 a.m., and I creep into the bedroom as quietly as I can. Amber is sleeping. The television is still on, but it's muted. She always mutes the commercials when she's watching TV, but sometimes she gets so tired that she ends up falling asleep, like she has right now. The light from the screen washes over her face making the scar under her right eye appear more pronounced in the shadows. Half her body is over the comforter, and the other half is tucked under the covers. I take off my shoes, socks, pants, and shirt, and slither into the bed next to her. I don't dare to turn off the TV because I know the change of lights within the room will wake her up. I sneaked around the whole medical center tonight, surely I can slip into a bed undetected.

"So, you're gonna help Holston?" she mumbles.

I tighten my eyes and crinkle my nose. She's up.

Great.

"M-hmm," I answer quietly.

She exhales in frustration.

"Why?" I ask. "Why is it a big deal for you?"

"It's not, I guess. I don't know. Seems like a big waste of time, is all."

"I don't think it is. I think it's a good thing."

She swoops the exposed half of her body underneath the covers and curls up in the fetal position with her back to me. I reach my hand and try to rub her arm, but she juts her shoulder away, and I retreat. "It doesn't matter, Griffin. None of it. All of it. It's all worthless and meaningless. I thought you understood that." Her voice makes a weird hitching sound every time she gets upset, and I pray to God, to any god, that she keeps it together long enough, so the tears don't start coming. I seriously can't stand to see her cry. She doesn't do it often, but when it does happen, it bothers me in such a profound way. Reminds me of my sister Sydney standing at the back door in our old home, begging me not to go off into the night, then rushing up to stop me. *Stupid kid. Got us both killed.* So, whenever Amber pulls her little wah-wah sessions, it grates on my every nerve; makes me want to gauge her eyes out and shove them down her throat.

"Stop," I say gently, trying to both convince her not to cry and to escape from my horrific violent eye-gouging thought. She quickly whips her body around. And there they are. The tears are glistening in her eyes against the light from the television. I hold my face as still as a statue in fear that my disgust will show through with my expressions.

"Do you wanna know what happened to me today?" she says, her voice calm and steady.

I look at her, studying her face, studying her crystal blue eyes that are so filled with fury and rage.

"I went out for food after you and Holston left. I wanted Chinese, so I went to the Chinese food place up on 60. I walk in, pick up a menu, circle a few items, hand it back to the cashier, she puts in the order, rings me up, blah blah blah. Anyway, the guy who cooked the food comes out with the order, puts it on the counter, takes one look at me, and snatches the bag away just as I'm about to pick it up. He starts yelling at the cashier girl in Chinese. Gets all up in her face, ya know. So, I say, 'Hey buddy, what's the problem?' And he says to me, 'We no serve you.'

"I didn't understand at first, like it didn't make sense to me. I looked down at myself and I said—get this, I actually said, 'I have shoes on'—like a complete idiot. He waves his hand all over and dumps the food onto the floor. 'We no serve you!' he screams at me again. I must have looked so confused, but the cashier girl looks at me and points to her cheek. *My* cheek. My scar."

I run my hand across the side of her face. "I'm sorry that happened to you today, Amber."

She grabs my hand and pulls it away, squeezing my fingers tightly together. "You don't understand. I was so mad, so infuriated, that I hissed at them. *Hissed* at them, Griffin. And that's not who I am! That's not who I want to be, *ever*. But for that split second, that one brief moment of losing control, I felt that power surge again."

"And you liked it," I say.

She turns her head to me and gives me an evil stare, but confirms what I said, "I loved it." The tears roll down her cheek and she wipes them away with her free hand. "I freaked out, drove home like a crazy person, and pulled out one of those old phone books that was sitting in the pantry from long ago. I look up plastic surgeons and call the first one I find. I just wanted to see. I just wanted to find out how much a scar revision would be, and maybe go in for a consultation or something."

I run my hand against the top of my head as if there were hair to grab. The prickly stubbles of my freshly shaved head grate against my palm. "Amber," I sigh. "You didn't..."

She ignores me and continues. "The receptionist asks me all kinds of questions, like 'Where's your scar? How big is it? What shape is it?' I answer her honestly, and she gets all quiet when she finally figures out what I'm talking about and says, 'Oh no, Miss, we don't perform those types of procedures on you people.'

"That's when I threw my phone across the kitchen floor. It broke. I need a new one."

That would explain why I kept getting her voicemail...

"Amber..."

She sits straight up in the bed and folds her arms over her chest. "No!" she yells, her blue eyes wide and crazy. "I want you to tell me what the point is, Griffin. What's the end game? What? So, you can be a graveyard shift janitor for the rest of your life, and I can keep getting stuck in basement mailrooms doing mundane clerical work? And don't give me that line of bullshit that *every race in history has had to overcome adversity*, because guess what? We ain't overcoming jack shit, buddy. You know why? 'Cause we can't even continue our 'race'! There's no 'generation to come' in any of our futures. We're the unholiest of unholies. We're less than human. So, doing Holston's bidding isn't gonna benefit nobody."

She huffs, like she's won a grand debate or something, and stares at the voiceless images on the television screen.

I pause, take in her words for a moment, and come right back at her. "Well, if anything, then for self-preservation. Think about it, Amber. Is suicide an option for you?" Her face darkens and she doesn't move a muscle. I know I've struck a chord. "It's not for me, I know that much," I continue. "And ya know what? I skimmed through Holston's files, and of all the people he's keeping tabs on, wanna know how many are dead from suicide alone? Twenty. That's not even counting those who died from other causes. *Twenty* took their own life. Is that what you want to do? Is that what you're telling me? 'Cause all this doom and gloom and there's-no-future talk is kinda leading me to believe that."

Another stream of tears opens up along her face. "No," she answers, her voice barely audible.

"And what about Holston? Above all, to respect a dying man's wishes. But he's not just any man, Amber. When you look at it from all angles, Holston is like our father. He's the only other person—besides each other—that we got. 'Cause I don't see my dad around anywhere. Where's your dad? Where's Mr. Fields beating down the bedroom door yelling at me to stop seeing his daughter?"

She inhales and rests her head against the backboard of the bed. "I ate him," she says breathlessly.

"Exactly. It's about redemption, babe. If we're truly defined by our actions, then it's about making it up to Josh, and Toby, and Sydney, and my mom, and your dad, and that Chinese dude's great-uncle, and the plastic surgeon receptionist's kid, and all the hundreds of others we killed or changed."

Without missing a beat, she sits straight up again in the bed, turns her face to me and looks me dead in the eye. "I never changed anyone. I always made sure they were dead."

Chills run throughout my body. I place a knowing hand on her knee, and once again I am reminded why I was drawn to her from the beginning. We are too similar, perhaps for our own good. But she gets it, she gets me, she understands, and we are connected more-so than any other two people can be. I was wrong about putting up a wall between us. She reminds me of a secret, and I don't think I want that to change.

If this is what love feels like, then...

I open my mouth to speak, but she beats me to it.

"I knew from the moment *I* changed," she says. "I knew it immediately. My sister Jayne and I were waiting for our dad to pick us up from the carline at school. It was so crazy. We didn't even hear them come up behind us. I knew something was wrong, that I was... I don't know... *changing*. But I kept still, kinda swooning from the chaos around me. Jayne was on the floor. I watched her get up and stumble around. And just like that..." she snaps her fingers and the crack echoes in the room like an ear-splitting whip, "... she pounces on some kid. That kid goes down, gets up, and attacks the teacher on duty who was hiding in some bushes in the front of the school. And that's when I knew. Even though the infection was working its way inside of me, I just *knew* I had to make sure they were dead. Next thing I know, my dad's getting out of his car, coming on over to me to see if I'm all right, and that's when... well, you know..."

"The hunger."

Her eyes drift through me, beyond me. "Yeah," she says, and her voice sounds so far away, like she's not really here with me in bed, like she's actually back in that moment—right there watching her dad come toward her and... "the hunger. That's all there was. And I sure was *starving*." Her eyes widen freakishly, and I almost get a sense of delight in her voice.

"Of course you were!" I joke, trying to break her from the bizarre trance she's in. "You're a friggin' *twig*!"

She blinks her eyes a few times, as if she were awakening from a spell. She lightly punches my arm and smiles. "Oh, shut up!" she laughs. "I could say the same for you!"

"Yeah, yeah," I say as I playfully roll my eyes. "I wasn't always this lean, ya know. I used to be r-r-r-r- ipped!" I put up my arms and flex my muscles, or whatever muscles are there, and she continues to giggle.

"Whatever am I going to do with you, Griffin King?" she whispers as she moves closer to me and curls up in the crook of my arm.

"I don't know, Amber Fields," I respond and pull the hair back from her face.

"Time for bed, my love?" she asks.

"Time for bed," I say.

I close my eyes. Amber's rhythmic breathing against my chest and the flashing lights from the images on the TV lull me right into a dreamless sleep.

4

I'VE NEVER BEEN TO A FORMAL FUNERAL BEFORE. NEVER been to an actual wake or memorial service. Never been to a celebration of life ceremony, or any other of those religious routines that people take part in when someone dies. For the first seventeen years of my life, I had managed to outrun Death and his icy grip. Then the Outbreak happened, and well, I sort of became the bringer of death. But as far as the *formalities* surrounding death—black clothes, ceremonies, over-abundance of flowers, crazy, old Italian ladies throwing themselves on top of their husband's coffins—I've never had the pleasure of going through that experience. Nope, never, nada, zip.

Until now...

Dr. Holston came to me two months ago and broke the news about his illness. He said his prognosis was six months. Well, someone along the line of communication must have been lying because it's been two months, and Amber and I are standing on the steps of the funeral home to pay our last respects to him. It could very well be that his cancer was extremely aggressive, and for a man his age to endure chemo and radiation just to extend his life by a fraction, well... he probably couldn't take it. They said he died peacefully in his sleep, which makes me happy.

It's hot. Muggy. Florida in July can be brutal at midday, and that's exactly the time on the big hand right now. Amber said that I had to wear a suit and tie because it's a respect and tradition type of thing, but I'm practically suffocating in this ridiculous get-up. Amber looks beautiful, as always. I guess women can get away with black sundresses and open-toe shoes as long as they have the right accessories and purse to match. She's all dolled up, maybe a little too much. Her hair is soft and bouncing with abundant curls, but her makeup? She definitely overdid it today. She has such flawless skin; I don't know why she feels the need to pile on so much foundation and blush and whatever it is that she cakes on her face. When she turns to look at me, a hint of sunlight catches the raised scar on her cheek, and it hits me... she tried so hard to cover up her mark. I kiss her gently on the lips and grab her hand.

"Ready?" she asks.

"No, but we don't necessarily have a choice, do we?"

She squeezes my hand tighter. "C'mon." She pulls me forward into the building.

As soon as the door opens, it hits me all at once—the super frigid air, and the powerful aroma of flowers. The scent gags me—grips the front of my nostrils and tugs on the back of my throat causing me to sneeze a few times in rapid succession. Amber reaches into her purse and pulls out a few tissues for me. "I'm fine," I say, sniffling. "Just caught me off guard."

"Me, too," she whispers.

The lights are dimmed, giving the large marble foyer of the funeral home an eerie nighttime look. Everything is decorated in gold and burgundy, with elaborate crystal chandeliers. This is a place where royalty would be memorialized, but I guess that's kind of the point, because when you really think about it, the dead don't need all this fancy stuff. These things are just for the living. For those left behind.

The room for Dr. Peter Holston is down the hall on the left. A golden plaque with his name engraved on it hangs next to the door. When we walk inside, the flower scent is even stronger, and this time, Amber sneezes. It's hard not to when you have supersonic senses like us.

I survey the room. Holston's coffin is at the front of the room. It's white with gold trimming and gold cushions on the inside. *A king's send-off*. There are soft fluorescent lights shining down on his body, giving him an illuminated essence—the appearance of being alive, just asleep. Chairs are set up in neat rows for all his friends and family, and there are about 20 people already here—lawyer types and doctor types and businessmen and women types. Nobody like me and Amber. No young adult types who wear black sundresses and open-toed shoes and a Salvation Army second-hand suit.

I study their wrinkled faces outlined by heads of salt and pepper hair, or their overly Botoxed foreheads frozen in time, and of the twenty or so people, regardless of age or countenance, not one of them has a scar. They're all human. Unlike Amber and me. Faces turn toward us, and my brain takes in their expressions and gestures—eyes roll, noses twitch and turn upward, steps taken backward. There's some silent bodily reaction to our presence, and it's certainly not a good one.

Amber's right there with me, 'cause she tugs harder on my hand, making my shoulder dip forward. "Do you see the way they look at us?" she whispers from the corner of her mouth.

"Uh huh," I mutter. "Do you see..."

"Uh huh. Just keep walking and find a seat."

"In the back," she says, dragging me over to a chair.

"Agreed."

Two Altered here for Holston. Two. After all he did for us, after all he continued to do out of the goodness of his heart and bank account. He just wanted to make the world safe. He wanted a legacy, some kind of acknowledgment and recognition for the *skatey-eight* times he saved humankind from extinction. And what does he get? A room full of snobs and a herd full of absent, ungrateful children.

Amber slides down into a row of chairs, and just as I'm about to take my seat, there's a tap on my shoulder. I swivel my head to see who wants my attention.

"Excuse me," a middle-aged woman says in a low voice.

I raise my eyebrows at her.

"Are you Griffin?"

My eyes narrow and I nod.

A smile comes over the woman's face and she extends her hand. "I'm Dorothy. Dorothy Oswald. Dr. Holston was my uncle."

I shake her hand, but I'm still confused. "Oh," I say. "I didn't know Dr. Holston had any family."

She releases my hand and looks down at the floor. "Yes, well, my mother was his sister, and she passed a long time ago."

"Oh, oh, I'm so sorry," I stutter, like a complete idiot.

"It's fine," she says with a kind smile. When I look at her eyes, I see a slight resemblance to Holston, and I smile back at her.

"I'm sorry about your uncle, as well. Dr. Holston was..."

"He was a wonderful person," she says, interrupting me. "A brilliant man. A dedicated scientist. He spoke very highly of you. I was hoping you would come to see him."

"Oh?"

She grabs both my hands firmly in hers, and stares me directly in the eyes, "You were part of his greatest accomplishment. He was so proud of the work he did helping you and the others. We all were so proud of him! Who can say that they created life but a mother and a father? For Uncle Peter, what he did was the next best thing. Griffin, I want to know if you would be okay with saying a few words during the memorial service."

I get tongue tied and my stomach starts to flip forward and backward, like I'm on some crazy roller coaster. "Um... I don't know. I... I... wouldn't know what to say, or..."

"It doesn't matter. Just speak from your heart. It would mean the world to me, and to my uncle."

I feel eyes on me. Human eyes of the crowd. Eyes that bore holes into my body. I'm damned if I do, and I'm damned if I don't. And suddenly, I go from never having been to a funeral service before to being the guest speaker deluxe. *Whoo-hoo. Dr. Frankenstein's Monster Speaks!*

Baffled by the request, I nod my head, and Dorothy's smile grows wider on her face. "Thank you," she whispers and kisses me on my cheek. "Listen, if you ever need anything, please don't hesitate to call me. My office is here in Tampa. I'm always willing to help." She smiles, hands me her business card, and walks away.

I put the card in my pocket and sit down in a fog next to Amber. She pats my knee and says, "You did a good thing, there. Holston would be proud of you."

"Easy for you to say. You don't have to get up in front a room full of people who hate you."

"Dorothy doesn't hate you. In fact, she looked quite... *smitten*."

"Oh, shut up, you! She's just an Altered Sympathizer. You know the type."

Amber giggles. "Not too many of those around."

"Nope, definitely not. I mean, how many people do you know who are on our side?"

"Hmmm..." she purrs and sarcastically tugs at her chin. "Besides Holston and the good niece? Nobody."

I stretch my arm around her shoulder. She nuzzles up to me and I bury my face in her soft raven curls. Her scent of coconut oil masks the pungent flower odor, and I close my eyes, breathing her in like a fresh summer day. The people around us talk in hushed voices—bees droning in a hive, the sounds carrying me off to a mini- daydream...

There's a tapping on a microphone, and I open my eyes to see what's going on. Amber sits up straight and runs her hands across her lap, smoothing out her dress. Dorothy is at a podium and addresses the crowd. "Everyone, we'd like to get started, so if you could please find a seat." The mumming sound from the crowd dies down as everyone settles into their places. It's all well-orchestrated. I assume many of these people have done this before.

"I want to thank you all for coming," she continues as she looks down at a piece of paper in front of her and reads, "My Uncle Peter loved and respected each and every one of you, and I know he would be smiling right now knowing that you were all here for him. My uncle was a great man. When my father passed away when I was just a baby, Uncle Peter did everything he could to help out his only sister, my mother. Even though he was always so busy with his work, we spent many holidays together, and even sometimes weekends when I was growing up. I remember him fondly. He was always so much fun to be around. I used to ask him what he did for a living, and he would tell me, 'I'm protecting the world.'"

A soft murmur of laughter rises from the crowd.

"Well, if Uncle Peter was protecting the world, then I knew I wanted to protect the world, too. He was my biggest inspiration for becoming a pediatric surgeon, and my biggest benefactor. I would not have been able to accomplish my dreams if it weren't for the love and support—emotionally and financially—of this great man." Dorothy puts her hand over her heart and looks up at us all. "Those of you who knew my uncle outside of a working capacity would know that he was a phenomenal storyteller. Many times, I told him to write his ideas down, or to try to get his stories published for children. But he never had the time. He was always too busy protecting the world."

Another round of laughter.

Dorothy smiles meekly and continues, "But there was one story that he told me, and I will never forget it because I think I made him repeat it about a thousand times. 'The Goblin and the Girl.' See, there's this goblin who falls in love with a young maiden..."

And he kidnaps her because he has to be with her forever...

"And he kidnaps her, because he believes that she is his destiny, and he needs to be with her forever..."

Wait. I know this story! I tap Amber's knee, but she grabs my hand and gives me her "stop it!" look. Dorothy continues the tale, but I kinda tune her out because I know this all too well. Mixed in with Holston's files, there are a few pages of nonsense. I guess it's not nonsense because Dorothy here is reciting the story pretty much word for word. I didn't read the whole thing because I dismissed it as the ramblings of an elderly man, but I make a mental note to go back and re-read it. Maybe there's a reason why he included his fairy tale with his medical journal and professional papers.

More laughter. Some women blot away their tears.

"But one of the greatest things my uncle has done is his work with The Altered..."

All of a sudden, an uncomfortable silence swoops over the crowd. Amber grips my knee. "... the Re-Assimilation Centers, the vaccines, Alt Home. He has given new life to..." The room is cold, frigid, but my hands start to sweat. "... one of his proudest moments—Griffin King."

Without thinking, I rise and approach the podium. "Just look at me," Amber mouths to me from the back of the room, but there are *eyes* staring at me, and the walls of the room begin to shrink. Holston's coffin is to my left, and I quickly glance over at his illuminated face. He's waxy and has too much makeup on. I wonder if the undertaker got the same makeup applying lessons that Amber did?

A sharp, high-pitched wail of feedback blares in the room as I step toward the microphone. I cock my head back to adjust myself to not make that sound again. I'm not gonna lie, I'm nervous as hell. But I inhale and begin. "Dr. Holston was a genius," I say, voice shaking. "It would take a lifetime to thank him for what he did for me." I pause to look at Amber. "For us." She winks at me. I guess I'm doing okay, and I start to relax a little more. "Dr. Holston did save the world. Probably more times than any one of us could know. He saved me *from* me and gave me a second chance when my first one was stolen. He will always be like family."

That's all I have in me. That's all I manage to get out. Besides, the overwhelming silence is more than unnerving. The crowd has no reaction to what I've said. No laughter, no applause, no standing ovation. *What the hell did you expect, dummy?* I scan the faces of the people one last time before I step down and go back to my seat next to Amber. From the corner of my eye, a familiar figure catches my attention and send chills up my back.

"You did good," she says with a smile. A fake smile. I was horrible. Emotionless. Like an alien trying to feign human emotion while wearing a glass mask. Like an *Altered*. But Amber's reassurance, no matter how manufactured, is comforting none-the-less.

A few more people speak about Holston—some old colleagues of his from back in the day. It's interesting to hear about him from other people—how they viewed him, what their relationship with him was like. All of them mention the great things he's done, tell anecdotes of his wild teenage years, and of his trials and tribulations in the lab. None of them mention his work during the Outbreak. None of them dare mention the Altered.

"I'm going to say goodbye," Amber says and motions to the coffin.

"Do you want me to come with you?" I ask. Isn't that what people do? Pay their respects together?

"Can you give me a minute alone?"

"Oh yeah, sure, sure," I say.

No sooner does she get up to kneel at Holston's coffin than a massive presence make its way next to me. A cloud of darkness looms in the corner of my eye, a hint of familiarity that makes my skin crawl, and the cologne scent that has been forever ingrained in my hypersensitive memory wafts gently in my nostrils. My heart feels heavy, like it's stopped for a brief moment and rewound time. I'm not here at the funeral home, mourning Dr. Holston, I'm back at the Re-Assimilation Center, sitting on a black leather chair, staring at a pair of manicured lunch-box hands, looking at the gelled-back black hair, observing the condescending tone of my enemy...

Graves.

He stares hard at me, giving me that look that I came to know and loathe. "Playing nice, 24?" he says, his deep voice rattling my every nerve.

All of the oxygen is sucked out of the room, and I'm afraid to respond; afraid that my voice will sound small and squeaky next to this monolith of a man. I slowly turn toward him to meet his gaze. "Only if you are," I manage to say.

He licks his thick lips and gives a quick nod of his head. My blood boils hard and fast and hot in my veins, and I do everything in my power to control myself from punching him in his chiseled jaw. I see it now: my hand connects with the side of his face, pushing it to the side a little, only for him to snap back forward and wag his finger "no" in my face like the T-1000 does in *Terminator 2*. I think he reads my mind, or something, because he grins that snakey-snake grin. I want to punch him even harder.

"I'm not surprised that you're here," he says coolly.

"Well, I'm surprised that *you* are," I answer.

Because really, that's the truth. He was the one who had the Re-Assimilation Centers shut down. He was the one who ended part of Holston's dream. Why would he be here if they had left off on bad terms?

He chuckles, and I clench my fists waiting for him to strike first. I have to be ready if...

"Why would my being here surprise you?" he laughs. "Peter and I were great friends. Because we disagreed on a professional level had no effect on our personal relationship."

I hate the way he makes me feel—like some dumb kid who is one step away from being crushed under his size 15 shoe. "Was there something you wanted?" I ask.

Graves inhales deeply. He towers over me like a dragon rising up from its slumber. I anticipate his wings to fold out any second to swoop me up so he can literally bite my head off. He smiles, and his perfect white teeth flash in the artificial candlelight. "Just wanted to catch up with a former patient, is all." He smirks.

I stand and anxiously rub my hands against my suit pants. I try to keep my emotions in check, but my height and weight are no match for a man of his size. "Okay," I say, trying to brush him off. "Consider yourself caught up."

He chuckles again, reaches into his pocket, and pulls out a business card. "I'll be back in town," he says as he hands it to me. "Setting up shop in Tampa. Not too far from the old Re-Assimilation Center in Brandon. Where did you say you were working again?"

Suddenly, I realize I'm collecting quite a few of these things. I take the card, fold it up, and put it in my pocket. "I didn't."

"Oh yeah," he says as he clicks his tongue on the top of his mouth. "The Brandon Medical Center. That's right. Yeah, we'll pretty much be neighbors."

How did he...?

"You know, there's still a lot of work to be done in the big cities," he continues.

My heart sinks.

"The big cities were hit the hardest, and they seem to be taking the longest to get back on track, but I'm confident my services will be greatly appreciated there."

"Services for *what*?" I practically spit.

"My practice. Don't you remember, 24? I *am* a psychiatrist."

He'll kill you, like he killed 2.

"How can I forget," I mutter.

He ignores me. "I want to help survivors. I feel that my best work is with them—helping them to cope with the events of the Outbreak and the aftermath."

"Oh, so you're getting out of the Altered business. Makes sense."

We lock eyes. I know that look. I know this feeling. He wants to leap over that coffee table and strangle the second life out of me. Only, we're not in the Re-Assimilation Center, there's no coffee table separating us, and we're certainly not alone.

An older gentleman walks up to Graves and claps him on the back. "Warren," he says as Graves pivots his body to meet the handshake of the man.

"Rick," Graves says, his tone completely changed. "When did you get in?"

"Late last night. I made arrangements as soon as I heard the news." The man eyeballs me up and down. "Everything okay over here?"

"Oh yeah. Fine, fine," Graves lies. "Just catching up with Peter's favorite patient."

"Oh, yes, yes," the man says in awe, like I'm some freak of a science experiment.

"Rick, this is 24, Griffin King," Graves says. A forced introduction. "24, this is Dr. Richard Trager."

Trager extends his hand, and I apprehensively shake it. So, this is Trager—the one who butted heads with Holston, the one who Holston stole files from, the one who Holston warned me about. He has light gray eyes, which seem to light up in the dimly lit room. They are in complete contrast to Graves's black, soulless ones. Trager must be in his mid to late 50s—younger than Holston, but older than Graves. Perhaps he was once a student of Holston's, and proved to be so good that Peter made him a partner. There is an uncanny resemblance in

Trager's mannerisms to the way Holston carried himself. Odd. I can't pinpoint it. I know they're not related, because I know the extent of Holston's family history. I don't know, something about Trager is off. Different. Altered. I just need to keep my guard up because if Holston didn't trust him, then I definitely can't trust him.

His hand is cold. Old man cold. "Pleased to meet you, Griffin," he says as he firmly bounces my hand up and down.

"Likewise, Doctor," I say, quickly pulling away.

"I worked with Peter on many, many projects back in the day. We were both responsible for the first vaccine for the U Virus, which I'm sure you're aware of."

I nod.

"Peter did great things for you people, and I assure you, I plan to continue on with his work to the best of my abilities."

I stare at him. *The hell you are.*

"It'll be a daunting task to sift through all of his paperwork. Lord knows Peter was a pack-rat!"

The two men chuckle a deep and phony chuckle.

"I will personally see that the volunteers Holston had running the Alt Homes will continue to do their jobs," Trager continues. He rubs his hands together and sighs. "I'm sure I'll be able to put the pieces of the puzzle together, so to speak."

Immediately my senses go into overdrive. Holston told me the Alt Homes would close after his death because money was getting cut, but Trager is going to see that they continue on? No way. Not buying it. He blatantly lied to my face and...

"Oh," I say with a hint of fake stupidity in my voice, "I thought Dr. Oswald would take over for Holston."

Trager's face slightly twists in shock. Graves doesn't notice it, hell, a normal human being wouldn't register the automatic expression, but I do. "Peter and I had an arrangement. A pact. Dr. Oswald is too married to her work to give the research of the Altered and the U-Virus her full attention..."

More lies. "You mean the Zorna-flu?" I interrupt.

Trager glances at Graves, then back at me. "Right, right..."

As if on cue, Amber taps me on the shoulder, startling me, forcing me to look away from the doctors. I have no idea how long she's been standing there, but by the look on her face I think she heard a good chunk of the conversation. "I'm ready to go," she says flatly.

"Okay. Let's head out."

"Pleasure to meet you, Mr. King," Trager says with a wide smile. It's phonier than Graves ever was or possibly could be. And he speaks with a weird lilt, like he's speaking with a British accent, but not. I wonder if he, too, will hand me his business card, but he doesn't.

I nod at him. "Graves," I say, and nod at him, too.

●

"I hate funerals," she snaps as she slams the car door.

"Technically, that wasn't a funeral," I say, trying to lighten the mood.

She exhales loudly. "Let's not get into semantics, okay? You know what I mean."

I turn on the car, pull out of the parking lot, and get on the interstate. Amber rests her head against the window and stares out. She's in her head right now. Probably replaying the events of Holston's wake, maybe thinking about what her life used to be. Whatever it is, it's not one of her nighttime dreams, because right now, she's not smiling.

After a little while of driving in silence, I ask, "Mind if I turn on the radio?"

"Sure. Go ahead," she answers, but I know she wasn't paying attention.

"Official Report from the UN states that the updated death toll from The Outbreak is anywhere from 50—60 million worldwide, the most deaths from any one event since World War II. Government delegates and representatives from the CDC..."

She snaps out of her trance and snaps off the radio. "Enough already!" she yells. "I'm so friggin' sick of hearing about it. It's been two years. Two years! Why can't people just move on and get over it."

I veer off at our exit, taking the long, winding road with palm trees and grassy areas on either side up and to the right. Before I get a chance to answer her, to tell her how I feel about what the government has to say, what I think of Trager, how Graves's reappearance rattled me, I slow down the car.

Did I fall asleep? Am I dreaming this? Did my heart really stop and reverse time?

"Why don't you ever have an opinion, Griffin? I say these things to you, and you never have..."

"Amber," I say over her, slowing the car down some more.

"I just sometimes wish that you, I don't know, *felt* a little more strongly..."

"Amber," I repeat, raising my voice, practically stopping the car.

She turns her head toward me. "What?" she yells angrily.

"Look."

And I point out the window to my left.

She gasps. Loud enough for me to hear it. I think I gasp, too. It's almost an unreal scene. *Too* real.

She digs her fingernails into the side of my arm. "Griffin," she whispers (as if she's trying not to be heard by an invisible person in the car), "Griffin, *what* is he doing?"

We both stare at the man in the grassy area of the exit ramp. He's on his knees, as if he's planted in the grass. His face and white t-shirt are stained with bright red blood and black bile. He moves his hands to his mouth, and as I inch the car closer, I see what he's doing. A headless rabbit is at his side, and he's eating it, indulging in it, savoring it... *like he's done this before.* Through the closed car windows, I hear his delighted moans, the all too familiar song of the zombie. He turns his eyes away from his meal and looks directly at us. His eyes are completely white with the haze of infection.

"Oh my God," Amber says under her breath.

Mesmerized, I can't stop looking at him. I'm fascinated by the way he engages his meal. There's something beautiful and serene in his movements.

And something stirs inside of me as I witness his carnage.

He slowly stands up, body covered in dirt and blood and black plague-ridden bodily fluids.

"Griffin, just go," she says, digging deeper into my arm. She can't look away, either.

He moans again, and against the light of the setting sun, I see a swell of a scar under his right eye.

"Griffin, please," she begs. "Please just go! Oh God! Just go!"

He takes a step forward in our direction. I step on the gas pedal, pushing the car forward as fast as it will go.

5

(From the personal journal of Dr. Peter Holston...)

I've managed to save whatever samples of the virus that I could. I put them in a separate container and labeled them **U Virus**. *That was the one thing that Rick and I actually did agree on—U Virus. This is an unknown strain, novel, and I am exceptionally perplexed by its nature.*

Approximately three weeks ago, the **New Mexico Veterinary Clinic**, *a veterinary lab in* **Albuquerque, New Mexico**, *contacted us with blood work from a German shepherd named* **Bear**. *Bear's owner,* **Dan Kahn**, *had brought the animal in after it had shown signs of lethargy, pain when moving, and a change in his bark. Mr. Kahn told the vet he had taken Bear with him on a camping trip in* **Black Canyon**, *near* **Santa Fe**, *and the animal began 'acting funny' as soon as they returned. I spoke with* **Dr. Anne Rennard** *at the animal clinic, and she said the tests came back inconclusive, but she was concerned, and contacted us at the CDC for another opinion. She wanted to know if she could send over Bear's files and blood reports so we could have a look.*

Rick and I flew out to **New Mexico** *the next morning, to be on the safe side. His theory was that it was* ***Yersinia pestis*****, bubonic plague**. *My theory was* **rabies**, *but in order to test positive for that, the animal would need to be euthanized. Dr. Rennard said the owner was against euthanizing the animal, so she quarantined it and waited for our arrival.*

Had it been rabies, Bear would have become violently aggressive within a day or two. Had it been plague, Bear would have had inflamed lymph nodes and the appearance of a bubo. When we got there, the animal had neither. He was gentle and friendly, and showed no physical sign of illness, save for his odd moan-like bark, and what appeared to be a craving to eat anything (even inedible objects).

For two days we drew blood and ran tests. Bear's behavior was slightly changing, but he had not entered the 'Mad Dog Phase,' which is typical in rabid canines. Rick was quick to throw out my rabies theory. At this point, I had to agree with him, as the animal was not presenting with any more symptoms.

On the third day, we noticed a lump at the base of its neck that oozed pus when prodded with the examination stick. Within five hours, the lumps had spread down the animal's spine. Rick and I were confused. There were symptoms from two different diseases—two deadly diseases that should have killed the animal at this point.

What was even more confusing was the blood analysis. The report stated that there was a presence of a virus, but what that virus was, we had no clue. It looked like **Rhabdovirus**, *with a* **flu-strain**, *with* ***Yersinia***, *with all types of other undefinable components. I would need the full capacity of my lab back in Atlanta to take on the task of isolating every last piece.*

My immediate reaction was to euthanize the animal and do a full body autopsy. If this was an unknown, a U Virus, my main concern was halting the spread of infection. Could it jump species? Where did it come from? Is it manmade? I wanted to be sure about what we were dealing with.

Bear's owner, Mr. Kahn, hung around a lot. He visited the animal every day for many hours at a time. The limitations of the New Mexico Veterinary Clinic hindered our moving forward with a proper diagnosis. Rick, still on his plague hunch, started the animal on a round of **Tetracycline** *without consulting me. The last few vials of blood I extracted from the dog became essentially useless because of the introduction of the antibiotic.*

After a week of us being there, the animal seemed to return to normal. His bark became normal and hearty again, his compulsion to eat anything in front of him stopped, he became active and alert, and all lumps had cleared up. Against my better judgment, Rick signed the release papers that Bear had a clean bill of health.

But I'm not sure the Tetracycline was a cure. In fact, I believe it was more of a mask, hiding what was really going on in the animal.

This disagreement put a strain on Rick and my relationship. He became even more ambitious and independent, and I became more distrusting of his judgment as a virologist.

A month after our encounter with the U Virus, Rick was offered a position as Head Virologist leading a team at the **Plum Island Animal Disease Center** *on* **Long Island, New York.** *I think it'll be good for him, as he's always had a high interest in animal diseases. In Rick's absence, I'm now able to begin writing my manifesto.*

~October 13

Contacted Mr. Kahn for an update on Bear. Mr. Kahn sadly informed me that last week, Bear breached the fence of the home and has not returned.

~October 24

Called the New Mexico Veterinary Clinic to follow up on blood samples from Bear and to see if there have been any reports of suspicious animal behavior recently. I was informed that Dr. Anne Rennard no longer is employed at the clinic, and there are no files or records of a German shepherd named Bear having been treated at the facility.

~November 10

Amber and I are both shaken up by what happened because Holston assured us we were immune, that we couldn't be re-infected, but we both saw his face and he had the mark. He was one of us, an Altered, most likely a Feral because neither of us remembered him from the Re- Assimilation Center. I don't know. I don't see how any drug could have done that to a person—make them act that way, do those inhuman things. I've seen people high on drugs before—a kid named Frankie Z used to come to gym class tripping on LSD all the time. What we saw the other day was beyond a drug high. The man's eyes were brimming with infection; there was no doubt about it.

And that's why this is extra scary for us. Was Holston wrong? *Can* we be re-infected? What does that mean? I feel kinda naked at the prospect of being *that* again. The sensation of being out of my mind, out of control, uninhibited...

Liberated...

I shake my head back and forth as if to shake the last thought from my brain.

We've become accustomed to taking what the media says with a grain of salt, so right now, Amber and I are conducting our own investigation. I scour through Holston's files looking for anything that would point to possible re-infection or a second Outbreak, and Amber is on her laptop searching the internet for any other reports that would seem odd or out of place.

"News reports say that the crazy man we saw on the side of the road devouring a rabbit was high on drugs," she says.

"Oh, so guess we weren't the only ones who noticed."

"They're comparing it to a case that happened in Miami back in 2012. Some guy, high on a drug they called "bath salts," stripped naked and attacked a homeless man on the MacArthur Causeway. They called him the "Causeway Cannibal," and they referred to it as a Zombie Attack."

"Well, yeah... the attacker ate the homeless man's face off!" I exclaim. "That's small time, baby. Talk to me about really eating people."

My comment doesn't amuse her, and she sighs loudly.

I look over at her. Her knees are curled up between her body and the edge of the kitchen table. Her eyebrows are scrunched together, and her fingers swiftly dance across the keyboard making gentle *tap tap* sounds. "Listen to this," she says, stopping her fingers' assault on the laptop. "This whole Miami Cannibal story is just weird. At first, they thought he had taken some synthetic drug and went all crazy."

"Yeah. You said bath salts."

"But the initial toxicology reports say they only found marijuana in his system."

"So, *no* bath salts?"

"Yeah, no bath salts. Weird. But then *later* on, it was revealed that, 'a number of undigested pills were discovered in his stomach but have not been identified.'" She straightens her back up tall and slams her palm on the table like she's uncovered some major mystery. "What do you make of that, huh?"

I run my hand across my stubbly cheek. I haven't shaved in a few days, and I'm due. "I don't know. Is there anything after that, like a follow up or something?"

"Nope. Nothing. They just let it go. The man who was attacked got pretty messed up. His eyes were gauged out, nose was deformed. And then, well, something else tragic must have happened in the world and the Miami Cannibal guy got forgotten."

"I never liked the nose," I say, thumbing through Holston's papers.

She looks up from the computer screen, white light washing over her pale face. She purses her lips and raises one eyebrow. "Don't even go there." And she goes back to her search.

I smirk to let her know I was joking around. Well, partially, but she doesn't need to know the real truth. I did hate noses. Too much bone and cartilage. Took too long to bite through. Now eyes were a different story! I always wished the human body had more than two because *I could pop those little gelatin suckers in my mouth all day long, and...*

I shake my head again and I feel my cheeks get hot. What the hell is wrong with me for thinking like that?

Focus, Griffin. Focus.

Suddenly, her eyes go wide, and her arms shoot up into the air. "I might have something here! Three days ago, the same day that we saw Rabbit Guy, there was a report of a man in California who attacked his wife out of the blue. It says: 'Perry Greene, of Santa Monica, is now in police custody after viciously attacking his wife and stepson in what authorities are calling a bizarre act of violence. Greene, 43, allegedly bit his wife on the shoulder following an argument, then chased his stepson through the backyard before police arrived. Mrs. Greene was treated for minor wounds, and Mr. Greene was being held for psychological evaluation. No word yet on whether or not drugs were involved. Mrs. Greene's son was not harmed in the attack.'"

I click my tongue against the roof of my mouth. "Doesn't mean anything," I say, and she looks back at her computer and goes back to *click clicking* at the keys. "People are crazy. They do crazy things. That's the way of the world."

"Mmm-hmm," she answers with a suspicious tone. "How are your little catch-up dates with the people in California going?"

"Fine. I really don't think there's a connection between the Greenes and the Altered from..."

"Oh no? Well, what about this?" Again, her arms shoot up over her head and she claps her hands together. "Out of Long Island, New York. Two days ago, a day *after* Rabbit Guy. It says, 'Orient Point, Long Island. Two individuals are being held in custody after a supposed bird torturing spree. Miles Walton, 27, of Riverhead, and his cousin, David Pettigrew, 28, of Safety Harbor, Florida, are accused of capturing, torturing, and killing a nest of bluebirds. Police were alerted to a disturbance at the Orient Inn where the two men were vacationing. That was when they found Walton and Pettigrew engaging in what authorities describe as "bizarre behavior." The birds were found decapitated, and their wings appeared to have been bitten off. Both men are being charged with aggravated animal cruelty and endangerment of a protected species. Bluebirds are a commonly found on Plum Island, which is just two miles from Orient Point, and are protected under the New York Audubon Society. At this time, it is unknown how the men were able to acquire the animals.'"

"Bird eaters? That's all you got for me to work with?"

"What? You don't think that's strange?"

"I do. I definitely do. But..." My voice trails as something in my memory awakens. Something hits me. Something about what she said from the New York report.

"And both reports say, 'bizarre behavior.' What do you think that means?" she continues.

"Wait. Did you say Plum Island?"

"Yeah, why?"

"Holston mentioned a Plum Island Animal Disease Center in one of his journal entries. I think Trager works there, or at least he did."

She perks up again. "Do you think there's some kind of connection?"

"Could be. Not sure. Maybe you should find out all you can about Plum Island. Find out anything you can about Rick Trager, too. I have a feeling that Holston was trying to tell me something, and..." Her face darkens, and I stop in mid-sentence, "What? What's wrong?"

"Be honest with me, Griffin. Do you think we're gonna turn again?"

I shake my head no. But the look on her face tells me she doesn't believe my half-hearted effort.

"You're not doing very much to convince me, ya know."

"I'm sorry. No. I don't think we can turn again."

"That wasn't my question."

I cock my head to the side. "Well, what was your question?"

"Not do you think we *can* turn again, but do you think we *will* turn again?"

I shake my head 'no' once more, and she nods in acknowledgment, but I know she's not convinced.

Truth is—I don't know if I am, either.

6

I'M SHAKEN AWAKE OUT OF A NIGHTMARE WITH SWEAT dripping down my temples and neck. I'm kinda rattled because sleep has been a constant dreamless cycle, and this one really got to me. The good thing about this dream is I can't remember if it was something that actually happened, or something that my mind manufactured. I was running and screeching around the cul-de-sac of my old house, and in my right hand I held a fistful of hair. It was a long, blonde ponytail with half of the scalp and fragments of skull bone still attached to the end with a pink hair tie.

For a few moments, I try scanning my conscious memory, searching for a pin-point moment that would confirm or deny the validity of the memory-dream, but nothing comes through. I'm still in that half-asleep, half-awake phase where the part of you that is still in the dream world is fighting against the realization of self-awareness. I wonder if I'll always feel like I'm trapped between two worlds: dreaming versus reality, killer versus hero, human versus Altered.

Amber sleeps next to me with her legs curled up to her chest. There's a pile of papers scattered at the edge of the bed that has spilled onto the floor. She stayed up late doing her "investigative" work. I close my eyes and try to go back to sleep, but the construction crews are in full swing, and there's no way I'll be able to rest with all the noise and rattling within the apartment. It's 7:30 a.m. I guess six hours is all the sleep I'm gonna get for now.

I've lived in this one bedroom, one-and-a-half bathroom, 700-square-foot apartment at The Luna Vista Apartment Complex since I left the Re-Assimilation Center, and from day one there has been some type of restructuring going on. Brandon is a fairly big town on the outskirts of Tampa, but because it wasn't as heavily populated as the big cities, the overall landscape wasn't hit too badly. Businesses were hurt the most because of the looting. If people had just stayed in their homes and rode it out, they would have been okay. There are a lot of apartment complexes in Brandon, too, and most survivors sought refuge on the top-level floors of the buildings and were fine until help came. See, zombies can't climb stairs. I would know...

I'm restless, like my body is yelling at me to get up and start the day, so I slowly pull the covers off, roll over on my side, slip out of the bed, and sneak out the door so as to not disturb Amber. A low hunger growl rises from the pit of my stomach, but I ignore it and make my way to the kitchen table. It's littered with Holston's papers, and Amber's laptop is still opened up. I sit down and begin sorting through everything. Holston's personal notes have been the most interesting to me because I don't have to decipher too many medical terms. He wrote it the way he spoke, and I feel that I get the best insight into his thought process by reading it. At least that's what I tell myself.

●

Since Drs. **Joel Williams** *and* **Adolph Schultz** *have joined the team, we've been making significant progress on a prototype vaccine. Williams is a brilliant man who has a true knack for working with chemical compounds. Schultz is more of the gregarious type and sometimes lets his charismatic nature overshadow his keen insight. I am glad to have both men working with me on what could be the most important venture of my career.*

~November 8

●

Joel and I are now testing my **prototype vaccine** *on four female cats that were exposed to the U Virus. They're responding well.*

~January 15

•

All test subjects expired within five days of being injected with the vaccine. One suffered heart failure, the other three died from their severe seizures. Adolph thinks we need to adjust the **albumin** *to make the serum more stable. We are all in agreement that the U Virus is* **not zoonotic** *and can be contained to the animal kingdom. During one of our breaks, the three of us spoke about a possible mutation of the U Virus that could jump species. I am so tempted to consult Rick Trager on this case, as he has knowledge of the virus. I think I'll suggest to my team we take a trip to New York, even though I can't stand Northern winters.*

~January 30

•

All right. All right. I confess. I sit here going through Holston's journal, wanting to tear my own face off, not because I want to torture myself with boredom, but because I'm avoiding the inevitable—the file that follows the journal, the one with all the names of the Altered, the one that tells where they live and what they're up to and if they're dead or alive. And there's one in particular who I've been purposefully avoiding.

Eugene Watkins.

AKA: 16.

There was something off with him when we met at the Re-Assimilation Center. His overall aura and vibe was sketchy and erratic. I'm glad I didn't know him before the Outbreak. Guys like him were always a mess—drugs, burglaries, and whatever other kind of mischief tweakers get into. I considered myself lucky for not running into him, but for as much as 16 sickened me with his greasy hair and his twitchy eye, I felt bad for him in a way. Was he like that because he reacted badly to the serum, or was he like that because of the way he lived his life before he was infected?

I can't even imagine what his life was like Before, only because mine was so charmed. I took for granted my loving parents, the nice home they provided, my sister—even if she was a brat—the fact that money was rarely an issue in the King home. Even my last name—*King*. A name to describe just how we lived. Like kings. Now, I think of how stupid I was for not being more grateful for what I had.

The notes on Eugene Watkins confirm my original hunches: he attended few meetings of Alt Home over the last few years, his address seems to change every three months or so, no phone number on file, yet he manages to get his blood work checked at the clinic as per schedule.

Must be afraid of a relapse.

The address that's listed for him is in downtown Tampa, and I'm not at all excited to head out that way for a visit. Before all this, I rarely ever went into Tampa, and now I'm not too anxious to see what has become of the city. However, the only way I'm going to be able to check up on Eugene is if I physically get over there and make an appearance. I write Amber a quick note and leave. 'Cause if I think about it for too long, I'll psych myself out and not go. Guess I just need to rip the Band-Aid or bite the bullet or do whatever those stupid expression that fits this scenario.

Heightened voices come through on the car radio telling me of yet another bizarre attack. Like the ones that have been happening recently. The tones of the broadcasters sound worried, almost panicked. Those are emotions that they get paid to hide, because no matter the situation, they are to report the facts with no tonal inflection that would indicate their opinion or emotion. But I catch on to it. The slight upward sound of an "a" at the end of a sentence, making it sound like a question rather than a statement. Or a little touch of shakiness in the words "bizarre behavior." To the human ear, these miniscule nuances wouldn't even register, but for me and my Altered perception, I hear everything. And everything is telling me there's trouble enough to rattle even the most stoic of reporters.

"This latest attack out of Kansas once again prompts officials to advise any and all Altered to report to their local clinic for a blood screen."

Why? To round us up for the internment camp?

"... in addition to the Altered survivors who were initially treated at the now defunct Re-Assimilation Centers, Homeland Security estimates there is an additional five to ten thousand Altered within the population that did not receive treatment directly following the Outbreak."

Oh, that many? I had no idea...

"The CDC, in conjunction with both Homeland Security and The World Health Organization... all untreated Altered survivors to voluntarily step forward and register with your local Alt Home facility to receive proper counseling and rehabilitation."

"Really?" I say out loud. I'm so distracted by the news report that I nearly miss the turn off. I jerk the steering wheel to the right and follow the directions from the file.

I slow down when I reach the pink, one story home with boards covering the front windows. My stomach turns over, and for a second I think about hitting the gas pedal and going back home. I hesitate for a few minutes then pull into the broken concrete driveway. Paint peels from the stucco, broken glass from the shattered windows litters the front walkway, the grass and trees are overgrown practically swallowing the side of the home. Can this even be called a home?

I breathe in letting a fresh wave of oxygen fill my lungs. My chest puffs out and I exhale slowly watching it shrink back to normal size. My knuckles barely touch the cracked wooden door when it flies open revealing the darkness within. A figure emerges from behind and peeks his head out just enough for the morning light to reveal his face.

16. Eugene.

His head darts side to side surveying the area, his straggly brown hair swishes against his face and strands get stuck at the corner of his mouth.

"Eugene?" I say.

He looks at me and ducks head down. "You alone?" he whispers.

"Uh... yeah."

He jumps out and grabs my arm. "Good, get in!" He pulls me into the house and quickly slams the door behind him.

We stand in a cracked tile foyer, and he pats me down. "Whoa! Whoa! Whoa!" I exclaim, backing up.

His eye twitches at me. "Just gotta be sure. Just gotta be sure." His hands shake and he swats at the scar on his face. It's larger and more pronounced than any other Altered I've ever seen, and I figure he must have put up quite the fight when they injected him with the serum.

CHAPTER 6

"Eugene," I say calmly. "Do you remember me?"

His neck involuntarily jerks to the side, and he puts a hand on my shoulder. "Of course, 24. Of course!" His smile reveals a mouthful of missing and rotted teeth. It's a knowing smile, like the one you would give your best friend from elementary school at some 20-year-reunion party. He scratches his head and flicks something onto the floor. "Man, what in the hell are you doing here? How did you find us?"

"I'm helping the doctor. Dr. Holston, not Dr. Graves," I say quickly. "Dr. Holston died about a week ago, and he asked me to make sure everyone was okay."

He crosses his arms over his chest and starts scratching at his shoulders. It looks like he has track marks up and down his arms, but I can't be sure. Some look old and scarred; some look fresh and scabbed over. They're too jagged and oddly shaped to be track marks, though. Who knows what kind of drugs he's into these days!

"You work for them?" a voice calls from a room off the foyer.

Startled, I bend in closer to Eugene and try to avoid his rotten breath smell. "Who's here with you?" I whisper.

"Oh, don't worry 'bout Jimmy. He's Kool and the Gang, if ya know what I mean. He's a Feral, but don't say that to his face, or else..." His face twitches up and he runs his forefinger horizontally across his throat. I get the message, so I nod.

"You alone?" he repeats.

"Yeah. Nobody with me," I say. "Is it just you and Jimmy staying here?"

Eugene waves his hand in the air wildly. "Dude! No way! We're like a family, ya know? Gotta keep it all together. Gotta watch out for each other."

"Eugene, you know this guy?" Jimmy says as he materializes from the other room.

Eugene takes a step back and extends both his arms. One hand touches Jimmy's elbow, and the other touches mine in a communal and welcoming gesture. "Jimmy, man," he closes his eyes, "this is 24. 24, this is Jimmy."

Jimmy is about my height. His dark hair is long and matted with dirt and knots. He has a lanky build that kinda slouches to one side. His long face reminds me of a horse's snout with deep-set elongated nostrils and frayed whisker hairs protruding from his chin. I take back what I thought before about Eugene's scar. Jimmy's is even bigger, almost like a giant, raised flap of skin with a pronounced hole on the side of his face.

I put out my hand to shake his. “It’s Griffin,” I say.

Jimmy doesn’t accept the offer of a handshake, and after an awkward moment, I retreat my hand and put it in my pocket.

Jimmy stares at me hard. His upper lip curls slightly as if there’s a foul smell in the room. Well, the only foul smells are coming from him and Eugene and this dilapidated house, but I’ve learned that people can’t really smell their own scents. Regardless, he’s giving me this *look*. He’s disgusted with something, and that something is *me*.

“You’re a RAT?” he hisses.

“Excuse me?”

“Dude,” Eugene interjects, “RAT—Re-Assimilation Treated.”

We’re rats to them. *RATs*. You would think that we’d all be in the same boat, the same family, the same race, but even among us Altered there’s a division that I’m seeing for the first time. Jimmy hates me—not because I have a job, or I’m clean, or I own a car, or I have a pretty girlfriend, or because I’m a young, white male. None of that matters. Hasn’t mattered in two years. Jimmy hates me because I was treated, and he was left behind. In his mind he must think that makes me privileged or something, like I’m some kind of Altered snob—The Inhuman 1%. If only he knew what really went on at the Re-Assimilation Center! At least he didn’t have to endure test after test, and let’s not forget the psycho-bullshit stylings of Drs. Warren J. Graves and Wendy O’Hare!

“If that’s what they’re calling us these days. You do know Eugene was there, too, right?”

Jimmy balls up his fists at his sides and lowers his head to better meet my gaze.

There’s a part of me that wants to say, “Come at me bro,” but there’s another part of me that wants to run back to the car and get the hell out of there.

“Jimmy, Jimmy,” Eugene coaxes. “It’s all good, man. 24’s on the level.”

“But he works for them, Gene,” Jimmy protests.

“No. I don’t,” I say. I hesitate. “It’s complicated.”

Jimmy runs his fingers through his hair, and I notice he’s got those strange track marks, too. “Nah man,” he says. “Ain’t nothing complicated.”

CHAPTER 6

"Dude," Eugene says, "We're at war, man. It's us against them. We gotta all lay low for now. Do our thing, ya know."

No, I don't know, but I say "yeah" anyway.

Something crashes to the floor in one of the back rooms, and in perfect time with each other, the three of us swivel our heads.

"Who else is here with you?" I ask.

Eugene nods in the direction of the noise. "Come with me." And I follow him and Jimmy down a dark hallway into a kitchen. A woman cleans milk from the floor, while next to her is a toddler strapped in a highchair.

She stops when I enter the room and her eyes go wide when she sees me. She recognizes me, and I recognize her right away as well. It's 7.

"Crystal?" I say.

Crystal tenses up and freezes. Her gaze is like the stare of a deer caught in a car's headlight. Slowly she gets up from the table, walks over to Eugene, and whispers in his ear. Jimmy sits at the table and pets the little boy's hair.

"Dude," Eugene says to me, "she wants to know if you're here for Troy."

The baby. The two year old. The little boy too big for the highchair, but who sits obediently anyway. "No. No way."

"'Cause man, that time when that lady came over to the house on North 26th, she was all about examining Troy, and poking Troy, and she was all like, 'let me take him overnight for medical observation and stuff.' We hightailed it outta that joint as soon as she left."

"DCF came to take the baby away?" I ask.

"What's that, man?" Jimmy snarls.

"The Department of Children and Families. They're a social services group that shows up when they think a child is being abused or something," I say. I stare straight at Crystal, and she cowers behind Eugene. How could she subject her child to this kind of life? This is exactly what Holston was trying to avoid with Alt Home. My temperature starts to rise, and I have to control my anger. A sensation in my stomach brews, like I want to leap across the table and rip out her throat for being such a crappy mom.

Eugene takes a step forward and extends one of his arms behind him as if to shield Crystal. "Hey man, it wasn't nothing like that, okay. Troy's in good hands, you hear? Besides, that lady that was snooping around wasn't no social worker or nothing. She didn't have no badge or government ID."

"Yeah, that bitch's only ID was her scar!" Jimmy chimes in.

"She was Altered?" I say, puzzled.

Eugene's shoulder spasms forward two times. "Yeah, she was *something*."

"How long ago did this happen?" I ask.

"I dunno," Jimmy answers. "Month or so."

Crystal has not stopped staring at me since I walked into the kitchen. She backs away from Eugene and walks over to the high-chair. "Come up?" she whispers to the boy, and he stretches his arms waiting for her to free him from the seat. As soon as she dips down close enough, he latches on to her neck instantly, and she slides his long body from the baby chair.

I gingerly move forward as if I were approaching a wild animal—delicate and slow movements so not as to frighten the creature away. Crystal's grip on Troy tightens when I get closer. I extend one hand out to touch her shoulder and the other to touch the boy's back, the same way Eugene did to connect me to Jimmy, as if to say "it's okay, we're family, we're Kool and the Gang." She relaxes at my touch and smiles a closed mouth smile.

"He's beautiful," I say.

Her green eyes brighten, and her smile opens up, and I smile back at her. There's no other word to describe the child. He's beautiful, and I can't help but stare at him. His skin is shimmery, like someone spray painted a thin coat of gold all over his body. He doesn't have that gray-skin look like Eugene and Jimmy. His hair is a mass of platinum corkscrew curls that contrasts his against his tanned skin tone. But the most extraordinary feature is his eyes—two unusual crystal jewels, white and green, infected and cured, all at once. He's unlike anything I've ever seen—human and Altered—a perfect combination, an anomaly, an aberration, something that shouldn't or couldn't possibly exist in this world.

More Altered than Altered.

Crystal whispers something in his ear and he looks right at me, hypnotizing me with his magic eyes. "Hi, Ten-ty Foh," he says and giggles.

His voice makes my heart warm, causing any anger I felt toward Crystal to melt away. I can't help but chuckle at the surrealism of it all.

"You can call me Griffin," I say, my voice raising a slight octave higher, ya know, how you lift your tone up when you speak to little kids.

He reaches out and touches my cheek. His soft forefinger rubs over the bump under my eye. "Giffin," he says and looks at Crystal. He does the same to her scar. "Momma," he says.

"And where's Gene?" Crystal says in a high-pitched mother voice.

Troy playfully crinkles up his button nose and points at Eugene. Everyone exclaims "Yay!" in unison, and Eugene goes over to give him a high-five.

"Where's Jimbo, little man?" Eugene continues the game.

Troy snorts with laughter and points to Jimmy, and again, everyone shouts "Hooray!" and claps.

Troy wriggles his hips and slides down from Crystal's embrace. She pats him twice on his bulging bottom and he waddles off into the other room. She quickly follows after him.

"Diaper change," Jimmy mutters.

Eugene pulls out a chair. "Sit down, man."

"Ya know, Eugene," I begin as I take my seat, "you guys really oughta think about getting yourselves a phone."

Jimmy throws his head back and slams a fist on the table. "Out of the freaking question."

"No way, man!" Eugene chimes.

"But, don't you think with the baby and all. What if something happened? What if there was an emergency?"

"Like Gene told you," Jimmy snarls, "we take care of it. Phones never did nobody no good."

"Dude, Jim's right, man. They can use your phone to track you and stuff. It's better off that we're phone-free, ya dig?"

"I just don't want..."

"End it, buddy! You heard Gene. No phones."

"Okay, okay. Got it. No phones."

There's a moment of silence as the three of us stop to listen to Troy playing with something in the other room. His laughter fills the run-down house with a temporary joy that I can't explain.

Eugene's eye twitches something awful, and I sense that he wants to tell me something. He shifts in his chair, scraping the legs across the laminate flooring until he finally hunches over to get closer to me.

"So, you checked up on us," he says. "Do we 'check out' ok?"

I nod slowly. "I'd say so," I say. "As long as you guys are keeping up with your blood tests, Troy is safe and healthy..." my voice trails a little because I really don't believe that.

"Then you should be on your way, right?" Jimmy snarls.

I nod again. "Uh, yeah. I'll be getting out..."

"Jimbo!" Eugene scolds. "C'mon, man. 24 is our guest. You could be a little nicer to my old friend."

"Yeah, yeah," Jimmy scoffs. "Once a RAT, always a RAT, right Gene?"

"Dude, it ain't even like that and you know it!" Eugene says with an almost defeated tone. Like, they've had this conversation many times before. The one where they debated who was better off, and who was more privileged than whom, and how their war-stories compared, and who was the 'harder man.' All posturing bullshit, if you ask me.

Eugene leans in closer to me. "Do you ever wanna go back, man?"

"Eugene!" Jimmy yells.

Eugene waves his hand in Jimmy's direction as if to silence him.

My eyebrows scrunch. "What do you mean?"

"Do you ever wanna feel that... that... *rush* again?"

Jimmy stares a mad-dog glare at Eugene. "Don't even go there, Gene!" he warns.

"I told you, Homeboy is all good in the hood, Jimbo. Trust me."

"What rush? Go where?" I repeat like a stupid parrot.

Eugene cocks his head to the side like he can't believe I don't know what he's talking about. "C'mon, 24," he sings, "don't you play dumb with me! Haven't you ever just thought about that feeling? Like, ya know, the feeling when we were changed." He smirks and reaches into his pocket.

I know exactly what he means...

"I guess so, I mean, I don't know. Maybe? I have dreams and all that, but..." I'm stuttering, like an idiot. I guess being here for as long as I have has rubbed off on me. "I've heard stuff on the news about people getting crazy acting infected, but..."

Eugene goes into a closed-mouth giggling fit like a little kid. *Like Troy*. Apparently, his laughter is contagious, because even hard-ass Jimmy starts to chuckle.

"What's so funny?" I ask.

"Yeah, guess the plague is really catchin' on," Jimmy says, and the two of them are now in a rip-roaring state of laughter.

Eugene pulls out an orange medicine bottle from his pocket and slams it down on the table in front of me. "This, my man, is Black Death." He pushes down the top and twists it open. Inside the bottle are black oval-shaped pills. He reaches two grimy fingers inside, pulls one out, and holds it up to my face. "My guy in New York comes down and hooks us up every couple of months." The pill drops into his palm, like a magician performing a magic trick, and he quickly puts it back in its bottle. "You only go back for a little bit, but when you're there..." he pauses to close his eyes and breathe in "... ain't nothing like it, man."

Jimmy nods his head, reveling in some kind of ecstatic memory.

Eugene puts the bottle back in his pocket. "Of course, we do it in a controlled environment. And we make sure everyone is safe and secure. We can't be re-infected or nothing, right? So, we help each other out."

Jimmy extends both his arms. "That's what family's for."

Close up, I realize what I initially thought to be drug-inflicted track marks are actually *bite* marks.

Bite marks. From each other.

I stare in disbelief. Mouth opened wide. Throat getting dry.

There is a drug. A drug that turns you back. And I don't know how I feel about this.

Eugene clicks his tongue against the roof of his mouth, breaking me from my trance. "So, if you ever, ya know, wanna get wild again, just come on by and see your old friend 16!"

7

I LEFT EUGENE'S SOON AFTER AND WENT TO THE MEDICAL Center for my shift. I left my phone number with him, just in case anything happens. Anything, like what, I don't know. I figured it was okay to give him that info because they don't have a phone and it's not like he's gonna call me to chit-chat. I more so wanted to give him the option to call in case anything happens with Troy. I couldn't care less about the others—Eugene, Jimmy, Crystal.

On the drive over to work, I called to check in with Patient 320, Calvin Banks, from the Texas Re-Assimilation Center. He yelled and cursed at me. Said he was fine. Said to leave him alone. Said to "tell the bastard doctors to go to hell." I told him that I had just visited two ex-patients at a crack house who were worse off than he was, and that he ought to be thankful for what he *does* have. He proceeded to tell me to go to hell, too, and do other things to myself that I'd rather not repeat. Oh well. Can I blame him for being angry?

Once I got to work, I *got to work*. Seeing Eugene and Crystal, and meeting Jimmy and Troy completely added a new layer of vision for me. *Especially Troy*. Holston had said that Troy's blood was different and interesting, and I wondered if he had gotten the chance to actually meet the child. I wanted to get a better understanding of what Holston was talking about, so on my nightly mission to the blood lab, I pulled Troy McKenna's entire medical history and made photocopies so I could evaluate it at home. Doing that was risky because I had to get the timing of when I got in and out of the lab just right, and I was *this close* to being spotted by one of the other janitors on duty. Getting arrested right now is not top on my priority list.

Hopefully, when I get home, I can find something in the records that will jive with Troy's medical chart, but who am I kidding? I have no idea what I'm doing! I don't even know what I'm looking for. I'm just going under the hopes that maybe something will magically jump out at me and make sense.

What didn't sit well with me was what Eugene said about the woman wanting to take Troy. She was Altered, and that situation was super shady. I'm starting to think maybe Eugene is right about not having a phone...

The lights in my apartment are off now, and I step into the darkness like stepping into the pit of the unknown.

"You left a mess on the table when you went out," Amber says. I track her voice to the couch. It's 1:30 a.m. Usually she's asleep at this time.

I snap on a lamp light, and in the dim shadows I can see her makeup is smeared under her eyes. She's been crying. A lot.

She jumps up when she sees me and latches onto my waist. I take a step back to catch my balance and throw one arm across her shoulders. "I'm sorry," I say. "I'll clean it up later, no biggie."

She pulls away from me. "No. No. I took care of it this afternoon. Which is a good thing 'cause..." She pauses, and I brace myself for the onslaught. This is what I have dubbed 'Amber Tirade Mode,' and it's about to happen in 5, 4, 3, 2... "Graves and Trager came to the apartment today. They were looking for you. Said they were cleaning out Holston's apartment and offices and they noticed that some of his things were missing. Some things of his that were 'paper in nature.' That weirdo actually said that. Paper in nature. He must think I'm a freaking idiot! And then, yeah, so they said they were covering all their bases, and they knew you had recently been in touch with him, and they wanted to see if you knew anything, and it's a good thing I cleaned up your stupid mess because no sooner had I put all that crap in the manila folder, those two goons were knocking at the door, and..."

I hold up my hands in a surrender pose. "Okay, okay," I say gently. "Slow down. Slow down. Breathe, baby, you're turning blue."

Tight-lipped, she noisily sucks in air through her nose.

"Now, exhale," I coax.

She squints her eyes and lets the air out the same way it came in. "Start from the beginning, okay?"

She plops herself onto the couch, props her elbows on her knees, and holds her face in her hands. "They know, Griffin," she says, muffled in her palms. "They know what you have." She looks up at me. "They know what you have, and I think you should give it to them."

Her words stab me. "No way!"

She looks up at me wearily, broken, defeated, tired. "Do you trust Graves?" I continue. "And that Trager guy? I know you sensed something was off about him. Holston didn't trust him. He specifically told me to keep his files out of Trager's hands. Something's going on, Amber."

"Yeah, I know! I read some of Holston's notes today. He thought that Trager-man stole samples of the U Virus from him, and that's why Holston stole Trager's notes and hid them in the pages of that stupid fairy tale he wrote. Have you read that yet? Super creepy. Look, at this point, I don't care if Trager organizes a second Outbreak. It wouldn't matter to us, right? We can't be re-infected! So, who cares? Let everyone else burn. I'm just so over it."

I don't respond. The look on my face is all she needs to change her tone.

"We can't be re-infected, right?" she says again, but this time with less certainty.

"I'm not sure that's entirely true," I say.

She perks up, sits straight up at attention, and lowers her eyebrows in concern. "What's going on, Griffin?"

"Something's not right. The attacks, Graves setting up shop in Tampa, Eugene and his crew..."

"Who's Eugene?"

"16. There was no phone number listed for him, so I went to visit before work."

She places her hands on her knees and leans forward. "And?"

"It was just... weird. The house, the people, I don't know. 7 lives with him, and some Feral guy named Jimmy. I met the baby, too. Troy."

"Okay, but what led you to believe..."

"They have a drug. Something they call the Black Death. Eugene says he gets it from some guy in New York every couple of months or so. I don't know all the details about how it's made or anything like that, but the gist is this: it turns you back. Temporarily, of course, but whatever it does to you, it turns you back. Infected."

She jumps up from the couch, runs her fingers through her hair, and paces back and forth in front of me. "Rabbit Guy?"

"Yeah, Rabbit Guy."

"How long does it last? Do they go out and kill people? Oh my God! Griffin! We need to report this..."

I grab her arms to stop her from moving. "No. We don't need to do anything like that. They do it in a safe place, like they babysit each other and stuff. 16 and that Jimmy guy had bite marks on their arms, so I'm guessing when they do it, they bite each other. I don't think they go out killing people, Amber. I don't think the drug lasts that long, anyway."

She shifts her head up to meet my eyes. "Don't think? You didn't do this drug with them, did you, Griffin?"

"No! No! Not at all!"

She pulls her arms hard from my grasp and takes a step away from me. "Did you *want* to do it? *Do* you want to do it?"

I don't know what to say because I'm not sure how I feel about the Black Death. The worst time of my entire life was when I was infected. The thought of being like that forever was worse than a death sentence. The things I did... the horrible, inhuman things I did will haunt me for the rest of my life. But the *feeling* of being infected... of having strange blood course through my veins... the prospect of feeling that way again... temporarily...

"This is a game to you, isn't it?" She puts her hands on her hips and leans to one side. "You get off on sneaking around at your job and making your little phone calls. You don't give a shit about redemption!"

She catches me off guard with her accusation. "That's not true," I say, but the tone of my surprised voice doesn't do much to convince her. Or me, for that matter.

"When we get spit on, or turned away at restaurants, it doesn't bother you. When the news people say things like 'concentration camps' and 'Altered' in the same sentence, you don't even blink an eye, do you?"

"I don't know."

She taps her bare foot on the hardwood floor. The thumping sound penetrates me, rumbling in my calves. "You don't know? You don't know?" Her voice rises with anger. "How does it make you feel,

Griffin?" She spits out the dreaded looney-bin doctor mantra. Now she's crossed the line.

I clench my fists. "Don't try to psycho-analyze me!" I snap.

"Wow! That's a first! Finally, some emotion from you. So, you *can* get angry!"

Her condescending tone grates on my every nerve, and my vision starts to change. A filter of red trickles in front of my eyes. I take a step forward and my boot thuds hard on the floor in a menacing way. It startles her. Her shoulders tense for a split second, and she takes another step back. I sense her breath quicken in fast spurts of inhales and exhales, like she's afraid...

...Of me.

"It's like you're living in some kind of fog, Griffin," she continues, her fear softening her voice a bit. "Like, you're not even alive. You're walking between worlds in some kind of zombified haze. You're more of a zombie now than when you ate people, you know that?"

"Real nice," I say sarcastically. "Nice to know what you really think of me. I'm glad the truth is finally coming out."

"I say these things because I care about you, Griffin. And I care about *us*. You're with me, but you're not. Not really. Would you even be with me if not for this?" She points at her scar underneath her right eye—the raised bump of hardened flesh protruding from the side of her face like a permanent Scarlet Letter. "Am I even the type of girl you would have dated before the Outbreak? Do you even love me? 'Cause we've been together for nearly two years, and I don't think you know a thing about me from Before."

Yes. I care about her.

Yes. There's a part of me that does love her.

We share a bond. A common ground. A secret. But that special secret we share is no longer enough for her. She wants more. I don't love her the way she wants me to love her, or rather, I *can't l*ove her the way she wants me to love her. She wants me to love the high school cheerleader with lots of friends, and good grades, who'll probably go to an Ivy League school. She wants me to love the 'good girl with a bad streak,' who goes to drinking parties and flirts with all the guys, and the girls, just for the fun of it. She wants me to love the do-gooder animal shelter volunteer who tries so hard to give back to the community.

But I don't.

I can't.

I can't because I don't know that person. That person no longer exists and will never exist again. The Amber Fields of Before is gone. There is no more Before. The sooner she realizes that, the better.

I look at her with a pained expression. "Amber, why do you have to go there? I thought we were happy. I thought we were on the same page. Can't we just be happy with..."

Now *she t*akes a step towards *me*. Her fear has subsided, replaced with a new emotion. "Happy?" she screams. "Happy with *what*, Griffin? Happy with being outcasts? Happy with being public enemy numbers 24 and 25?"

I throw my hands up in the air and shrug my shoulders. "What can we do?" I yell back. "Storm the White House and demand change? Get in our DeLorean and go back in time?"

She takes another step towards me and with both fists clenched she pounds on my chest. "I'm serious!" she yells as she hits me again. "Stop making a joke out of everything! Every time we start talking about something serious, you make some kind of sarcastic remark, or crack some corny joke. I'm sick of it, Griffin! Can't you be serious for once? You're either numb or joking! I can't take it!"

Her hands rise up to go at me a third time, but I grab her forearms in mid-air and squeeze her so hard that the lower part of her body dips to the side in hope of a release. I don't let her go. I force her to look at me. "Stop it, Amber!" I command, but she flails around, trying to break free.

"Let me go!" she wails and continues to writhe.

I tighten my grip, my short fingernails dig into her thin flesh. She squeals from the pinch. "Are you gonna stop hitting me?" I say forcefully, digging at her arm a little harder.

"I said let me go!" she spits back.

"Are you gonna stop!" I scream again, my voice filling the room.

She stops wriggling, and her body goes limp. I ease up my hold on her, but I don't let go. Her head dips down in the space between us and her shoulders bounce up and down with every sob.

"You can't even tell me if you love me or not!" Her cries are muffled, and I barely make out what she says.

"What? What are you talking about?"

She lifts up her head. Streams of tears roll down her face the second she locks eyes with me. She breathes in to compose herself. "You can't even tell me if you love me or not," she says calmly.

"I don't love you," I say, and her body kinda dangles in my hold for a second. "I don't love you from Before. That's not going to ever happen, Amber, because you're not that person. But I do love you Now. This. The strong-willed woman who's not afraid to challenge anyone in this world. I love you Now. The You, Now. The ex-killer with nighttime secrets, whose eyes twinkled a little when I talked about the Black Death. This is who I know. This is who I want to know."

She stares at me with her crystal blue eyes. The lamp light catches the corners of them, and the light refracts from the line of tears. She looks so sad. Lost. Beautiful.

Delicious.

We say nothing to each other. We don't have to. Our gaze says it all. I tighten my grip on her arms and pull her closer to me. She lets out a startled squeal but accepts my kiss when my mouth locks on hers. Unlike the other parts of our bodies, her lips are warm, and I savor the heat from them, bending down and continuously going back for more, as if the warmth of her lips will somehow transfer heat to my own Altered temperature. I let go of her arms, wrap my hands around her back, and pull her even closer. She throws her arms around my neck and holds on to the back of my head, as we continue to kiss—passionately, violently.

I move my head to her neck and continue my mouth's assault there. I pull the strap of her tank top down her upper arm and my teeth gently graze the flesh between her collarbone and shoulder, making her shudder with goose bumps. Her breathing becomes shallow, almost panting. She's breathless. And my heart pounds at the sight of her bare shoulder. Peach-colored skin with a patch of freckles on the top side. I continue to kiss her mouth, her neck, her shoulder, moving up and down her right side, while all the while resisting my primal urges to bite, to chew, to *consume...*

"I know you want to do it," she whispers in my ear. "You can fool yourself and try to fulfill whatever oath you promised to Holston, but I know."

I stop to look at her. I narrow my eyes and she leans in close to my ear again. "Black Death." She bites at my earlobe and uses her teeth to move down the side of my neck. This time, I'm the one who shudders. My eyes roll back as an electric wave passes through my body. I grab her hair and pull her head back, forcing her to stop, forcing her to kiss me again. Her nails dig into my shoulder blades, and once again, I open my mouth, bare my teeth, and scrape them down the side of her neck and down her upper arm.

"Do you ever wonder what I taste like?" she says breathlessly, seductively.

Without even thinking about it I answer, "Always."

She pauses for a second and pulls her body back slightly from our embrace so she can see my eyes. "So, why don't you try me?" she says as she moves and glances at her shoulder.

I can't help myself. My hand massages the back of her upper arm. I tug at the flesh, roll it back and forth between my fingers, relishing in the dichotomy between the tight skin and layer of juicy tissue beneath. Her body tenses and she closes her eyes.

She breathes heavily when I kiss her neck again. She moans when I lick the dip in her collar bone.

She whispers, "yes," when my teeth nibble the top part of her shoulder.

And she screams when I bite into her bicep.

8

I NEVER DID DRUGS IN MY FORMER LIFE. THE IDEA OF being out of control and not in my right mind never appealed to me. My best friend, Josh, and I would sometimes go out into his father's garage and steal some beers, but that was the extent of my 'experimentation' years. In middle school, this kid—Frankie Z—started smoking pot. He formed his own little stoner clique and thought he was a bad ass because he was twelve and getting high all the time. Meanwhile, he looked like an idiot every time the teacher called on him to answer a question and he was so stoned he didn't even know what day it was. Anyway, Frankie Z graduated from marijuana to cocaine to LSD and eventually to heroin. I remember this one time in eleventh grade—I was in the media center doing some research for some English report. He comes waltzing in, high as a kite, sits down and sparks up a conversation like we were best buds. Somehow, during the course of his babble-fest, I asked about his drug use, and why he was always hopped up on something. I remember clearly as day. He answered, "It was fun at first, but now I'm just chasing the dragon." Being a non-drug user, I didn't understand what he meant. As a matter of fact, I just took it as some drug-induced mumbo jumbo. But now? It all kinda makes sense.

Chasing the dragon.

You get a taste for something. Something that completely fills your soul and whets every imaginable appetite you may have. It feels good, whatever it may be. It feels so good that you don't ever want the feeling to end. When the experience is over, the memories haunt you. The memories are so strong and so clear that if you close your eyes long enough, you can feel the warm sun beating down on your face, or smell the gray sky ready to snow down upon you, or feel the rush of the rollercoaster zipping you into oblivion, or the thrill of meeting a new girl and bringing her back to your place, or the supreme head change from an injection of heroin in your veins, or the taste of hot blood exploding in your mouth as you bite through a piece of flesh. So, you want more. And you do everything you can to reclaim that feeling.

You chase the dragon.

Only problem is this—the dragon is a dream, a myth, a fantasy, because nothing will ever feel as good as the first time you had it. Even the memories are sometimes sweeter than the reality.

Amber swishes in front of me in the kitchen. She's busy packing up an old-fashioned picnic basket for our 'special outing' today. It's August 4th, my 20th birthday, and she says that she wants us to have some normalcy in our lives, so she's prepared a traditional picnic lunch at some remote woodland area or park or whatever, and that we're going to relax and enjoy the day like a normal couple. The thought makes me cringe. I fear she's once again grasping at the invisible straw of the past.

Normal couple? Is she serious? We're anything but normal. The facial scars we have scream to the world that we're not normal. The little yellow sundress she's wearing forces the world to see that we're everything but normal, because as she glides happily across the kitchen floor, I catch a glimpse of the wounds on her legs—human teeth marks that would make any normal person do a double take. When she bends at the waist to grab something from underneath the sink, a piece of a bandage on the back of her thigh pokes out from underneath her dress.

Memories of me chasing the dragon.

I'll play along because I know it'll make her happy, and she really is trying hard to make sure that *I'm* happy.

We drive out on I-75 to a place called Lettuce Lake Park. It used to be a county-run park that boasted hundreds of acres of natural preserves. It used to be a place where newly engaged couples would have their professional photographer take pictures of them out by the sprawling lakes, or families would go to spend the day enjoying the wonders of nature right in the middle of an industrial city. All of that changed when the Outbreak occurred. Lettuce Lake Park was sectioned off as a refugee camp for survivors in the area. They had tents set up and a makeshift outpost with guards patrolling 24-7. From what I've heard, the CDC came in and used the park as one of their gassing control points without knowing there were encampments in the woods. They gassed the area and pretty much killed all the survivors who were stationed there. The humans. On a mission to capture one, maybe two, Infected people, they ended up killing nearly 100 humans. There wasn't an Infected soul to be found.

When the realization of what they did hit, they essentially sealed off Lettuce Lake Park for good. No one's allowed in. No more picture-perfect scenes for young, attractive couples. No more camping and day trips for the average family of four. Just let whatever animals are left roam free and throw up some warning signs with a biohazard symbol that reads "No Trespassing, Restricted Area."

Of course, we ignore the warning signs and climb over the chain link fence to get in. Amber leads me down an overgrown path, holding my hand and smiling brightly at me. She breathes in through her nose, and exhales with an "Ahhh."

"You know where we're going?" I ask.

"Oh yes," she says cheerily as she swings the picnic basket at her side like a little kid.

"Been here before?"

"Yeah. My parents used to take me and my sister here all the time." She points to her left. "Over that way, behind those big old trees, is the observation tower that looks over the lake. It's like a big wooden fort with three platforms. When you climb up to the top, you can pretty much see the entire park."

Great. I was right.

She's taking me down her memory lane, a place and time from Before, and I honestly and truly do not want to make this journey. My stomach feels sick and growls. Not from hunger, but from agitation.

Her head perks up to one side. "Was that your stomach?"

I nod.

"Hungry much?"

"A little," I lie.

She smiles wide, flashing me her perfectly straight teeth. In my head, I envision her at twelve years old, bucking in pain against the dentist's strong arm as he pries the silver train tracks from her teeth. *Nobody's teeth are that naturally straight.*

I get agitated again, and my stomach roars.

She giggles in her hand. "Oh, don't worry," she says. "We'll take care of that tummy in no time."

Great.

She holds on to my hand and guides me to a small wooden walkway that snakes around the greenery and natural surroundings. Everything is dense—the trees hang over, heavy with green leaves, providing ample shade from the morning August sun; the grass has worked its way through the wooden slats of the bridge, tickling my ankles as I pass through; and the animals and bugs are in full swing—there's scurrying and wing shifting sounds all around us. I have to admit, it's all pretty in this unkempt, overgrown state. It's natural. Normal. Without the touch of human hands. Without the stomping of human feet—the way it was intended to be.

We come to an open clearing surrounded by Black Mangrove and River Birch trees. The only reason why I remembered the names of them is because I had to do a report on Florida agriculture in the fifth grade, and my teacher, Mr. Cruz, was all into nature and wildlife. It kinda startles me to remember pieces of information like that. Those memories come to me at the most bizarre moments.

Amber opens the picnic basket, pulls out one of our bed sheets, and lays it on the ground. "This is a good spot, don't cha think?"

I sit down and fold my legs over in what my little sister Sydney used to call 'crisscross-applesauce.' Looking around I say, "Yeah, it's nice," but I've lied again. Honestly, it doesn't make a difference to me either which way.

She sits down across from me, propped up on her knees, and begins unloading the picnic basket. My stomach muscles get tight as I anticipate the façade of normalcy to cover me like a blanket of broken glass. Bottle of wine, cheese slices, buttered rolls, pepper spray...

Pepper spray?

I do a double take. There's no wine, or cheese, or rolls, or little apple slices with caramel dipping sauce! Amber lays out a vial of pepper spray, a rolled-up line of rope, a kitchen timer, a first aid kit, and a bottle of water. She smiles and hums like she's so proud of herself.

I raise an eyebrow at her. "We're not having a picnic, are we?"

"Well, yeah, sure we are," she says coyly.

"So, you wanna explain to me..."

There's a rustling over by the trees, and two figures emerge from the thick foliage. "Found ya!" a voice says.

Amber claps her hands together, "Excellent!" she squeals. "Right on time."

Now I'm completely confused. Amber stands up and races over to them. I stand up to get a better look at who it is that's so excellent to be here.

Eugene and Jimmy.

Like a little kid, Amber skips back over to me. Her dress rustles up showing her cut up knees. In her hand is an orange medicine bottle. I'm starting to see the bigger picture.

"Close your eyes and put out your hands," she says smiling.

I'm not five. This game is not amusing to me, especially since I already *saw* what she was holding. But she looks so happy, so pleased with herself that I can't help but play along.

I oblige her request, and when I feel the bottle drop in my palm, I open my eyes and try to appear as surprised as I can. "What's this?" I say with mock surprise, because I know what it is, and quite honestly, it scares me a little.

She leans in and kisses me on the cheek. "Happy birthday!" she says.

I bring the bottle up closer to inspect it. There are four pills within and a label on the side that has some doctor's technical instructions (probably fake), and as I scan the fine print, the word *Zombaxin* jumps out at me...

"Surprised?" she asks.

A line from an old movie pops into my head: *"If I woke up with my head sewn to the carpet, I wouldn't be more surprised than I am now."*

Surprised isn't even the word. A tumult of emotions passes through me: Surprise. Anger. Fear. Anticipation. Hope.

"Hey man, your lady here says it's like your birthday or something," Eugene says as he and Jimmy reach our spot.

"Uh huh. Sure is," I say nodding my head.

Amber's face twists. "You're mad. You're mad at me."

I clutch the orange bottle in my hand. "No. I'm definitely not mad."

"Okay, so what's wrong? I thought you would be happy."

"He's friggin' scared!" Jimmy bellows.

I glare at Jimmy like I'm going to kill him, and Eugene's head starts to twitch, sending his greasy hair back and forth in front of his eyes.

Amber looks at them, then back at me. She wraps her hands around mine—around the one that's cradling the Black Death. "I want to know you," she says in a low voice. "I want to share that experience with you. I want to know you like only *I* can know you. Does that make sense?"

Her eyes gleam with excitement. And it hits me.

I've had it all wrong with her.

Amber's version of Before, and my version of Before are two totally different ideas. She doesn't want me to love the person she was before the *Outbreak*. She wants me to love the person before she was *Altered*. She wants me to love the *Infected* Amber, the crazed lunatic Amber, the killer Amber. The need has been inside her, too—brewing, churning, stirring, *aching* in the very pit of her soul. She's suppressed those feelings for far too long, and all of our biting and eating games that we play when the sun goes down can never be a real substitute for the feeling of being infected.

She moves in closer to my ear, taking my lobe in her mouth before whispering, "I want to hunt with you." Her words send chills throughout my body that both frightens me and turns me on at the same time.

"We're here to babysit you guys," Eugene says. "But just know we'll call on you to return the favor some day!"

I look over at him, down at the supplies on the blanket, and nod.

Jimmy folds his arms across his chest. I know he doesn't want to be here because he sees me and Amber as nothing but RATs. It makes me wonder why he was able to connect with Eugene? Eugene was in the same exact position as Amber and me, and yet Jimmy doesn't seem to have the same contempt for him. "I'll set the timer for two hours, 'cause that's usually what it lasts," he says, his voice gravelly and deep.

Eugene closes his eyes and waves his hands in the air. "Might be longer, though, Jimbo. They're first timers, remember?"

Jimmy moves to the blanket and picks up the timer. "I'm still setting it for two hours, Gene. That's what the pepper spray's for."

"Wait? What?" I quickly interject.

Eugene shakes his head wildly and snuffs. "Don't listen to him, dude. It's just a precaution. Just in case we can't get you to settle down. You'll be fine, just fine. We've never had to use the pepper spray."

"But we did have to tie that one guy up!" Jimmy laughs.

Eugene laughs back, his body bends forward and he puts his head between his legs. "Oh, man! Oh, man! Stop! Stop! Why'd you have to bring that up, man! That was the funniest thing..."

Jimmy's laughter is nearly out of control. "And he took that thing and..."

"And you... you... you were all like 'get the bastard!' And he dropped to the floor with it *still* in his mouth!" Eugene lifts his head up to breathe. Laughter tears stream down his face. He wipes them away and breathes out a "Whooo, whooo," to catch his breath and settle down.

Amber and I exchange a puzzled glance.

"Oh, don't worry about us, guys," Eugene says when he's composed himself. "Just reliving the glory days."

I look back at Amber. She unfolds up my fingers, takes the medicine bottle and opens it up. "You in?"

I nod, and she gently taps the side of it to release two of the four black pills into my palm. She looks over her shoulder and calls to Eugene, "How long before it kicks in?"

"Not too long," he replies.

"Could be quick, 'cause ya know... you guys are first timers," Jimmy says with a snarky smirk.

She plucks one of the pills from my hand and puts it to her lips. "Here we go," she says and pops it into her mouth. She swallows hard, puts the orange bottle back into the picnic basket, and motions for me to follow suit.

And I do.

I hold the little bit of Black Death between my fingers. My hand shakes something awful and I'm afraid I'll drop it. It looks like a piece of valuable onyx—a precious gemstone, a most sought-after commodity. I waste no more time, place the pill on my tongue, muster up as much saliva as I can in my mouth, and swallow it down.

The lump descends down my throat, and almost immediately I feel a pulsating heat radiate throughout my chest. "What the hell..." I mutter as the first wave of a drunken feeling sways me stumbling to the side. I look over at Eugene and Jimmy, but my vision gets fuzzy, like it's blurring in and out of focus. They're standing by a tree, smiles on their faces, pointing at me and Amber.

Amber's on all fours. Her face is in the grass and she's coughing. A black substance trickles out the side of her mouth, and...

All at once my muscles tighten up, like they're caught in a metal vice, and I, too, drop to the ground hard on my back. My head bounces off the grass, and I try to control it, but I can't control it, and the waves of electricity start to shock me and jerk me around and my lungs are tight, and my heart is on fire and my lungs can't catch any air and I'm convulsing, convulsing, convulsing. My eyes sting. I hear music in the distance, but I know there's not really any music, it's just the sound of my blood pumping the poison throughout my body, but the song is wonderful and inviting and temporarily lulls me out of this torment. But I could only be so lucky, because a heartbeat later, I roll over onto my stomach, uncontrolled, natural reaction. The metal taste rises up my throat and spews onto the ground. I shut my eyes, they sting so much!

I'm dying, all over again, this is the death. The Black Death. The hands of time to cradle me away and walk me to my fate and lead me to the watering hole, the watering gate, where I will sing with the butterflies and dance with the chickens and...

I can't focus. My mind swirls. Electric fire races through my limbs. I throw up one more time. It's thick, like the gak stuff a kid gets in those supermarket quarter machines, and it makes me gag. This is it, this must be the end. I can't stand the heat and these convulsions and this goo coming out of my mouth and the feeling of water in my ears. I roll on the ground and dig my nails into the brown earth and scream from the pain when....

It all stops. Just like that. The onslaught of torment ceases. The torture of the change releases its electric grip on my body.

And I open my eyes.

My new eyes. My quasi-infected eyes. And unlike the first time, I take it all in.

I stand up, and the familiar feeling starts to take hold—*run.* But I remember to control myself. I remember to hold back and put one foot in front of the other. Eugene and Jimmy are still by the tree. Babysitters. Slick brown hair like olive oil coated brownies. I inch over to them.

They're not afraid. They don't smell of fear or chicken or human smells, but they aren't odorless, that's for sure. I don't want them. At least I don't think I do. There's a hissing sound in my ears, and realize it was me actually *hissing*. At Jimmy. Jimmy. Jimmy. Smells like metal. A copper penny. Penny. Like metal medicine. Eugene, too. Not like people and their tasty food smells. Like metal. Hard. Cold. Steel. Metallic.

Eugene puts his forearm out to me like a police officer does with a training canine. He looks fuzzy and hazy and gray. I shut my eyes. Open them. Shut them. Open them. They are talking to me, but I can't make out their words. I hear them. But I don't. I want to tell them to speak louder, but when I open my mouth, only the guttural moans come out. I see them laughing at me, and my anger surges. I clamp my mouth on Eugene's arm, bite down, and tear away. His blood pours into my mouth and down my throat and I spit it out. It's vile. Like antiseptic. Like drinking hydrogen peroxide. A small chunk of his skin falls at my feet.

"Dude!" he yells through his laughter. I hear him now. "24 got me good!"

Jimmy laughs.

I stare at them. I know I'm moaning. They're still laughing.

Jimmy waves his hand in the air. "Go, man!" he screams. "Have fun!"

Is he smiling at me?

Then I remember—we're in an abandoned park! The only other people around are tasteless Altereds and my infected girlfriend. I have the run of the park and the animals within. Not wholly satisfying, but I might as well indulge temporarily.

I take off, howling like a wolf, and race deep into the woods.

While different from being truly infected, this is the closest feeling to it. I free my mind from the shackles of responsibility and just *go with it*. As I sprint, it's as if my legs are barely moving beneath me. I push passed the hazy veiled vision and inhale the scents of the forest, trying to locate a meal, because the rumble sounds from the pit of my stomach can only mean one thing...

I'm hungry.

Starving. Like I haven't truly eaten a thing in two years. All the processed foods and home cooked meals are no substitute for what my body craves, has been craving—flesh, blood, sweet fluid filled organs. To sharpen my teeth against exposed bone again just...

A foxhole.

Someone, somewhere, long ago asked the question about what kind of sound a fox makes. Well, I don't know anything about that, but when I reach my rigid hand down into the den where the babies lay waiting for their momma to return, the only sound I hear is the crunching and ripping and tearing and gurgling.

When I'm done with them—*one baby, two baby, three baby, four*—I head back into the forest, ready to indulge on some other delight. Animals seem to fall into my lap. Duck. Cat. Snake. I don't discriminate. I gorge. I feed. I fill my aching belly until I can stand no more. In the blood swoon, I stagger, barely a moan from my throat. I collapse onto my back at the lake's edge and notice a wooden observation tower before I close my eyes.

Must be the one Amber told me about. I'll have to remember to tell her I saw it.

9

I KNOW THAT SOME TIME HAS PASSED BECAUSE WHEN I wake up at the edge of the lake, the sun has shifted in the sky. The pulsating heat of midday no longer breathes down on my skin. If I had to guess, it's late afternoon—still hot, but less oppressive. I lay on my back in the grass right beside the big lake. Ants crawl up and down my arm, and when my vision comes into focus, I swat them away.

My vision.

I can see just fine. Normally. No more pseudo-infected fog gloom. I'm back to my old self. The drug has worn off. Well, that's not entirely true because I'm feeling some weird type of after-effects—my heart beats like a jack rabbit and there's a terrible, tremendous pain in my stomach that makes me want to...

I sit up and lean over into the lake to vomit. Black bile lays on top of the water like a poisoned oil slick. I try to stand up, but my legs are shaky and I'm afraid I'll fall into the lake.

I'm just gonna rest here for a little while.

I look down at my shirt. I'm covered in blood and gore from my drug-induced killing spree. As I begin to remove my shirt, I hear voices yelling my name in the distance. Eugene and Jimmy charge through the woods, screaming for me. I try to stand up, but a dizzy spell rocks me, and I plop back down to the grass. "Over here!" I say, but in my head, I screamed it. In reality, it was barely a whisper. My throat is hoarse and scratchy. It hurts to talk. I pray to someone that Eugene's Altered hearing heard it.

CHAPTER 9

"Oh God! There you are!" Eugene says frantically when they locate me. His face is twisted and they both race towards me. Jimmy puts his hands on his knees and lets his head fall in between his legs as he pants, trying to catch his breath. "Dude! Are you okay?"

I rub my temples. The sound of his voice echoes in my ears and makes my head pound. "Yeah, I think so."

"Alright, man. You gotta come with us! We gotta get the hell outta here!" Jimmy reaches over and starts grabbing at me to get up.

"Wait, wait!" I say through my dry throat. "I can't..."

"Jimmy, help him up!" Eugene commands. Jimmy glares at him like he either doesn't want to be told what to do, or he doesn't want to help me. "C'mon, man! We gotta get the chick and we gotta motor!" Jimmy bends down and hoists my arm around his shoulder.

The chick?

"What's going on?" I ask.

"No time! No time!" Eugene says quickly. "C'mon, man! Your lady is all messed up. We gotta go get her!"

I will myself to my feet and act upon instinct. I ignore the tightening pain in my stomach and hobble along with Jimmy as Eugene takes off ahead of us. We jog behind him for about 150 yards when I start to see blood splatters on the grass. At the base of the wooden observation tower, it's a massacre. I let go of Jimmy's grip and dart to the first set of steps to meet her.

Amber is sitting up, half-dazed, with her head in her hands. I call to her and she jerks her head in my direction as soon as she hears my raspy voice. When I reach her, she throws herself sobbing into my arms, almost knocking me off balance.

"What happened?" I ask. "Are you okay? Are you hurt?" I pet her head to try to calm her down and say, "It's okay. It's okay," even though I don't know what the hell is going on.

She buries her head in my shoulder and continues to cry. Eugene comes into my view, and I hold my hands up as if to say, "What happened?"

His face goes white, and his eyes open up. "Dude!" he says in a low voice. "Didn't you see? Look around you..."

I glance down over Amber's shoulder and the first thing I notice is that the back of her shirt is completely blood-soaked. I continue to pet her hair, but as I lift up my hand to stroke her again, I see there's wet blood on it as well. Then I look down to a pool of red. My eyes take in the horror of limbs and flesh and bone fragments strewn up and down the stairs. Blood coats the wood like a fresh glaze of reddish-brown paint, and in the corner of the square platform I see the heap of a body, or rather what used to be a body. *What used to be a human body.*

I put my hands on her shoulders and pry her away from me. "Amber? Amber?" I say, trying to get her attention, to get her to make eye contact with me. Her eyes are glazed over, and she looks at me, but she's not really *looking* at me. "Amber!" I say again, this time louder, raspier.

Her eyes snap to life. "Huh? What?"

"What happened?" I ask as I look down at the front of her. She moves her hand up and wipes the side of her face. Dark red smears up the side of her cheek.

"He wasn't supposed to be here, man!" Eugene says, pacing back and forth.

"What do you mean?" I say to him.

"Some homeless guy," Jimmy grunts as he climbs up the steps. "He shouldn't have been here."

She looks over her shoulder and lets out a blood-curling scream.

I pull at her and turn her face back toward mine. "Don't! Don't look!" I say.

"This is bad, man! Totally bad. What are we gonna do?" Eugene babbles.

Jimmy huffs again. "We ain't gonna do nothing. Stupid guy. Shouldn't have been here. Guess he couldn't read the biohazard signs."

Amber throws herself at me again. I hold her close, gripping her tightly.

Jimmy and I lock eyes. "As far as I'm concerned, your woman here did a good thing. We should just kill them all!"

"Really?" I snap at him. "That's not who we are! Let's not be who they think we are."

He laughs. Not a laugh, but more of a sinister chuckle. "Okay, RAT," he says, "you keep telling yourself that. But you know the truth. You took that pill just as fast as it came into your hand."

"Hey! Hey!" Eugene jumps in. "This ain't the time for that! What are we gonna do about the dead body over here?"

My head swims. I'm still trying to process the whole scene unfolding around me.

"Leave the damn thing," Jimmy growls. "Let's just get the hell out of here!"

"They're gonna find me. They're gonna arrest me. My blood is all over it," she whispers in my neck.

She's right.

Her blood is on file. She's a registered Altered and she's being tracked. Any little thing they find to use against her—against any of us—they'll nail her to the wall. We need to leave this place and get her as far away as possible.

"He's a homeless guy? Are you sure?" I say.

"Yeah, yeah," Jimmy answers. "Why else would someone be hanging out in a quarantine zone?"

I raise my eyebrows.

"Well, you know," he responds. "Other than doing zombie drugs. What's your point?"

"This is actually not a bad thing," I say, trying to rationalize the situation. "Who else is gonna be looking for him? No one. It's like he probably doesn't exist."

"Yeah, yeah!" Eugene chimes his face lighting up. "Who's gonna know? She can come stay by us for a while, until everything settles down, ya know?"

Jimmy opens his mouth to protest, but Eugene shoots him a look.

It's a bad idea. A horribly terrible idea. But right now, it's the only one we got, and in a sick way, it makes sense. I grab her shoulders and shake her again. "I want you to stay at Eugene's for a little bit," I say, looking directly into her eyes. She blinks a couple of times, and I shake her again. "Do you understand? You're gonna go with Eugene and Jimmy and lay low. Just until this all disappears. When I think it's safe, I'll come for you."

"Hey, hey, hey!" Jimmy yells, waving his hands in the air.

"No, she's going with you guys," I assert. "You're the only ones who are off the grid. And you know what'll happen to her if they find out. You know what'll happen to all of us."

We'd be tarred and feathered, for sure. They would round us up and quarantine us. Public hangings. Firing squads. You name it. For two years, a vast majority of the people have been looking for something—anything—to prove that we Altered are a threat to society. Amber just wrote all of our names on a full magazine of bullets for them.

I know he hates to admit it, but Jimmy nods. "Not so off the grid."

I narrow my eyebrows.

"Gene keeps telling the clinic our address every time he goes for his blood work."

"Well, they keep asking!" Eugene defends.

Jimmy huffs. "That woman came to the house the other day again, wanting to see Troy and stuff. Thank God Crystal had him out shopping with her, 'cause I told her that they weren't living with us no more."

"Yeah, man. We're packing up shop again. Found a place over on Nebraska Avenue."

"Fine, fine," I say, not really paying attention. "You just had your blood taken, Eugene?"

"Yep. Me, and Crystal, and the baby."

"Okay. When you get to the new place, make sure you only give the old address out. Don't let anyone know where you are. Lie, okay?"

Eugene nods, and his slimy bangs fall into his eyes.

Amber looks up at me. "What about my stuff?" she says in a low voice.

Her stuff? Her stuff? She just tore a man to shreds and she's worried about her stuff? I realize that she's not in her right mind right now, but please!

"It's all good," Eugene says reassuringly. "Crystal can take care of you. She can help you out."

Her eyes widen.

"It'll be fine," I say, trying to convince both of us.

We make our way to the car, leaving the murder scene behind us. I have Amber strip off all her bloodied clothes and put them in the picnic basket. I wrap her up in the bed sheet she had brought for our outing. She curls up in the backseat, and Jimmy sits next to her, but as far away from her as he can. Eugene is in the front with me. He doesn't buckle his seatbelt, and while I want to say something to him about it, I have a satisfying vision of getting into a car wreck and him being shot out from the passenger seat onto the concrete pavement, so I let it go.

"What the hell is that stuff, anyway?" I ask after driving for a few minutes.

"What? Black Death?" Eugene answers.

"Yeah. What's Zombaxin?"

"Oh man, that's just the clinical name for it, I guess." He puts his feet up on the dashboard and reclines his seat.

"How did you get turned on to it?"

He rubs his chin thoughtfully. "Bottom line is this, man. About a year ago, I was fiending for some meth. Like hardcore, dude! Me and Jimmy were tapped the hell out. So, I'm all crashing parties and stuff. Hitting the underground and all. Seems everyone was dry. So, Jimmy knows this Altered girl over on Kings Street who was having an AFO..."

"A what?"

"An AFO. It's like some weird Altered fetish party. So anyway, Jimmy says 'let's go.' And I'm like, 'okay.' So, I'm working the crowd, trying to get the feel if anyone's got any Ice..."

"Ice?"

He sighs, "Meth, Dude."

"Sorry, sorry, go on."

"So, I see this big dude in the corner of the living room, just hanging out and all. I ask Jimmy if he knows him. Jim's like, 'nah man.' So, I give him the head nod. Big dude nods back and I see his scar, so I turn my head to kinda show him mine. He nods again at me and tilts his head for me to follow him. Well, off I went! I follow him into that Altered chick's bedroom. It was all pink and glittery and shit, really stupid looking. Anyway, he whips out these pills... the Zombaxin. Says it's better than anything I've ever had. Better than pot, or coke, or meth. And at first I was all like, 'nah, I don't think so,' but he told me what it did and convinced me real good and I paid him like twenty bucks for two pills."

"Wait," I interrupt. "Where did *he* get it from?"

"Just listen!" he says, agitated. "So, I say to him, 'Big Dude! Where'd you get this from?' And he tells me this story about a guy in New York who knew some doctor who worked on the virus and stuff. Big Dude has all kinds of connections."

"Doctor? Did he ever tell you the Doctor's name?"

"Nah, nothing like that! It's all super secretive stuff, ya know? Big Dude hooks us up like every three or four months."

"Right after your blood tests?"

Eugene laughs. "Exactamundo, my friend!" and he turns the dial on the car radio.

"... on the US government's official position," it blares. *"Members of the AAC, the Anti-Altered Coalition are filing suit in court this afternoon to reverse parts of the Altered Protection Act that states any crimes committed in an infected state cannot be prosecuted criminally or civilly. Virologists, government officials, and even Altered sympathizers have pushed Congress since the Outbreak two years ago for laws to protect the Altered population. The Altered Protection Act has been the first step toward reform, but the AAC states that with the high number of unregistered Altered individuals, there is still a threat to the general welfare of society. This continues to be a prominent issue in the upcoming Presidential election this November, and both candidates are expected to..."*

I turn off the radio.

"Why'd ya do that, man?" Eugene wails.

"My head is pounding, Eugene. I just need some peace."

"I was infected," Amber says from the back seat. Her voice is thin and quiet, and I'm not sure if she intended for us to hear her.

"Yeah, darlin'," Jimmy says. "We all were."

"No. No. I mean, today," she says, her voice a little stronger. "I was infected *today*. The law says I can't be prosecuted for what I did. That counts, right?"

Jimmy chuckles at the stupidity of her logic. "No, baby girl, I don't think it counts when you purposefully turn yourself into a zombie and go on a killing spree..."

I shoot him a look in the rearview mirror. "Easy!" I scold. "Ease up on her!"

"Yeah, yeah," he relents.

I pull up to the battered house, get out of the car, and go around to Amber's side. I open the door and help her out making sure that the bed sheet is secure around her body. I hand Jimmy the picnic basket. "Burn this and that bed sheet when you get her into some clothes," I say.

Eugene knocks out a pattern on the front door like Morse code, and it cracks open. Crystal darts her head out, looks from side to side, and ushers us in. The house is dark and smoky, and there are a handful of people in the living room. I put my arm protectively around Amber and kiss the side of her face.

"Gene? What's going on?" Crystal says.

"I'll explain in a little," he answers, kinda brushing her off.

Troy pops out from behind Crystal's legs. He gives me a big smile and reaches his arms as if to be picked up. "Giffin!" he squeals.

I can't help but smile back at him. "He remembers me? How is that possible? We met once, like a few weeks ago."

"Oh, this kid remembers everything, man," Eugene says. "You tell him something once and it sticks in his little head. Photographic memory, or something."

Or something.

"Look, 24," Jimmy says, and as soon as he says my number-name, the people in the front room stop talking and start listening, "you probably should get going. Rip the Band-Aid, if ya know what I mean."

For as much as I hate him, he has a point. I need to get out of there. And not just for legal reasons. My unsettled stomach is starting to act up something awful, and I'm afraid I might not make the drive home without having to pull over and throw up.

Amber tenses up in my arms. "It's okay. You'll be safe here. Crystal will help get you cleaned up. You'll be fine," I say like I'm talking to a lost and injured child.

Her eyes swell with tears, but she nods through them. "Okay. Okay," she whimpers. "When are you coming back?"

I don't want to leave her. I don't feel safe leaving her with the tweaker Eugene, the timid mouse Crystal, and the Feral Barbarian Jimmy and his band of angry former-men. "As soon as it's okay to come back. Eugene is gonna take you to a safer place tomorrow, and when I can, I'll pick you up there."

It's pathetic. She's so out of it, I doubt she'll even remember this conversation. Jimmy nods at me, and I manage to get out a "thank you" before I leave.

I barely make it to the car, my stomach hurts so much. I close my mouth tight to prevent the vomit from coming up my throat, start the engine, and peel out of there as fast as I can—praying that I'll make it home alive.

As I come up the side stairs to the second floor, I pass one of my neighbors—some guy with a big gut, who I've seen around the complex many times. I'm having trouble getting up the staircase, but he doesn't even ask if I need a hand, or if I'm okay. Does he ignore me because he knows I'm Altered? Or does he ignore me because he sees the dark brown stains on my clothing? Or both? A normal person would offer a helping hand, right? Especially if you know the other person in some communal capacity like say, oh, an apartment complex! The little old lady needs help carrying her groceries up the steps and Big Gut Guy is probably the first person on deck to help her out. But me? I'm *clearly* in pain, *clearly* struggling, the blood on my shirt could possibly be my own. I could be stabbed, or shot, or dying, or....

...infected.

I stumble into the apartment clutching my stomach, doing everything in my power to keep the bile, and whatever else wants to come up, from coming up. I think my body is rejecting everything I ingested today, because my stomach keeps knotting up, contracting, and trying to force the strange and foreign substances out of it. The body is a miraculous place, when you think about it. Right now, mine knows that I was bad to it. I fed it a chemical poison then gorged on raw animal meat and blood. No wonder I'm in so much pain. My body must be so mad at me right now.

If I could just get to the bed and lie down...

But I barely make it through the living room when the inevitable happens, and I double over and puke on the hardwood floors. I curse at the mess and the thought of having to clean it up, but I think my body is finally calming down.

I breathe in through my nose, slow my racing heart, and settle myself down. I feel better. I sigh out loud and stretch out on the floor next to the mess. The sun is starting to set, and I look at the shadow shapes on the ceiling. I want to get out of these clothes and get cleaned up. Should probably call work to tell them I'm sick and not coming in. The smell from the floor makes me queasy again, makes my stomach ache and turn and...

...growl?

I can't be hungry! There's no possible way! I sit up and pause, as if I'm listening to my body—listening to the inside highways of stomach fluids and blood and breathing patterns and... there it goes again! Plain as day. A hunger growl! But this time it was more of a roar. And it hurts. The hunger pain actually hurts! I suppose it's plausible. I haven't really eaten human food in some time, and now, after expelling my stomach contents, it's really no surprise that I would actually be hungry.

I get up and walk into the kitchen, or should I say drag myself into the kitchen. Everything that happened today has definitely taken its toll on me, and I'm now feeling the after effects. I'm weak. I guess anyone who ran and hunted foxes and other animals for over two hours would be tired, too. I open up the refrigerator and freezer doors at the same time to see what's inside. Not much happening in the food department, but my stomach rumbles again and I know I need to just pick something to satisfy the beast.

Mudpie Madness Ice Cream. My favorite.

I open the carton and dig in with my fingers and start to eat, but this isn't what my body wanted. The cold ice cream almost burns, and the artificial sugary taste is like acid as it goes down. I rush to the sink and spit it out, pawing at my tongue to rid it of the taste. I go back to the fridge to start over again.

There's really nothing—a package of frozen peas, some cheese slices, a two-liter bottle of Pepsi, a package of steak from the butcher defrosting for my birthday dinner. The cellophane package oozes red on the sides, ready to be cooked up and eaten. I instinctively reach for it, almost mesmerized by the swirling red color against the plastic, and put it on the counter next to the stove. I pull out a pan, turn on the gas burner, rip open the package, and dump out the contents. The meat sizzles as soon as it hits the pan, and the juices bubble up all around it, the smell reaches my nostrils and my stomach growls again, telling me "Yes! This is what I want!" I stab at it with a fork, letting extra juices flow out in a sputtering pool of blood. I lick the fork, and the meat taste on the metal prongs makes my heart start to race.

I don't know why, but my stomach screams again.

I don't know why, but I turn the stove off.

I don't know why, but I pick the barely cooked piece of meat out of the pan with my bare hands.

I don't know why, but I bite into the raw steak—hot juices dribbling down my chin.

I don't know why, but my body finally feels satisfied.

10

FOR THE NEXT WEEK, I SCOUR THE INTERNET, AND KEEP both the radio and TV on all day. The only time I leave the apartment is to walk to the corner deli so I can buy as many newspapers as I can. I've told work that I have the flu. They didn't believe me at first, because who actually gets the flu in August? But when I said that my doctor thought it might be related to my "condition," the human resources woman clammed up right away and said to "take as much time as you need, dear." Anyway, I haven't heard a thing about the homeless man in the park. There have been reports of minor incidents, of people demonstrating "bizarre behavior," but no one has reported the death of another person. I'm surprised that the media people are not connecting the dots on this one. Well, maybe they are, and they're just not saying because they don't want to panic the regular people. Whatever the case may be, Black Death is definitely making its way around the country.

"Man Attacks Pitbull in San Diego."

"Teenage Girls Attempt Break-in at Bronx Zoo."

"Woman 'Stumbles' in Apiary."

And I start to wonder... all these instances of "bizarre behavior" involve animals or insects. Hell, I even had the sense to hunt for animals when I was high on Zombaxin. And the Rabbit Guy on the side of the highway, and the Bird Guys in New York. Of course, none of these cases have been confirmed to be Black Death related—I'm just assuming so because of the weirdness of them, and from what I witnessed and experienced first-hand. However, there was that one dude who attacked his wife, but that seriously could have just been some random psycho going nuts in a domestic dispute.

And now I'm puzzled with the thought of Amber. Why didn't she have the capability to reason with her instincts? Why wasn't she able to discern between the right and wrong? *Humans, no. Animals, yes.* When I think back to when I was really infected, ya know, bitten, changed, the whole nine, even then I was able to say to my slowly wasting brain—*Humans, no. Animals, yes.* It was only when the disease had been in me for too long that I lost control. When we did Black Death, it felt like the first waking moments of infection. I knew what to expect. The feelings were familiar. I *knew* them, if that makes any sense. When I was really infected, I was running wild for three months, but with the Zombaxin, it was more like three hours, certainly not enough time to have a complete and total mental break from reality.

But Amber did.

Whatever the drug did to her, it tapped into her old killer instinct. I don't know anything about Amber's timeline of infection—how long she was infected, how she handled the infection. Nothing. Nada. She's never really offered up those details, and to be honest, I never asked. The only person she probably would have told was Graves. 'Cause I know how he rode me, prodded and poked my brain, digging for some semblance of his version of the truth. And she's kinda a baby, ya know? She would have caved in to his questions and accusations. Now, I start to think that maybe I should have had those conversations with her. I should have talked to her openly and honestly about our experiences instead of just assuming we were one and the same. The only time she really talked about specifics with me was when she told me about her change. She told me she *knew* she had to make sure they were dead, so that means she *had* to be sentient, right? What kind of soul must a person have to just... just... *let go* like she did?

The day after I left her with Eugene and the Gang, I got a call on my cell phone, I'm assuming from Jimmy. I didn't recognize the number, and figured he was calling from a pay phone. He said, "At the new house. Everyone's good. Talk soon," and hung up. I haven't heard anything since, and it's been a week.

A week since the incident. A week since my girlfriend killed a man with her bare hands and ate him. A man was mauled, and no one knows about it. No one cares. He was just some transient, some homeless guy—nameless, voiceless, faceless (now literally). A week, and whatever was left of his remains are probably in the bellies of the creatures who roam those woods. All these stories of "bizarre behavior" are barely making front page news. Barely making a blip on anyone's radar. Is it possible that we got away with it? Everyone is just so wrapped up in which celebrity is cheating on her husband, or the upcoming Presidential election, policies of the country, and *the rally that's about to take place in Washington...*

The Anti-Altered Coalition is holding some kind of protest in front of the Historic Courthouse in Washington, D.C., today. They're the group that wants to put strict regulations on anyone who's Altered. I watched the group evolve over time—the first time I saw any action of theirs was when I was able to watch TV for a brief moment at the Re-Assimilation Center. Back then they were just a handful of angry survivors of the Outbreak, but now their numbers have amassed, and they actually have a strong voice in the media and the government. Who would have guessed that American people would be so outraged and non-accepting of mindless killers roaming around?

I chuckle at my own stupid sarcasm, but in all actuality, had the shoe been on the other foot, would *I* have been associated with the AAC? *Probably not.* I wasn't much for paying attention to politics and world issues when I was a human, and if I had survived the Outbreak, I probably wouldn't have batted an eye at those issues afterward. That's what happens when you're a privileged kid. That's what happens when you're a self-centered person without a clue. A bite on the shoulder really did change everything for me.

I turn up the volume on the TV. The amount of people gathered on the steps of the courthouse is alarming. They're out in full force today, that's for sure! Picket signs, custom t-shirts, hats—the whole nine—all lined up the steps of the front entrance. They're all about making waves, making noise, getting their name out there, being on the front of every newspaper, trending on every major internet site, and being the top talking point on the journalism TV shows.

"Justice for our dead!" they chant as the camera pans the crowd. It's their 'go-to' mantra.

The ticker on the bottom of the screen says that their big beef today is apparently the topic of 'registering' all Altered people. I'm already registered, says so on my driver's license—*Griffin Patrick*

King 024. Amber's registered—*Amber Justine Fields 025*. Eugene's registered—*Eugene Watkins 016*. But there are the Ferals—those who weren't initially treated in the Re-Assimilation Centers. Above anything, Ferals scare the AAC (and probably everyone else in the world, but that's another story), and they are trying so hard to get the government to pass a law making it mandatory for all Altered people to get registered.

Not just register, though. They want all Altered people to register and be *tracked*. Monitored. Which would mean, anyone anywhere who might get a little scared or 'uneasy' by us, could ask for our IDs. And because the words 'scared' and 'uneasy' and 'uncomfortable' are so subjective, it leaves giant question marks on human and non-human rights. Like Nazi Germany. "Show me your papers, please." As if showing them an ID card with a government issued number and sticker will make me any less dangerous of a non-person.

And it would be completely legal.

These are the types of things that Holston fought for us—to be freed of discrimination and stereotypes. He was a champion for the Altered—one of the few voices who rallied for us. Now with him gone, these lunatics might actually get their way, but all hope is not lost when I see a familiar woman walk through the crowd—Dr. Dorothy Oswald, Holston's niece. I know she's there to take up the torch for her beloved uncle. And if she's anything like Holston, I know she'll put up a fight in front of the judge.

The camera pans the crowd again. They've switched their chant to, "Why hide? We're on your side!" and I literally laugh out loud. The type of legislature they're trying to get through says just the opposite. I may be blind to politics, but I know what's really going on here. My momma didn't raise no fool!

"I'm on the steps of the Historic Courthouse today," says newscaster Jessie Holmes. She's a pretty little woman with short blonde hair wearing a soft pink business suit. She's one of those field reporters, so I see her on the news a lot. For some reason, though, today she looks out of place. Short. Tiny. Like a little kid in the center of a crowd of adults. Like the throng will swallow her up if given the chance. On camera, her voice quivers a bit. Nervous. Like she doesn't want to be there. Like she's never done this type of reporting before. But I know her! She's no rookie. I see her all the time covering late night car wrecks and SWAT team drug busts. She's been in there with the worst of the worst. But today? There's something off about her. The way she stands. The way she holds her mic. The way she curls her fingers on her right hand and rubs them against each other. Every now and then she glances over her shoulder to her right, and as the camera moves around to get a long shot of the entire crowd, the source of her nerves comes into full view.

Off camera, to her right, is a metal barricade guarded by police officers. Behind the metal barricade is another swell of people with their arms crossed in front of their chests, scowls on their lips...

...and scars under their eyes.

The Altered have shown up for the demonstration, too.

So, there she is—poor, sweet, little Jessie Holmes, smack dab in the middle. To the left, there's the chanting mob of the AAC, and to the right, there's the silent throng of the Altered. No wonder she looks so unnerved.

She walks up the courthouse steps, her puppy-dog of a camera man following obediently. She sticks her mic in a middle-aged man's face. "Sir? Sir? Can you tell me what you hope to accomplish today? What does the AAC hope to gain?"

The man blinks and looks at her with a blank stare. "Uhh... I think it's pretty obvious," he says. "Our government has let these people run loose for far too long. It's time they took better measures to ensure the safety of the American people."

"And how can the government do that?" she asks.

"We need to track these people! We need to make sure they are monitored all the time!" He gets a little agitated as he says it.

"But it's been two years and there really hasn't been any indication of a widespread threat," she says, playing typical journalist devil's advocate.

He looks at her like she just said the craziest thing in the world. "Well, I don't know about you, sister, but those things killed my whole family. And I'll be damned if one day they decide to wake up and do it all over again." He lifts up his head and howls to the crowd, "Tag 'em, or bag 'em!"

What the hell does that even mean?

Apparently, it means something to the crowd because they all join in. The camera flashes over to the barricade, and the Altered remain silent and still, but I feel their aggravation, and it's mounting.

CHAPTER 10

Jessie Holmes hops down a few steps and flutters over to a black-haired woman holding a sign on a wooden stick. Her sign says, "Justice for Our Dead." Jessie sticks the mic in her face. "Ma'am? Ma'am? Why are you here with the AAC? What do you hope the AAC can get accomplished today?"

The woman grabs the mic and puts her mouth directly on it. A muffled sound comes through the TV. "C'mon, people. Wake up! We're on the verge of disaster, *again!* Let's put these animals back in their cages!" She pumps her fist in the air then screams, "Whoooooo!!" and the group of people in her vicinity pat her on the back and clap for her, cheer for her.

Tag 'em, or bag 'em? Animals in their cages? What is wrong with these people?

Jessie Holmes walks down the steps, separating herself from the roaring crowd. "Are the concerns of the AAC warranted?" she asks into the camera, then looks down at a notecard in her hand. "To date, there has been no *activity* since the virus was isolated and contained. However, AAC members fear that without proper investigation, the virus might somehow mutate and cause another Outbreak. Virologists from the CDC are divided on the issue, and no clear answer can be given."

The live feed cuts out to a pre-recorded interview with a doctor wearing a lab coat in an office. The ticker reads *Dr. Adolph Schultz.* I know that name. He was on Holston's original team. "There is no way to tell what this virus is capable of," he speaks with a deep German accent. "Like any virus, the nature of Hz7RNA—the Zorna flu—is a very tricky one. There are many questions still surrounding its genesis. Its containment has been a blessing, but because this is a novel virus, we are unsure of its future. Mutation is always a possibility, as with any virus, and we have crews working round the clock to study every last aspect of its makeup, of its genetic code. For us scientists, this is quite an exciting time." He smiles and lets out a slight chuckle. "We're working with something so powerful and so awe-inspiring to the human race. To have something so magnificent in the palm of your hand..." he sighs—proud and truly in amazement, "...is beyond anything I could have ever imagined."

The feed goes back to Jessie Holmes. "That was an interview last year with one of the top virologists in the country. Dr. Adolph Schultz was one of the first researchers of the virus and helped to organize the initial efforts for containment."

The crowd behind her gets louder as a judge swiftly walks up the steps and disappears among the swarm and into the courthouse. Jessie Holmes touches her earpiece and says into the mic, "I'm getting word that Judge Chelsea Marin has just arrived and will prepare to hear the motion of the AAC. This is unprecedented and goes against all formal proceedings—yet another indication that this situation could be brewing to a head." She looks to her left, tentatively, and touches her earpiece again. "In a prepared statement earlier, Judge Marin said that she was open to hearing both sides of the case but would *not* allow any *non- registered* Altered people into her chambers. If that's any indication of how this hearing is going to play out then..." She stops, and a wave of terror washes over her face. She nods. "Okay, okay," she says still nodding away. "Let's see if we can shed some light on the other side of the issue," and she gingerly walks over to the guarded barricade. The noise from the AAC members lessens as she gets closer to the stoic silence of the Altered.

There must be thirty or forty of them. Ferals.

Jessie Holmes practically tiptoes to the barricade and sticks the mic up to the first woman she reaches on the front line. The microphone wobbles in her hand. She's beyond nervous, and it's starting to show. Any normal human would be able to see that now. The Feral woman doesn't even look at her. She shifts her hips and re-crosses her arms in front of her chest.

"Excuse me, ma'am," Jessie says with a quavering voice. "Ma'am? You're an Altered, correct?"

The Feral woman lowers her eyes downward and glares at Holmes. Holmes looks like a tiny ant next to the tall woman. I brace myself for the moment when the Feral raises her hand and swats the pretty little news reporter out of her way. But that doesn't happen, and I'm left watching, uncomfortable in the awkward silence.

"What are your feelings on the AAC's position? Are you yourself a registered Altered?" Holmes continues to no avail.

Holmes touches her earpiece and walks away from the woman when she realizes she's not getting a response. She approaches an Altered man, and tries the same round of questioning, "Sir, what are your thoughts? Do you have anything to say about the AAC's demands?" She's met with continued resistance. The Altered are quiet, calm, and most of all—pissed off.

It's painful to watch.

When she realizes she won't be getting answers from the opposing side, she reluctantly turns her back on them to face the camera. "I think their silence speaks volumes," she says. "This particular group of people has been through the unimaginable, and many wonder if they will ever be able to reclaim the life they once knew."

Another pre-recorded interview materializes on the screen; this time of a young black man sitting in a black leather chair. His head is completely shaved, and although the angle is from his mid-chest up, it is obvious he's wearing a hospital robe. There are tears in his eyes, and the bump of his scar sits just below his bottom eyelash line. *Too close to his eye*; *I'm surprised they didn't damage his vision when they injected him.* The graphic at the bottom of the screen reads, "Antoine Freeman 028." I vaguely remember him from the Re-Assimilation Center. Never had any sessions with him or any interaction at all, for that matter. *I have yet to check up on him, too.* The video footage is old, though. *And familiar.*

Graves's office at the Center.

I hear Graves's deep voice off camera say, "And then what happened?"

The tears in Antoine's eyes explode, and the camera zooms in close on his face making his scar look like a mountain of flesh protruding from a bushel of eyelashes. "I don't know!" he wails. My heart sinks for him. "I didn't want to hurt those people! I didn't want to hurt nobody! But I couldn't stop!" He sniffles and repeats in a whisper, "I couldn't stop."

Jessie Holmes reappears. "See, as the tension mounts, the two sides of the issue..." Her voice trails as the noise from the AAC group gets louder. The camera zooms in to reveal that some of the members have taken a blow-up doll with a black "Z" on its chest and start passing it around as if the doll were crowd surfing. As the doll passes from hand to hand, the members punch at it violently, spit at it, curse at it. One man punches the doll so hard, its blowup face smushes in and deflates.

The camera quickly swivels back to Holmes, who has not moved from in front of the Altered's barricade. She swats at that stupid earpiece, trying to hear instruction from her home base, when I suddenly notice some movement from the Altereds behind her. They had been like stone statues this entire time, but now, some of them were dipping their heads in toward each other and whispering. Probably talking about their formal statement or finalizing what they will say to the judge in appeal. A few of them reach into their pockets. Holmes continues to chatter away, but I keep my focus on the scene behind her.

I feel bad for them. They're probably taking out their drivers' licenses and determining who will be allowed to go into the courthouse to speak to the judge. It's kind of sad—my people being discriminated against in this way. It kinda makes me feel...

One Feral moves his hand from his pocket, up to his mouth, and swallows something. The two next to him do the same. My heart nearly stops as I watch this. *Then another*. Because I fear I know exactly what they are doing. *Then another*. And I have an urge to scream out "no!" to the television. *Then another*. But it's no use. No one will hear me. The damage is done.

In slow motion, the scene unfolds. One Feral crouches low, then the next, then the next. Heads go between knees. And a collective gurgling sound starts out low but gets increasingly louder and louder as the seconds pass. The noise from the AAC is so overwhelming, that no one even notices the inhuman sounds coming from the Altered group—the Ferals have ingested scores of Black Death, and are changing one by one by one by one... The cameraman notices something because he backs up, and the live video feed goes wonky. Jessie Holmes looks at him, puzzled, and a large box cuts to the screen at the studio. The news anchor there asks, "Holmes, what's going on over there? We're noticing..."

Jessie Holmes's box gets bigger again when the cameraman stabilizes. "Nope. Nope. We're okay over here, just some technical..."

A newly infected Feral jumps over the metal barricade, and latches onto the back of one of the police officers. He dips his head into the officer's neck and pulls his head back up releasing a red fount of blood onto the concrete.

The others take their cue from the first, storm over the barrier, and race toward the steps of the courthouse. Jessie Holmes screams as the camera zooms out to show a mass of Infected barreling into the AAC crowd. Like rabid wolves, they seem to glide up the stairs, and pounce on their prey. At once, bodies collapse to the ground in a heap as the horde descends upon them, painting the cement staircase with their blood. Deafening screams fill the air, people run in all directions, and shots ring out off-screen as the two remaining officers try to control the massacre before them.

My stomach wrenches into knots. I am dizzy. I want to look away, but I can't peel my eyes from the horror. One side of me is sick with disgust, and one side of me is cheering my brethren on.

The cameraman stumbles and the equipment falls to the ground on its side. He's either run off or been attacked. Voices from the studio come over the TV. One says, "Cut away!" Another says, "No! Keep rolling!" They must agree to the latter, because the sideway carnage continues.

Jessie Holmes stands in her spot between the steps and the overturned barricade. She's dropped her microphone. Her eyes are shut tight, body tensed up, hands balled into fists and clutching her own body. Like a lost little child in the middle of complete chaos. She's frozen. Can't move. Welded in her position by pure fear.

"Authorities are on their way to the scene..." the studio news anchor says in a clear, calm, voice, but others yell over the anchor to Holmes, "Holmes! Get out of there, now!" Holmes shakes her head wildly from side to side creating a swirling blonde storm around her face.

Then a wandering Feral snatches Holmes's hair from behind, yanking her head all the way back so that her torso is arched. Another Feral steps in front of her and plunges his hand deep into her stomach cavity. The last thing I hear before transmission ceases is the poor, sweet voice of Jessie Holmes, begging for her life.

"No! Please! Stop!"

And the screen goes black.

11

THE REST OF WHAT HAPPENED AT THE RALLY IS STILL A blur. There was chaos and screaming, and blood... *lots of blood everywhere.* Surprisingly enough, after Jessie Holmes was attacked and her cameraman's equipment was trampled and blackened out, another news team was dispatched to the scene almost immediately. *God forbid the American people miss out on the carnage!* When the new crew arrived, they kept a quasi-safe distance from the action, but their super-zoom lenses were able to capture images of the Ferals storming down the doors of the courthouse, people screaming and running for their lives, police and SWAT mowing down anything that moved, and the blood, blood, blood, blood.

In the end, the death count was at 54. That included AAC members who were attacked, three police officers, Ferals who were 'put down' by police, Jessie Holmes and Dwight Dillinger, her cameraman, and two AAC members who were accidentally shot in the crossfire. No one in the courthouse building was harmed, just shaken up. There were 12 lucky Ferals who made their way into the building and were able to escape the shoot-out on the front steps. Surely they were hunting for the higher ups, but somehow they managed to find their way into the various rooms within and hide out until the Black Death wore off. Unfortunately for them, those super-zoom camera lenses were able to reveal their identities, and within an hour, they were arrested and publicly hauled off to jail. I'm sure that normal people would not have objected to a bullet to their Altered skulls the second they walked out of the building, but that would kinda be against the law, now wouldn't it?

CHAPTER 11

They may not always get the initial facts correct, but I gotta tell ya, our media works *fast*! Within an hour of the ordeal, every channel had some type of coverage going on. News graphics and tickers said things like:

"Altered Attack at AAC Rally Confirms Possible New Outbreak"
"Are the Altered Waging War?"
"New Drug Suspected in AAC Massacre"
"Zombaxin and its Deadly Effects"

So, the jig is up. Black Death is out there, known to the public. Whether the government was aware of its existence beforehand and was just keeping it a secret from the general population doesn't matter now. They know. Everyone knows.

I can't look away. I'm glued to the television like a mindless drone. It's horrid and horrifying and shocking and unbelievable and yet so beautiful all at the same time. There's a conflict brewing within me, because, well, been there, done that. On the one hand, I know those Ferals hate me for whatever ideology they govern their lives by, but at the end of the day, we're all Altered. We've all gone through the same type of experience, and felt the same range of emotions, and suffered the same human injustices today. I feel proud of them for having the moxie to stand up for their rights, *our* rights, in such a frenzied public way. On the other hand, the way in which they handled it was completely mortifying. Innocent lives were lost. While the people of the AAC may have hated us, they didn't deserve to suffer and die the way they did.

Watching the brutality on the television really makes me evaluate everything I thought I knew and understood. I knew that hunger. I knew that feeling of starvation and liberation. I knew that burning fire vein-heat behind my eyes and that insatiable desire to feed. I revisited it not too long ago. I've been on *that* side. When I was bitten and infected, my humanity was taken from me, like a thief in the night snatching a small child from his bed. I did everything I could to maintain my sense of right and wrong, but in the end, the infection won out and eventually I was left without any control over my actions. I had no choice. What was done to me was done to me, and it wasn't my fault.

But to be an outsider watching the effects of infection? Well, that's something different all together. It was stomach turning to see the pools of blood collecting at the base of the courthouse steps. My brain still can't wrap around hearing someone scream one second then hushed into silence the next—never to scream again. The camera zoomed in real close to a Feral with whitened eyes and a gaping, bloodied mouth savagely tearing into the throat of her helpless victim. The Feral looked exactly like that—a feral animal, rabid with madness and hunger, soulless and devoid of any humanity. *Zombie*. It's also stomach turning to witness the bloodbath over and over again like our media outlets know how to do best. The footage is replayed numerous times on every news station and internet streaming service.

White eyes.

Bite.

Zombie howls.

Tear.

Blood.

Screams.

It's only 2 p.m., what must the children at home be thinking?

Black Death is a conscious choice. I know. I made that choice.

And it was wrong.

It was wrong. It was wrong. I know this now. I see this now. I knowingly and willingly infected myself. Even if it was only for a little while, the knowledge of my "return" played a role into that decision. When I took the Black Death, I knew it wouldn't last. I took it, and I let go. I enjoyed it. And even though there was a *sense* of infection with Black Death, there definitely was a major difference from the Hz7RNA virus. It wasn't the same. Black Death only mirrored the feelings of infection, like my brain knew it wouldn't last, but something else *inside me* knew it wouldn't last, too. With Black Death, there was almost a giddy feeling. Like I said, I enjoyed it. When I had the virus pumping through me, there was only pain, fear, anxiety, and hunger. I definitely *did not* enjoy that.

And for me, that's the devil of the Black Death. The fact that it *is* something of a recreational drug for us Altered doesn't make it right. When I did it, I was somewhat reserved, but when Amber did it, when those Ferals did it, it turned out drastically different. Just ask that homeless guy at Lettuce Lake Park or any of those AAC members today.

Oh wait, I can't...

No wonder people hate us so much.

I realize I never want to be like that again—whether it be involuntary or not. Despite cravings, anger, or curiosity, I will never put myself in the position to be infected. I need to take Holston's words to heart, and I need to follow through. He had the foresight to know the devastation that was upon the human race, and he entrusted me to see to it that measures were taken to prevent that from ever happening again. I promised him, and I have to take that commitment seriously and not treat it as some super-secret spy mission, like Amber called it.

Amber.

The thought of Amber overwhelms me, and I have a sudden urge to find her wherever she is and hide her away. The news is saturated with the AAC rally disaster, but I catch a glimpse of the bottom ticker (the place where they need to insert snippets of everything else that's happening in the world right now, but just isn't deemed important enough to get full coverage) and in a quick blurb I read, "Human remains found at Lettuce Lake Park... police investigating..." My stomach drops. We haven't gotten away with it, after all. I need to find her and get her some place safe—away from Eugene and his gang of Ferals and all the dangers they pose. As a matter of fact, I need to get Troy away from them, too. Me, Amber, Troy. We need to go. Need to get out of here. Of course, I don't know where we would go, or where we would even *think* to go.

Maybe Dr. Dorothy Oswald could help us? Holston's niece is definitely an Altered sympathizer, maybe she could help to point us in the right direction?

I should just go through some more of Holston's notes. I probably should have read the entire journal by now, but all of his entries were just shoved haphazardly into the thick manila envelope in no particular order. Hopefully, I'll pick up some clues or insight there anyway. Maybe he knew something about Zombaxin or Troy or a second Outbreak or something...

... anything...

Sequence parameters:

$P\,n<20\%\ \text{or}\ P\,m>80\%)\quad LogLD50=X_K-d\,(\sum p - \text{unknown})$
$LD50=Log^{-1}\,LogLD50$

<u>Subject variations</u>: *white mice, osprey, fetal pig, adult cat, sea bass, unknown?*

<u>Time frame</u>: *six weeks, start to finish*

<u>Components</u>: *U Virus, U Virus Variant 1, Vaccine Injectable 1, Vaccine Oral 1, Vaccine Injectable 2, U Virus Variant 2 (?)*

●

I've come across some of Trager's notes hidden within the pages of Holston's mish-mosh. There are pages upon pages of calculations, codes, and things that make no sense to me whatsoever. I flip through them all, coming up short, trying to figure what all of it means. It feels random to me, like Holston scooped up different papers and reports from Trager's desk drawers. Little of this. Little of that. Words that I do recognize are *U Virus*, and of course *vaccine*. And it doesn't take a scientist to figure out that Trager had samples of and was working on both. Being the head of a government-run animal research facility was the perfect environment to work his researching magic.

In Holston's journal, he goes deeper into what I've already assumed:

I hate to play tit for tat, but Trager has given me no other alternative. He wasn't shy about his dealings with me. He played coy at first, but like any child who can't lie to a parent, the truth came out. I knew right away he had taken the U Virus samples from the lab. To him, he justified it as 'equal work,' that they weren't mine to begin with. I explained to him that in the medical field, he should know better than to take research or anything of that nature without first consulting his team. He laughed it off, and half-heartedly apologized, saying it was an innocent rookie mistake. Rick Trager is a lot of things, and stupid rookie isn't one of them.

I unfortunately had to "return the favor" on my unplanned visit last month. And while I do not have any of his physical findings in my possession (I knew better to leave the lab undisturbed), I have obtained crucial code and sequences. Trager and his new team have been culturing the U Virus in many new and exciting ways. Their manipulation of the disease is both frightening and exhilarating at the same time. There are components for the first possible vaccination for the germ, and construction of the 1st viable oral form. I know in my heart this is all Trager's doing, and his "team" is nothing more than his underlings.

Trager is the brains of his operation, a true master of his craft. I can't deny that. He has been one of my best students and colleagues—thirsty for knowledge and a healthy appetite for the unknown. On paper, he is a true contemporary of mine. But Trager takes too many chances. He pushes the envelope too far. He stretches the rubber band beyond its limitations, and I'm afraid he's going to snap. In my later years, I've learned that sometimes the risk is not worth the reward, and sometimes pushing that envelope has severe consequences. I fear that Trager is going too far.

~August 7

Trager did an interview with the New England Journal of Medicine *last month. It was damage control for the recent scandal the Plum Island Animal Disease Center is enduring. One of the workers on the island blew the whistle on the Center saying that it's unsafe. Trager had him fired from his contracting job and he is suing. Since Trager is the senior virologist, he's been put on the frontline to take the brunt of it. This is something he is good at. PR. He assured the interviewer that the research on foot-to-mouth disease is crucial, and that the safety of the facilities is their top-priority. He provided data and inspection notices from third-party companies—documentation to satisfy the leeriest of believers. In the course of his interview, Trager said something about a new drug he's developing called "***Baxinalin***" which would be the answer should some of these diseases they work with ever "accidentally jump species."*

Baxinalin. I will keep my ear to the ground on this one.

~May 6

If the Hz7RNA virus (Zorna flu) ever mutated, I'm afraid of what the ramifications would be. Transference swifter. Infection more rapid. High resistance to antibiotics.

Troy McKenna may be the answer we are looking for. The end all and be all of infection. Should Zorna mutate, an antidote derived from the child's blood could put a stop to it. In fact, anything derived from McKenna's blood would be revolutionary.

Brief history of Troy McKenna: Troy's birthmother, Crystal McKenna, was approximately three months pregnant when she became infected with Hz7RNA. Birth father, unknown. Ms. McKenna was given the second iteration of antidote and became Patient 07 at the Re-Assimilation Center in Florida. She was approximately six months pregnant when she received the serum. Child's progress was closely monitored in utero. Child was born at approximately 36 weeks. Both mother and child were discharged from the Re-Assimilation Center shortly after the birth and are still under observation.

McKenna is a healthy child, showing no signs or symptoms of abnormalities. Physical features are that of a Melanesian child of the Solomon Islands, except with lighter skin tone. Eye color is completely unique, but the most distressing factor is his blood.

Upon observation, I have found that McKenna's blood possesses the typical Rh factor antigen. He does not have the A or B antigen, which would lead one to assume that he possesses O. This is not the case. What the child has is unprecedented. He has an O variant, something that upon first glance appears alien-like.

The child is a miracle in my eyes, as he has endured the unimaginable: human conception, infection of one the deadliest diseases known to man, and vaccination all before birth. One can only think of what it has done to his genetic makeup.

I would like to eventually run a full genetic code map on his DNA, however, I'm more concerned with his blood type. H.

H+ to be exact.

It just might be the permanent solution I am looking for.

~September 1

I put the papers down when my cellphone rings. I pray to someone that it's Eugene or Jimmy or Amber. I can't shake this feeling that I need to get her home. I need to stow her away somewhere—hide her away forever.

The caller ID reads "Brandon Medical Center." Just my job. Just the nurses calling me to probably see if my 'flu' has gotten any better. Maybe they're calling to tell me that I no longer have a job. Fired. No Altered allowed. I figure I should be feeling the backlash of the D.C. attack right... about...

I let it go straight to my voice mail, and when the notification dings indicating the caller has left a message, I swipe my finger across the front of the touchscreen and type in my code.

I expect it to be Nurse Edie and her sarcastically cheerful voice but am stunned when I hear the voice on the other end say, "Um... this is Dr. Graves. If you get a chance, please call me back. There are a few things I need to discuss with you."

12

I WRESTLED WITH THE DECISION FOR A FEW DAYS, AND ultimately, I made the choice to come in to Graves's office. He pretty much hassled me all weekend with his non-stop phone calls. After the fifth call from him, I decided to answer and see what he wanted. I guess my curiosity got the best of me. And he's no dummy, either. He knew that if he had told me what he wanted in one of his messages that I would have completely blown him off. Even when I answered his phone call, he was vague and mysterious-like. Said he wanted me to come into his office to 'talk.' Said he had some information for me and wanted my opinion on things that were 'going on.' So, I bit the bullet, so to speak, and came into his new office in Tampa. And of course, like a sign from Satan himself, the second I pulled into the parking lot, the thunder clapped, and the skies opened up, drenching me with a late summer storm.

I could only be so lucky.

His secretary ushered me right into his office the second I said my name. She got all flustered and jittery, like she was taken off guard or something. "Follow me! Right this way!" she said quickly and scooted me into his room. "Can I get you anything?" she asked, which I ignored. When she realized she wasn't going to get a response from me, she said, "Dr. Graves will be with you in a moment," and shut the door.

The office screams Graves. The furniture, the décor, everything in the room reflects him. Everything smells new, too. The tight leather arms of the black couch, the gray Berber carpet that has scarcely known feet, a fresh coat of cream-colored paint on the walls. There's a small black desk nestled in the corner of the room, offset by a small picture window outlined with navy blue sheer drapes, I assume some designer stuff. Graves has had it decorated to suit a man of his tastes—lots of clean lines and minimalist decor, and probably worth more than anything in my apartment. The paintings hanging on the wall are the kind that look different, or give you a different feeling, each time you look at them. This is all part of his Psych 101 game. Like the game he played in the Re-Assimilation Center, only now he's not in the government's house, and he can show off his flashy, expensive style. I know this game all too well, though, and I'm not about to let him Psych-101 me today.

I sit down on the black leather couch, lowering my body gently onto the thick crunchy cushion. I cross my right leg horizontally over my left knee and kick back a little, listening to the sound of the couch with my every movement. There's a coffee table in between an oversized leather chair and where I sit. The chair has a high back and the arm rests spill over and around the sides. It looks like a black throne, one that Lord Hades would sit upon if he were a shrink. I bet Graves feels like a god when he 'psychs' his clients.

Against the wall, to my right, is a small black bookshelf. It's stacked with all sorts of books that I've never heard of, but what catches my eye is a frame with a picture of a teenage boy in it. I squint my eyes to get a better view of the image. The boy is about 15 in the picture, dark hair, dark eyes, stocky build. Looks a little like Graves. And then I realize this must be a picture of his son! The one who got infected. The one who Graves had to kill. I look and I try to picture the scene in my head of the Infected boy coming after Graves and Graves having to stomp his own son to death with his size 15 shoe. And the more I look at that picture, I see that this kid, this son of my hated enemy, kinda looks a little like me.

For a split second, I actually feel bad for the guy. For a split second, I have a wave of sympathy for Graves and for what he went through during the whole ordeal. For a split second, I think, 'Hey, gee, Graves might not be so bad after all...'

But those split seconds deflate the instant he walks in the office with his strong cologne, and his clipboard in hand.

He sits down in the chair directly across from me and shuffles his left leg in the same exact position as mine. His suit is black, with a black shirt and a red silk tie. He looks back and forth between me and the clipboard in his makeshift lap. Yes. Hades must be trapped here on Earth. His eyes are blacker than ever, as cold as I remember them to be, and he sighs, "24," to acknowledge my presence.

My stomach drops as a sickening wave rushes through me. A familiar feeling of helplessness and disgust that I haven't felt since my days at the Re-Assimilation Center—since my days of sitting across from Graves in my psycho analysis sessions. "Graves," I respond, nodding my head forward.

The two years that have passed have been relatively kind to him. His skin still glows, probably from a facial or the numerous products he uses. His build has remained the same; I assume he works out daily for at least an hour to stay in such good shape. But what I notice in the light of the office that I hadn't noticed in the dimness of the funeral parlor is that Graves's slicked-back jet-black hair is starting to show speckles of gray at his temples. I don't know why, but this makes me smile. You're not immortal, after all.

"I asked you to come in today in light of the recent events that have been happening," he begins.

"Yeah, about that. Why did you call me from my job?"

He crinkles his nose. "How else was I supposed to get your number?"

I want to bite his nose clear off his face. Damn you, Graves! Damn you for making me feel like...

"Anyway, as if the Altered community hasn't been scrutinized enough, this whole Washington Incident sheds a different kind of light on the situation."

"So, what does this have to do with me? You told me yourself that you're out of the Altered business. You psycho-analyze survivors now, isn't that right?"

Graves doesn't look at me. He thumbs through the papers attached to his clipboard and ignores what I've said. "We've been asked to collaborate. All the doctors, personnel, staff, anyone who has had extensive contact with the Altered in the past are getting together to compare notes, so to speak. We're looking for behavior patterns, blood sample patterns, bits of conversations—anything that anyone has documented or can remember."

Holston. Everything goes back to Dr. Holston, the Architect of the Now.

I exhale. "So, where do I fit into your little think tank?"

He still won't look at me. Instead, he pulls out a chart from the back of his clipboard and places it on the coffee table between us. He leans forward and holds the paper in place with one of his thick sausage fingers. "I examined all of you here in Florida. I consulted the other psychiatric professionals who were stationed at the other Centers. We've compared notes and audio and video, and the one conclusion that we determined was that most of the Infected were not sentient. At least not for long. In the very beginning, in the first moments of infection, yes, there were some remnants of their former selves, but that lasted only for a short period of time." His eyes scrape up slowly from the paper to meet mine. "Except for you," he says accusingly as he taps his finger on the paper with a loud *thud*.

Like in a cheesy horror movie, a clap of thunder shakes the room at that instance. I can't help but smile and shake my head. This derision doesn't amuse Graves in the least. He leans back in his chair and smooths out his pants with his hands.

"That's not true," I say flatly.

"What's not true?" he answers, aggravated.

"That I was the only one who was aware. Everyone was."

He breathes in heavily through his nose and clasps his hands together in front of his mouth. His nostrils flare out behind his fingers like tiny demon wings rattling. "Did you not hear what I said?"

"Oh, I heard you," I say, keeping my composure. "But you're wrong. They were all afraid of you, didn't you know? They told you what you wanted to hear." There's a cockiness in my demeanor now, because I think I rattled his cage a little, and I'm not his patient anymore, and I can't stand the way his black eyes stare through me like I'm not even a person, and I honestly have nothing to lose at this point in time because he made it quite clear that he and the entire world hates me, so why not? Why not be a little cocky? Why not give him an attitude? Show him I'm not afraid of him. Show him I'm not playing his stupid game. I chuckle. "Didn't you ever hear the little song that we all sang? 'He'll kill you like he killed 2.'"

He rears his head back and closes his eyes in disbelief. "What in the world are you talking about?"

"Um... ya know. Patient number 2. You talked him into suicide during one of your sessions at the Center."

Graves pauses and smiles slowly, methodically, like there's warm pride spreading across his face. He laughs through his nose and rubs at his chiseled chin. "Oh. Is that what you all thought of me? That's good to know. Thank you, but no thank you. I'm not as good as good ole Hannibal Lecter. Number 2 was beyond repair. Simple as that. I didn't talk anyone into doing anything. If I had that kind of power, don't ya think I would have used it more often?" He nods his chin upwards at me 'cause he means "me."

A cold rush of defeat enters my lungs. "Me." He would have talked me and the whole lot of us into killing ourselves. He wouldn't have risked his life-long friendship with Dr. Holston by having the Centers shut down. If he had it his way, he would have played those pipes until we all fell over a giant cliff.

"It's nice to know you all thought so highly of me." He folds his hands into his lap and rests his head on the back of the chair. He smirks in victory, his thick bottom lip protruding out in a sinister sneer.

Yes, a suitable throne for Lord Graves.

I have nothing else to say to him right now. I drop my leg down to the floor and let my elbows rest on my knee tops.

"I will say this much, though," he goes on. "Holston saw it in you immediately. And it wasn't anything that he did; it wasn't attributed to his serum or treatments. It was pre-vaccination. There was something inside of you that set you apart from the other Altereds. I looked at the case files from New York, watched the tapes from California, conferred with the doctors in Texas. It's all the same. Within days of being infected, all sense of self was erased. But not you. You claim otherwise. And Holston took such a liking to you, and put so much trust in you, that now, in hindsight, I can't overlook that."

Wait. Is he complimenting me? Is he saying something nice *to me?*

"What I don't understand is—what makes *you* so special?"

"Gee, Doc, for a second there I thought you were actually giving me a compliment."

"So, I reviewed every last detail from our sessions, and the conclusion I made is this—you spent a lot of time watching the Infected. You observed them. You observed their behaviors, took note of their patterns. You watched them."

I did. I did watch and observe. I made it a game. I pretended that I was some army general scoping out a military operation. I watched how they ran, and shambled, and ran again, like they were trying not to run, but couldn't help it. I listened to their moans and screams and dirges of agony as they tore into neighborhood wildlife, or other neighbors for that matter. "From my second story window," I mumble, in a trance, in a memory.

"You and your family were pretty secure in your home, weren't you?"

"Yes. For a while. We were just lucky, I guess." I run my fingers slowly across the top of my head, savoring the stubbles of my fresh shave.

He stands up and walks over to his desk. He bends down, puts something in his pocket, and then stands straight up again with the heads of two plastic bottles of water dangling from the fingers on his right hand. He saunters back over, sits down and offers me one. I reach for it, open it, and take a long drink. Rain pelts against the side of the building, rapping on the glass of the picture window with a hypnotic summertime song.

"Not many people were as lucky as you," he says conversationally, then drinks from his water bottle like we're two old friends having a drink and catching up on old times.

I nod. "We were beyond lucky. The world was being torn apart all around us, and for some crazy reason, we were kinda blind to it all. Sydney read books and magazines in her staircase cubby. Mom tried to keep things normal in the house by cleaning and straightening up or organizing the food supplies. I watched the Infected people like I was watching some kind of reality show on TV. It was all surreal. Like it wasn't really happening to us."

"Did you ever talk to your mother and sister about the possibilities of what was happening? Did you ever speculate about the nature of what was going on?"

I think for a second. "No," I say in a faraway voice, remembering the time I spent with my mother and sister, trapped in our house like prisoners.

Graves grabs his clipboard and flips some pages. "There was a girl who stayed with you. Toby, right? You said that she upset the dynamic in your home when she came to stay with you. You said she was your first kill."

I nod again.

"Did you ever discuss what was going on with her?"

Toby.

God. I haven't really thought about Toby in ages, maybe because there's so much about her and that time that I desperately want to forget. But to answer Graves... yes. Toby and I did talk about what was going on.

Especially when we were at the 2nd story window.

13

"GRIFFIN!" TOBY'S BLEATING VOICE RESONATED throughout the house followed by my mother and sister 'shushing' her. "Griffin," she repeated, lowering her voice.

I walked to the top of the steps and poked my head down the staircase. "What's up?"

"Your mother made food. Come down."

I put my finger up in a 'one minute' gesture, turned away and went back to the window. I had hoped she would walk away and go into the kitchen, but she didn't. I heard her delicate feet against the carpeted steps, and in an instant, her bleached blonde hair appeared in the threshold.

Aggravated, I rolled my eyes. "What's up?" I asked again.

She slid up next to me, smiling. "Whatcha doing up here?"

"Same thing I always do."

She placed her hand on my arm and my whole body tensed up. She peeked her head over my shoulder to get a look of what was happening outside and bopped her face up and down to see between the slats of the Plantation shutters. "What do you think is wrong with them?" she asked, breathing close to my ear.

This was the first time she had taken any interest in anything I was doing. Toby spent a lot of time with my sister, mostly because Sydney would braid her hair and paint her nails. She really got the full-on spa treatment with Syd! Toby also hassled my mother, asking to borrow her clothes or makeup or perfume so she could dress up and look pretty, or maybe just feel normal. But it was different with me. Toby only seemed to buddy up to me when it was food time.

During meals or snacks she would sit right next to me, chat me up a bit, act like she really wanted to know me, bat her eyes and flirt. I was such an idiot because at the end of almost every conversation, she would ask so sweetly, 'Oh, could I get that last bite?' or 'Oh, can I get a sip of your drink?' and of course, I would hand over the last bites or sips of whatever I had. Now, she was upstairs in my hiding spot with me, asking me about the crazy people on the streets? Was Miss Youngblood having a change of heart about me?

"I don't know. I have no idea," I answered.

"It's like one of those movies. Ya know, where the dead people come back to life and start eating people and make more of themselves. I never really watched horror movies, but my sister liked them. Then she would have nightmares and wet the bed!" She snorted. "Could you imagine? Sixteen years old and wetting the bed? I told her she needed to stop watching those stupid movies, but she didn't listen. She made me promise not to tell anyone about that."

"Well, you just told me, so I guess you broke your promise," I snapped.

She turned her head and looked at me seriously. "Yeah, well, when a person's dead, I guess there aren't any more promises to keep, now are there?" There was a biting sadness in her voice. She looked back out the window.

I had to admit it, she had a point. There were no more rules, and I suppose even the tradition of honoring the dead kinda got thrown out the window. I suddenly felt sorry for Toby. She must have felt so out of place with me and Mom and Syd. Could she have been so blind to not notice that we were all a little annoyed that she was with us? No. She was selfish and conceited, not dumb. And I know it was my decision to let her join the fold, because of my own stupid guilt-trip for letting Josh die, but honestly, I was regretting it more and more as each day passed.

I decided that I needed to change my attitude toward her if we were all gonna survive the end of the world with some ounce of sanity left. I relaxed my shoulders and adjusted the shutters so she could get a better look. She noticed this, and slid closer to me, so we were practically huddled cheek to cheek.

Below us, an Infected woman shambled in the cul- de-sac. One side of her face was torn open revealing the side of her jaw and all its white-tooth glory. The woman carried the body of some small, mangled animal, possibly a bunny or a squirrel. I couldn't tell because it was badly damaged, and barely recognizable as a former anything. Toby shuddered as a chill ran through her body. "My God!" she whispered. "What is she doing?"

A twisted smile came over my face, as if I had seen this TV show one too many times. "Right on schedule," I said.

"Huh?"

"I call this one Pearl."

"What? You named them?" she yelled.

The noise must have traveled down to the street below because the Infected woman stopped walking and looked slowly from side to side. Quickly, I grabbed the top of Toby's head and pushed her down to her knees with me. "Shuuussssshhhh!" I said forcefully. "Can't you keep your voice down?"

"Sorry! Sorry!" she said in a hushed voice. "You just freaked me out, that's all!"

I popped my head up to see if we had made enough noise to garner any attention, but stupid Pearl went right back to her afternoon stroll around the rotunda, and I breathed a sigh of relief. "It's okay," I said. "And I only nicknamed a few that hang around the neighborhood."

"Oh," she said, joining me in our viewing. "Did you know her? Ya know, like when she was alive?"

I shake my head. "No. I don't know who she is. She might have been a relative of one of the neighbors who was staying here on vacation. And, I don't think they're dead."

"Why do you say that? Don't the movies say they're dead? Zombies?"

I looked at her and gave her an 'are-you-serious?' eyebrow raise.

"What? If they're not dead, then what are they? Why do they eat people and stuff?"

"I just think they might be sick or something. Like, watch her. She walks around that circle like she's looking for something, or someone. Maybe waiting for her ride to come and pick her up. It's almost as if she has some kind of memory left in her."

"Holy crap! You're right! Look at her face. She looks almost..."

"Lost?" I said, finishing her thought.

"Yeah! Yeah! She looks lost and," she paused and her face twisted, "and kinda lonely. I almost feel sorry for her."

"She's attached to that animal in her hand. I haven't seen her let go of it since she started coming around."

"Pearl," she said to the window. "Wait! Why Pearl?"

"Um, look at her face."

Toby gently punched me on the arm. "Ohhhh, I see. Pearl. As in pearly whites. Her teeth. Har har, real funny, Griff!"

I smiled. "She's one of the regulars. There are five of them that frequent this area."

"Why do you think they do that?"

I thought of a quote from one of my favorite zombie movies and chuckled to myself. "I guess it *is* memory. Assuming that they're not dead."

Toby shook her head back and forth. "I still don't understand why you think that."

"I don't know," I repeated. And just then, a crazy person came running and screeching through the cul-de-sac from one of the neighbor's backyards. Toby tensed up, and a small hiccup sound came up in her throat, but she remained steady and calm. "We're safe up here," I said as I put my arm around her shoulder.

She breathed in. "I know. I know. I just hate the sound they make."

Again, she had a point. They made this high-pitched screeching sound that seemed to echo. It was almost like a double voice, like they had a microphone machine in their throat to amplify their gurgles and screams. It was definitely a sound that I had a hard time getting used to hearing.

The screecher raced across the grass of the rotunda, nearly barreled through Pearl, and took off through another yard. "That's so weird," she said.

I kept my eyes fixed on the scene outside, but tilted my head toward her, questioningly.

"That guy ran. He was all crazy. Like the ones that chased me. Ya know, in the beginning and stuff. But Pearl? She's all walking about, all lackadaisical. She's not running. She's not making that horrible sound. So, what's the difference?"

"Oh, Pearl runs. Believe me. You're just seeing her on a slow day, but she has her moments where she's probably the fastest on the block. Look! Look!"

Just then, a group of three Infected people came slowly from behind a house. They were covered in fresh blood, holding furry limbs in their hands and mouths.

"Jesus!" Toby gasped at the sight of them. "Those poor animals."

"Never mind the animals," I said. "What about those poor people?"

"I know. I know. Griffin? What the hell is going on out there? Is this the end of the world? Do you think this is the end of the world? Be honest with me. I trust you."

"You trust me?"

"Of course, silly!" She slapped my arm again. "You saved my ass from those crazies. I'm in *your* house, eating *your* food..."

"Well, technically, it's my mom's house, but yeah, come to think of it, you *do* eat my food!"

Toby laughed. A *real* laugh. Not one of her fake, sarcastic chuckles. It was probably the first time I had ever heard her give a genuine, honest to goodness laugh. Her face brightened up, and for once I was able to see past my mother's caked on makeup, and her seven-inch dark roots. The laughter made her a real person to me, and not just some caricature of the typical dumb damsel in distress.

"Seriously, Griff. Lay it out on the table. Tell me what you're thinking."

"Is it the end of the world? I don't know about that. I have to believe that there is some kind of hope out there. Like Santa Claus—how he doesn't really exist, but he's out there bringing happiness to people. I guess that gets me through the day."

She narrowed her eyes. "Well, you kinda lost me with that one," she said as she stood up. "How do you think this started? Like, were we invaded by aliens?"

I raised my eyebrow again, and she rolled her eyes.

"You know what I mean," she huffed.

"I don't believe in the supernatural. I believe in what I can see. And right now, I see a group of crazy people sitting in the circle of my cul-de-sac feasting on... oh, one's got what looks like a black racer snake, one's got a mouthful of blue feathers, and the other one has what looks like a dog's tail in his hands. I see sick people with a very, very bad infection."

"Gross," she said, sticking out her tongue.

"Yeah. He's going to town on it like a rack of ribs."

Her body twitched and she hopped to the top of the steps. "Ewww. Stop!"

I laughed. 'Cause, really, if I hadn't laughed, I probably would have screamed in fear.

"Still have an appetite?" I asked as I got up and joined her.

"Why? You gonna let me have some of your fruit snacks?"

"I might have to," I said, bumping her shoulder with mine, "you might get hungry enough to start eating my fingers!"

"Griffin! You are so disgusting! All I know is this—I don't ever want to be like them! Like Pearl! Ever! I tell you what—you do whatever it takes to keep me from getting infected. You have my permission."

I think when I became infected, I remembered what she had said. Because when I encountered Toby in my infected state, I made sure I granted her wish. Maybe all my observations of how the Infected acted influenced how I acted when I turned. Like, the others who turned, turned so quickly with no real knowledge or understanding of what was happening. Their bodies were just working so hard to fight the virus that their minds were not able to function correctly. But I had a deeper understanding of it. I had observed their actions and behaviors for weeks. Maybe my prior knowledge was what helped me to consciously hold on to my moral compass for as long as I did? Who knows?

As if someone turns off a faucet, the rain ceases its assault on the building. I hear a *click* sound and look up to see Graves setting a tape recorder down on the coffee table between us. I plant my face in my palm when I realize I've been sitting here blabbing away while he recorded the entire thing. I promised myself I wouldn't let him Psych 101 me, and what happens? I'm such an idiot for falling into his trap.

"What did you just do?" I ask.

He smirks his snake smile at me. "What do you mean?" he says with a sarcastic, condescending lilt.

"Did you just tape me?"

"Of course I did," he says as if I'm the crazy one. As if I should remember some prior deal we made. "I told you, the team is trying to piece together..."

I close my eyes, shake my head, and wave my hand dismissively in the air. "Yeah, yeah, yeah. Whatever, man. You do what you gotta do." I feel like he got me again, like I can never break free of Graves's lunchbox handhold. It squeezes me at the base of my brain, and I can't seem to slither my way out. I stop moving my head around and open up my eyes. In the corner, I catch a glimpse of the picture frame on the bookshelf.

Something in me clicks. “It’s okay. Really it is.” My own sarcasm drips out of my mouth, like the words aren’t actually coming from me, but from some super-intelligent being. “You know, I’m not your son.”

Graves’s face darkens.

“When he was infected, he probably had no clue what was going on. He probably just... *went with it*.”

You know how authors write in books things like: ‘you could feel the tension building,’ or ‘the tension in the air was so thick, you could cut it with a knife’ or some other cliché with a corny line about feeling tension or the physical representation of tension? Well, I don’t know what an author would write to describe what happened in this room. Graves is silent. And still. Like one of those ancient Greek statues. And the air in the room *shifts*. Like a presence made its way into the abstract space between the leather couch and the leather chair. I gasp. I actually gasp! There was such a rage built up in Graves’s body that it completely sucked away any and all oxygen from the room. It felt heavy. Oppressive. *Tense*. Like holding your breath in anticipation for a building to explode.

After what feels like an eternity, Graves uncrosses and re-crosses his leg. “Is that what you did when you killed that man at Lettuce Lake Park? Did you just *go with it*?”

I try desperately to catch my breath.

He knows.

I can deny it all I want, because it really is the truth. I didn’t kill anyone. But he knows. And I will do anything to protect Amber.

“I don’t know what you’re talking about,” I say. “I didn’t kill anybody.”

“Oh, really? Then why don’t you tell me what you know about Zombaxin.”

I play stupid. “Zom-what-in?”

His nostrils flare out as he inhales sharply. “Zombaxin. Tell me what you know. I know you know, because *I* know.”

“Then, if you know everything, what do you need me for?”

Graves clasps his hands behind his neck and leans his body forward. The bones in his neck and back pop thunderously. One. Pop. Two. Pop. A line of boney dominos exploding against his skin and through his suit jacket. He sits straight up and straightens out his back, composing himself. "I know you think I'm the enemy here, but I'm not. If I was, I would have turned you in weeks ago. If you're open and honest with me, you won't get into trouble. I can protect you."

I stare at him blankly. *Does he really think I'm falling for this?*

"Listen," he continues. "You're a good person. Holston saw that in you. Just let me know who your dealer is, and we can get to the bottom of this. If you don't give me a name, more people are going to get hurt, and the Altered community is going to suffer tremendously."

Dealer? He thinks I'm a Black Death junkie?

"I didn't kill anyone," I repeat.

He uncrosses his leg and rests his hands on his knees. He leans forward a bit and lowers his voice. "An Altered was caught high on Zombaxin last night in New Jersey. He tried to attack his parents. They were able to barricade themselves in their bathroom and call for help, but not before the kid took a chunk out of his mother's arm. When help finally got there, the boy was out of control. They were able to subdue him and throw him in the psych ward. He didn't recover from the drug for about six hours. When he came to, he told the doctors that he had taken a double dose so that it would last longer, and he was sorry that he had attacked his parents. The mother's bite itself wasn't life threatening, but she's in the hospital in a medically induced coma. Within hours of the bite, she developed a fever and went into septic shock."

I continue to stare at him, my mind unable to fully process what he is saying to me and the tone at which he is saying it.

"Do you understand what this means? Dr. Trager thinks this might mean transference. And transference could mean the start of another Outbreak. That's why I need your help, Griffin. And that's why I can promise you protection."

This is the first time Graves has ever said my name, the first time he's ever asked anything of me, or even reached out to me in a humanly way. It's weird to hear. It's weird to hear his strong voice now fraught with anxiety, resentment, and a desperation I didn't think possible from him. I'm trying not to let the desperation in his voice deceive me. He's making me a promise, but I'm not so sure he can or will want to keep it.

I know how easy it is to break promises to the dead.

What would be the difference with an Altered?

14

THE WORD COERCION IS DEFINED AS: THE ACT OF forcing someone to do or say something via force or intimidation. But in all actuality, it's not so much an *act* as it is an *art*—an art form that Dr. Warren Graves has mastered so well...

I didn't feel threatened. I certainly wasn't forced. But for some strange and stupid reason, I kinda spilled my guts to Graves. Of course, he had me in his office for nearly four hours, and at first I was so sure of myself—sure that I wasn't gonna give in to him, sure that I was going to resist his barrage of questions, but I don't know what happened. One thing led to another, and one comment opened up another door, and before I knew it, I was singing like a jay bird. I had sound mind enough to choose my words carefully, but in hindsight, I shouldn't have had to choose anything! I walked out of his office feeling dirty, violated. Like someone had touched the deepest parts of my psyche. What he did to me wasn't Psych 101. Oh no, it was definitely a way more advanced course than that. And that's why Graves is a true artist of his psychoanalyzing craft.

So, what does Graves know? Well, to be honest, not much more than I do. I didn't mention anyone specifically by name. I basically regurgitated the story Eugene had told me about the group of Ferals that he had met at some Altered girl's house. Except, I told it as if it had happened from my point of view and not Eugene's. I also told him about the connection to the guy in New York, and how that was the suspected place of origin for the Black Death. Of course, I denied killing the homeless man, because in truth, I didn't. I told Graves I was at Lettuce Lake Park when it happened, but I wasn't sure who actually did it.

Graves assured me over and over that he would protect me, and that whatever I told him would be used to investigate Zombaxin and curtail its spread. He told me that I would be safe from persecution if I told him everything I knew. He asked me if I ever tried Zombaxin, and I lied. I told him I took half a pill to see what would happen, and that it had no effect. I don't think he believed that, but I really didn't care.

I shouldn't have said anything to him, but I just couldn't help it! When he first made his plea to me, he said something like, "Dr. Trager thinks this might mean transference...," and the way he said Trager's name sounded... I don't know... *off.* My senses kicked into overdrive when Graves said Trager's name. It was almost as if there was a hint of disdain in his voice. It was subtle, so subtle that a normal person would not have noticed it. But me? I picked up on it immediately. Maybe that was his plan all along, though? Maybe Graves knew that my super- acute senses would notice the little off-colored nuances? For as much as I hate the bastard, I can't deny him one thing...

...He's good.

It's 2 a.m. and I drift in and out of a dreamless sleep. Work kicked my ass tonight. Today's storm caused the roof to leak in the storage room, and it took two other janitors and me most of our shifts to get it cleaned up. If I don't see a curly-tailed mop for the next year, I'll be happy.

I pull a pillow over my face when my cellphone starts vibrating on the nightstand, and as much as I want to ignore it, Amber's absence in the bed rattles me to attention.

I reach for the phone and look at the incoming number. It's a weird 800 number, and I press the green telephone icon on the touch screen.

"Hello?" I say in a hushed and groggy voice, which is so completely dumb, because there's no one here for me to disturb or wake up.

"Dude!" the voice on the line says.

I rub my eyes with my free hand. I'm completely awake when I recognize the voice. "Yeah, Eugene? You okay?"

"Yeah, yeah. I'm fine, man. I'm fine."

In my mind's eye, I can visualize him on a corded phone, pacing back and forth in the back office of some dingy gas station. Probably begged the owner to let him use it. Maybe threatened him. Who knows. I can see Eugene, though, all twitching out and scratching at his arms in typical Eugene style.

"So, what's up?"

"You gotta come to the house, man!" he says muffled, like he put his hand around the receiver end. "It's so baaaaad!"

I sit up straight in the bed. He's definitely gotten my attention. "What's bad, Eugene?" I say forcefully, more alert. "What's going on?"

"Dude! I can't talk about it over the phone. You never know who could be listening!"

He's got a point. "Is it Amber?"

"It's everything! Just get here as soon as you can, okay?"

I get up out of the bed and fumble for my clothes. "Get where?"

"Take MLK to Nebraska. Pick me up at the gas station at the intersection, like *now*, dude."

"Okay, okay. I'm on my way."

Eugene hangs up the phone. I get dressed, put my phone in my pocket, grab my keys, and go.

At 2:30 in the morning, even in a big city like Tampa, there's little happening on the roads. Many storefronts are still vacant, and the line of traffic down Martin Luther King Jr. Blvd. is barely existent. I pull up to the intersection to see Eugene standing on the corner like some dealer-junkie derelict. He's disheveled, scratching at his arms like I knew he would be, and jerking his head back and forth up the street watching for my car. Any normal person would be afraid to walk within ten feet of him, especially after seeing his massive eye scar. I pull up to the side of the street and unlock the door. He jumps in, and screams, "Go!"

I don't ask him any questions, because I don't expect to get any answers. I just follow along as he directs me to their new abandoned home. It's no better than the last place they squatted in. Crystal opens the door as my car turns into the driveway. I'm barely in park when Eugene jumps out yelling, "C'mon! C'mon!"

As soon as I get out of the car, I hear moaning and yelling coming from within. My stomach sinks.

Inside, there are Altered people all around. Ferals. It reminds me of a crack-den from one of those 90s drug-bust movies. Crystal pulls me in the doorway and slams the door behind me. The moaning and yelling is louder once I'm inside.

"There was a bad batch or something, man!" Eugene babbles as he paces back and forth.

"Bad batch?"

He scratches at his neck, and his fingernails grate over his unshaven stubble. "Black Death, man."

The howling from the back of the house is ear-splitting as a door quickly opens and slams shut. Jimmy comes into the front part of the house and gives me a worried head nod. I don't return it. "Eugene," I say firmly, "what are you talking about? A bad batch of Black Death? What does that mean?"

I guess some of the other Ferals who are sitting on the floor of what would have been the formal dining room sense the anger and agitation in my voice. They get up simultaneously and walk over to us in a protective-like stride. Instinctively, I take a step back and put up my hands in defense. "Where's Amber? I just want to know what's going on," I say more calmly.

One of the Ferals, a big black guy with a small scar by his eye, hands Eugene a cigarette and flips open a Zippo lighter for him. "Thanks, Donovan," he says, and he takes a long, hard drag and exhales the smoke in my direction. I nearly gag from the smell of the cigarette and his foul breath. "We got our supply like usual, ya know? Everything was cool. Everything was fine. Then Marco was like, 'Let's do two!' and we all joined in. And we all lasted longer, 'cause we've been kind of immune to just a one-er. And we all came down, and Marco says, 'Let's do three!' Then three became four, and four became five. Each time was a little longer and more intense. Me and Jimmy tapped out at four. Marco said six, and your girl was all in. So, they do six, and the time goes by and by and by and no dice." He takes another drag, "No dice," he repeats with a puff of smoke.

"Wait. Back up a sec," I say waving my hands in air, clearing out the smoke in front of me. "Amber's been doing Zombaxin even *after* what happened in the Park?"

Jimmy chuckles. The sound from his throat is gritty, as if it will produce a cough any second.

I shoot him an angry look and straighten up my shoulders. "What's so funny?" I say, deepening my voice.

Donovan takes a defensive step forward, but this time I stand my ground.

Jimmy glares at me with a sneer on his lips. "Oh, yeah. Your girl can't get enough of it," he says, the words slipping from his mouth like thick slime coating a tree trunk.

I see red and attempt to move toward him. I want to tear out that useless, gritty throat of his and shove it...

Eugene steps in front of me, blocking my path. Donovan is right behind him. "Dude, stop," Eugene whispers. I jam my hands in my pocket to prevent any further temptation.

"Where's Amber?" I plead.

Eugene looks at me with a pained expression. "It's been three days, man. Her and Marco just won't come out of it." He grabs my wrist and leads me through the house to a small semi-circular hallway. The moaning gets louder. There are three closed doors, and in typical floor plan style, I suspect one to be a bathroom, and the other two to be bedrooms. However, one of the closed doors is barricaded with furniture. It doesn't take a genius to figure out what's happening. Amber and Marco are locked away in the barricaded room, still high on Black Death, still in an infected-like state. I scrape my fingernails against my legs from within my pockets, in hopes of calming myself down.

I point to the barricade. "She's in there?"

Eugene nods.

Jimmy, Crystal, and Donovan come up behind him.

"Did she hurt anyone else?"

He snorts. "She's got a pretty rough bite!"

I roll my eyes. "You know what I mean. Did she *hurt* anyone else?"

"Nah, man," Jimmy interjects. "Nothing like that."

"Open the door," I command in a calm tone.

Eugene's face goes white. "I... I don't know if that's..."

"I said, open the damn door!"

Jimmy pushes his way in front of Eugene and dismantles the barricade. "Your girl, your problem," he mumbles as he tosses pillows and books aside.

"Wut'you say?" I ask, knowing very well what he said.

"I think you heard me. She's your girl. She's your problem. I'm not gonna be held responsible for..."

"You're already responsible," I snap. "You gave her the pills. You did this to her."

"Look, man," Eugene tries to intervene, "it's nobody's fault. She's a big girl. She did this to herself. Jimmy's been good to her—trying to take care of her, getting her food and stuff, and... well, she's got a problem, man. A real, big problem."

"Ya know what, Eugene? Stay out of this," I say, eyes still fixed on Jimmy. "This is between me and him."

Jimmy narrows his dark eyes at me. How I wish I could go back in time ten hours or so. I wish I would have given his name to Graves. Pin the whole thing on him!

"Stupid RAT," he huffs and throws more of the barricade around.

"Excuse me?"

"Oh, I know you heard me that time..."

"Yeah, uh, I don't know. I think my RAT ears are clogged or something..."

Jimmy's in my face in a flash. Eye to eye. Nose to nose. I press my forehead hard against his as strands of his greasy hair brush up against my cheeks. Crystal lets out a small squeal. Jimmy presses back on my forehead with the same strength and ferocity. I realize that if this goes any further, he and I would be evenly matched.

Donovan comes up behind Jimmy and grabs his shoulders. He pulls him away from me, and Eugene waves his arms frantically in the air. "Enough, you guys! Enough! We're on the same side here!"

I stare hard at Jimmy.

"I don't think so, Gene," he says, still holding my gaze. "You guys weren't left on the street like some animal to fend for yourselves. You got all kinds of star-treatment."

I laugh. I can't stand this anymore. "Are you serious?" I say. "If you think the grass was greener on the other side, you're highly mistaken."

Jimmy kicks the last throw pillow down the hallway and turns the doorknob. "Your lady awaits," he says sarcastically, and he opens the door.

A low growl surfaces in my throat when I pass by him and peer my head through the opening of the door. The room is dark, but the light from a streetlamp lets me vaguely make out two figures huddled in opposite corners. Blood stains on the grey carpet look like black ink spots in the darkness among the various animal parts strewn across the floor. At least Eugene had the sense to feed them *something*.

Amber and Marco both moan that familiar lament of the Infected; the song that is one of agony and ecstasy all at once. She sits with her knees curled up to her chest. A long t-shirt covers her body, almost locking her in place. She looks up at me and our eyes lock. The white haze of her irises illuminates in the darkness. There's something peaceful in her gaze, almost happy. In the dim light, I think I see her smile at me. Does she recognize me? Is she cognizant enough to know that I'm here? I want to race over to her, tell her that it's going to be okay, that I'm going to help to find her way out of this. I want to cover her and protect her and scoop her up in my arms and take her home. I want to kiss her and rewind time to before the Incident in the Park.

She lifts her head and sniffs the air like a predatory animal sensing its prey. There's foam around her mouth—the frothy white substance catches the glow of the lamplight. Her nostrils flare out a few times smelling her surroundings. *Smelling me.* She looks at me one last time with a pained expression, a sort of macabre sadness. Then she lowers her head and goes back to singing her song and grinding her teeth on her shirt.

I'm not the kind of food she wants. The Infected won't eat the Altered.

I step out of the room, close the door, and twirl my finger in the air, giving Jimmy the signal to block it up again. There's a part of me that believes that this is what she wanted all along. To be *that* again.

"What are they doing in there?" Crystal asks quietly.

"They're just *waiting*."

"Waiting for what?" Donovan interjects.

"To eat? To go back to normal? I don't know."

"What if this *is* normal?" he asks.

Before I get a chance to respond, one of the other doors in the hallway opens up, and little Troy walks out, rubbing his eyes angrily, like he was just awakened from a deep sleep. Crystal hops over to him and tries to usher him back into the room. That's when I realize, he's been here all along, through everything. God only knows how much he saw or heard from these crazed junkies.

Don't let the files get to Trager, watch over the Altered, especially Troy. Those were Holston's exact instructions. I've done the first two, now it's time to do the last. I suddenly realize that Troy can't stay here anymore.

"Pack some stuff for you and Troy," I say to Crystal.

Crystal's eyes go wide with fear.

"They should stay with me for a little bit," I say to Eugene. "Just until Amber and your guy go back to normal. In the meantime, Crystal and Troy should stay with me, where it's safe."

"Safe?" Donovan scoffs, and Jimmy gives a little snort-huff noise of agreement.

"Yes. Safe," I reiterate.

"I don't know, man," Eugene protests. "That might not be such a good idea."

"It's the best idea. Troy doesn't need to be around all this right now. I'll watch over them. They'll be fine. Just 'til Marco and Amber come out of their trip. You really think it's a good idea for Troy to be exposed to..."

"Yeah, but, what if that *is* normal?" Donovan repeats.

"Then we'll just have to come up with something else."

15

IT TOOK QUITE A BIT OF ARM-TWISTING EUGENE TO LET them stay with me, but eventually I was able to convince him, and the others. Basically, I told him it was a trade: my girl for his girl. My ultimate talking point was that he was better equipped to handle the "Amber situation," and I was better equipped to handle the "Crystal situation." I laid it all out for him, explaining that it was probably in the best interest of Troy to not be around all that craziness right now. Donovan was cool with the plan right away, and I was shocked that Jimmy eventually agreed. Guess he's not so mindless after all. Even Crystal eventually got on board. Eugene was the last to give in, but only after Crystal convinced him. I'm not quite sure what his relationship with Crystal and Troy is. I know he's not Troy's biological father, but he most definitely is the closest thing that child has to one. I'm not sure if Eugene and Crystal are a couple, either. I mean, it's obvious that he cares for her, and the two have been close even going back to the Re-Assimilation Center days, but if there's anything 'romantic' between them, I couldn't tell ya.

It was almost sunrise by the time I got Crystal and Troy back to my apartment. They took over my bedroom, and I finished the rest of the night on the couch.

When I woke up at 3 p.m., I called work to say I was sick again and would be late. There was no hassle or resistance, partially for the fact that I don't think they really want me there anyway.

I turn on the TV in the living room and immediately adjust the volume so as to not wake up my guests.

"Tensions mount in the continuing threat of the Altered population," the news woman reports. "More reports are coming in from around the country of an alarming increase in the use of Zombaxin, the new super-drug that has been known to cause the Altered to revert back to what officials call 'a temporary infected-like state.' Known more commonly by its street name, Black Death has been linked to a recent rash of animal *and* human attacks the past few weeks, most notably the attack at the Anti-Altered Coalition rally in Washington, D.C., where 54 people were viciously killed after a group of Altered protesters are alleged to have consumed mass amounts of the drug. Surviving AAC members are pushing for stronger legislature concerning the Altered community and the effects of the Black Death."

"Back deaf?" a voice behind me says. I swivel my head to the hallway. Troy rubs his eyes and waddles his way into the living room. His hair is a disheveled mass of white blonde curls hanging in his face.

I quickly turn off the TV. "Oh, that was nothing," I say, and I realize my voice rises an octave higher when I speak to him. I guess that's how most grown-ups talk to little kids. I pat the space on the couch next to me. "Come here, buddy. Come sit down."

A big smile plasters on his face. He races over to me and jumps into my lap. I ruffle up his messy hair and he giggles. "You sleep okay?" I ask.

He nods and his hair brushes up against my face and into my nose. I breathe him in deeply and his scent is like the beach—coconuts and suntan oil. Salt water on metal. Sweet blood tinged with the smell of the sea. Like the perfect summer day for an Altered.

But he's not Altered. *He's something else.*

"Momma still asleep?" I ask.

He nods again and tilts his face so he can see mine.

"You like my bed?"

He smiles big again and nods his head frantically.

I laugh and tickle him in his armpits. "Oh yeah? Well, don't you go getting used to it, okay?"

He laughs back, his voice like a bell in perfect pitch. There is something so calming, so soothing about him. Sitting here with him on my lap is almost like being in some kind of magic bubble where the outside world doesn't exist.

CHAPTER 15

I slip my arms under his and stand up, placing him on my side hip. His legs seem to naturally conform around my waist, and he throws his arms around my neck. "Hungry?" I ask.

"Yep!" he squeals.

Funny. I'm not.

"Cereal?" I ask.

"Yep!" he repeats, leaning in and kissing my nose.

My heart melts at his pure innocence and I carry him into the kitchen and sit him down at the table. His chin barely touches the tabletop, so I grab an old phone book from one of the cabinets and set it underneath him. "This isn't like your highchair, Buddy, but this'll have to do for now," I say and start rummaging through the boxes of food Amber and I have. There's not much here. Pop-tarts, old crackers, cans of corn. Not very breakfast like. "No cereal in my pantry, little man. What about a granola bar?"

"Okay, Giffin," he sings happily. "Milk, peeze."

I give him the last granola bar from the box and scrunch up my nose. "Soda?" I respond.

He imitates me and scrunches up *his* nose.

"Water?" I offer, to which he nods.

His eyes are so bright that when he smiles, he brings new meaning to the expression 'light up the room.' Troy is a pretty neat kid. I think I could definitely get used to him being around. I envision day trips to the park, hanging out watching cartoons on TV, sneaking out to fast food restaurants and whispering, 'Don't let Eugene or your mom know!' This could actually be *fun.*

Who am I kidding?

I can't do this. I'm not equipped to do this. This whole 'taking-care-of-the-kid' is sweet and in a weird way, comforting, but this isn't life. This will *never* be life. Maybe Holston's cancer just wasn't in his pancreas. Maybe it had spread to other parts of his body, like, oh, *his brain!* And maybe it had affected him so drastically that he thought it would be a good idea to entrust *me*, an Altered, a science school experiment, with all his deepest, darkest secrets. Sure, I can handle making a few phone calls, jotting down some notes, sneaking around a laboratory and reading simple blood reports, but *this?* Taking care of the kid? I can't do this. I'm in way over my head with this one. I know I need help.

I rack my brain for any possibility. I can't go to the cops—they're completely out of the question. I can't go to Trager because I was specifically told not to. I won't go to Graves, 'cause I still don't trust him. Not many people out there are what you would call Altered Sympathizers...

Crystal saunters into the kitchen, as a plan starts to form in my head. She and I exchange glances, and she kisses the top of Troy's head before she sits down.

"Can I get you something?" I ask.

She just shakes her head, and I nod slightly. A knowing nod. I know how she feels. I'm not hungry either. I hand Troy a glass of ice water and join them at the table.

"Listen," I say to Crystal. I need to 'talk' my plan out loud to see if it makes sense for real, and not just in my head. "I want you and Troy to go to the medical center tonight to get his blood drawn."

She tenses up and her eyes widen.

I reach out my hand to touch the top of hers. "It's okay," I assure.

"We just had our routine visit," she says quietly.

"Don't wike needles," Troy huffs.

I smirk. He's too stinking cute, even when he's complaining. "Just tell them that the baby was sick."

"I not a baby. I not sick!" he exclaims.

"I know you're not, Buddy," I say, touching his arm with my free hand. "We just have to say it this one time, okay?" He's not a dumb kid. As a matter of fact, I believe he has intelligence beyond his years. His eyes shift to his granola bar. "You understand what I'm saying?" I say gently, and he nods.

She brings a hand over her mouth. "Why would I tell them that?"

"Because they'll see him right away. There's a star on his chart that indicates he's a top priority. If anything goes wrong with Troy, they want to be the first to know about it. So, just bring him in, say he was running a low-grade fever and not acting like himself. They'll draw blood in a heartbeat."

Troy winces at the thought of needles and I squeeze his wrist. "It's okay, I promise."

"But Eugene always..." she protests.

"Don't worry. I got it figured out. You guys come with me to work and hang out in the car for a little bit. Later, when they're done with Troy, I'll meet up with you and bring you back here on my break."

She looks down. It's obvious she's not comfortable with my plan, but I'm able to see the bigger picture. I know there is one person out there who is an Altered Sympathizer and who is equipped to help me—Holston's niece, Dr. Dorothy Oswald. Pediatric surgeon, Dr. Oswald. Altered Sympathizer, Dr. Oswald. Woman who gave me her business card that is now sitting in the top junk draw, Dr. Oswald.

About an hour into my shift, Crystal and Troy come to the front desk. She plays the part of concerned mother very well when she has to. I hang around the waiting room with my mop in my hand and my head hung low. I keep my back to the receptionist's desk and pray to God that Troy doesn't spot me and yell my name!

The receptionist is curt with them at first, but when Crystal says, "Troy is sick," the woman's tone completely changes. They are taken back to an examining room immediately.

I follow them and hang around the hallway, acting like I'm doing my job. The scene plays out rather perfectly, actually. I watch the doctor go in the room with a small medical cart. A few minutes later, he rolls it out into the hallway. Right before he goes back in, I stop him to ask if he needs any help. He hesitates. I see he's tired and frustrated with something. He agrees and tells me to take the cart to the laboratory. I smile. Not a problem at all. Happy to help! As I'm about to turn the corner down the corridor, I see Crystal and Troy leave the examining room. Perfect. Couldn't have planned this better. I stroll the cart to the lab, but on the way I pocket 3 of the 6 vials of Troy's blood and make some changes to the chart. I've been working here a long time, so I know the ins and outs of the system. I know which blood analyzers actually do their job, and which ones cut corners. I know what time they come and go. I've become a great sneaky snake. And I know that blood can be stored at room temperature for a few days.

In an excited thrill, I tell the head janitor that I'm not feeling well again, and he tells me to go home. Crystal and Troy are waiting for me in the car, just like I said.

It's only 9 p.m., not too late for us to get home and try to contact the good doctor.

I know exactly where I left Dr. Oswald's card. I see it in my mind's eye, and my hands dance instinctively in the junk drawer. I find it, dial the numbers, and cross my fingers.

"Hello?" the voice says on the other line.

"Hello, can I speak with Dr. Dorothy Oswald, please?"

"This is she. Who may I ask is calling?"

"My name is Griffin. Griffin King. I was a patient of your..."

I hear her voice catch her breath. "Yes! Yes!" she gasps, as if she'd been waiting all this time for me to call. "Are you okay? Is everything okay?"

"I... I'm sorry for calling you so late, but..."

"Stop all that. It's fine. What's the matter? Are you okay?" she repeats.

"Well," I stammer, "y... yes and no."

"What do you mean?" Her voice is stern with concern.

"It's just that I think I'm going to need your help with something."

"Okay. What do you need?"

"Well, I'd rather not say over the phone, and..."

"Say no more," she snaps. "When can I meet you?"

"The sooner the better."

"Tell me where and I'll be there tomorrow morning. Text me the address."

"Thank you, Dr. Oswald."

"Will you be okay tonight?"

"Oh yeah," I look over at Crystal and Troy sitting nervously on the couch. "We'll be okay tonight."

She hangs up on her end. I quickly send a text message with my address to the number on the business card. When it goes through, I throw the phone onto the rocking chair.

"Griffin, what's going on?" Crystal asks, her eyes filling with tears.

I kneel down next to her and put my hands on her knees. "Hey, Buddy," I say to Troy, "why don't you go on into the bedroom and watch some TV. Let me and Momma talk alone for a little bit."

He slithers off the couch and waddles into the other room.

I hold out the business card to Crystal. "This is the number for Dr. Dorothy Oswald. She's coming here tomorrow morning..."

Crystal jerks away from my touch as the tears stream down her face. "Troy? She's taking Troy?"

"No, no, no! Nothing like that," I say calmly. "She's going to help us. I trust her." I lie. I have to. The truth of the matter is, I don't know Dorothy Oswald from a hole in the wall, and I'm not a hundred percent certain that she actually will help me. But I have to keep Crystal in check and composed, so I tell a little lie. In all actuality, this whole little scheme of mine could blow up in my face. "Take this. You might need to get a hold of her in case something happens to me."

She takes the card and looks at it blankly. "How do you know she'll..."

"I just know. She's Dr. Holston's niece. I met her at his memorial service, and she offered her help to me if I ever needed it. I believe her. I believe she really will help us." She looks at me strangely. "I believe her," I repeat with more conviction.

"He was the only one that was nice to me," she says quietly, relaxing her shoulders.

"Me too," I agree, "and he asked me to look after Troy."

"So that's why you..."

"Yes. I wanted you away from that house. It was no place for him. You know that."

She lowers her head in shame. "I know," she mumbles.

"With Amber and that guy Marco not coming down from the pills, I don't have any idea what's gonna happen next. The news is talking about some bad things for us. For our people."

She looks up and wipes her eyes. Two big green marbles set against her gray-toned skin. She folds the business card in half and clutches her hand tightly. "I hope you're right. I hope she can help." She stands up and moves to the opening of the hallway. "They want to kill us, you know," she says matter-of-factly, her back still to me.

"Who wants to kill us?"

"All of them. Everyone. They used to tell me all the time when they..." her voice trails. She pauses and takes a deep breath. "Oh, never mind," she exhales and walks into the bedroom.

16

AN AWKWARD SILENCE SETTLES IN THE ROOM AS DR. Dorothy Oswald sits on the edge of my rocking chair staring at the three freaks of nature on the couch in front of her. If there were crickets in the room, their chirping would probably make us all deaf.

Sweet, rambunctious Troy is in between Crystal and me. His two-year-old short attention span forces him to fidget almost uncontrollably. Crystal puts her hands on his knees every few minutes in hopes of settling him down, but it's no use. He's a little boy. He wants to run, and jump, and play. The last thing he wants to do is sit here with three grown-ups discussing grown-up stuff!

Oswald has been here for about ten minutes now. We got passed the formalities and introductions, and the "ooh's and ahh's" of meeting Troy. I offered her a drink, like any good host would, which she declined. We spoke of the mundane, usually awkward stuff that you talk about when you initially begin conversation: "The weather was bad last night." "We haven't been to the new sushi place in Brandon! How is it?" "Counting down the days to the election. Can't wait until the barrage of political ads is over with."

The awkward babble always leads to this—the awkward silence.

Troy bounces on the cushion, so I lean down to his ear and whisper, "You wanna go play in the other room?"

He fervently nods his head so that his mass of white curls bunces like clouds shaking in heaven.

"Go on," I say as I pat his back. He slides off the couch, sets his feet firmly on the hardwood floor and is about to take off running.

"Wait!" Dorothy yells, and we all stop to look at her. "Come here for a second." She extends her arms as if she were to embrace him.

He pauses. Hesitates. Then looks to me for confirmation.

Not his mother, but me.

"It's okay," I assure him. "She's a doctor, Troy. She's not gonna hurt you."

He walks over to Oswald. She holds on to his hands and pulls his arms out to the sides as if she were inspecting high-priced merchandise. "Magnificent," she breathes. She lets go of her grasp and twirls him around. "Simply magnificent!" she gushes, and her resemblance to Holston is undeniable.

"There's everything," I motion to the packet on the end table next to Oswald. "I put all of your uncle's notes and paperwork together in some kind of order. There's all the recent blood reports, and I even made a separate stack of all of Troy's charts. There are three vials of Troy's blood. They've been at room temperature for almost a day now."

"Any hair samples?" she asks.

I hadn't thought of that. "No."

"May I?"

Crystal rubs her hands together nervously, and I scoot closer to her on the couch to try to calm her down.

"Yeah, sure. Whatever you need," I say.

She leans in close to Troy and says, "I'm going to pull a few strands of hair out of your head, okay? Just a tiny pinch and you can be on your way."

Troy looks back at me again with a nervous expression. I nod at him, to let him know it's all right. He turns back to face her and dips his head forward, as if to say, "go ahead, lady, take what you need." Oswald and I chuckle at his bowing act, at his perfect innocence.

She grabs a few pieces of his hair and plucks them out at the roots. "Thank you, sweetie. You go play now. Let us big people talk business," she says, and he takes off into the other room. She reaches for the package and places the hair inside.

"Your uncle was working on a vaccine," I say. "He was afraid of another outbreak."

Oswald sighs and runs her fingers through her sandy blonde hair. "I know. He told me about it every time we spoke. Even up to the night before he died. He said he was close to it but had a little bit of paranoia going on. Thought that people were watching him and had taps on his phones. I think the cancer and all the medication really messed with his mind in the last few weeks of his life."

"It's possible, but not completely out of the question. There were a few people that your uncle didn't trust, one doctor in particular. See, he kinda *acquired* some files of this particular doctor and..."

"Dr. Trager?"

I nod. "I put all of Trager's notes in one pile as well. Holston left everything in such a mess that I needed to organize the material. There's even a copy of his fairy tale in it."

Oswald smiles, big and bright, and puts her hand up to her chest. "Really? That'll be such a great treat to read from start to finish."

Troy starts singing along to one of the TV cartoons in the bedroom, and we pause momentarily to listen to him.

"So, tell me, what do my uncle's notes say about him?" she nods her head in Troy's direction. "What were his conclusions?"

"He's different, that's for sure. His blood type isn't... isn't... *human*."

Crystal's legs tense up, and Oswald looks puzzled. "What do you mean, not human?"

"He has a different blood type. It's not A, or B, or O, or any of those combinations. Holston said it resembled O, but it's different. He named it H. Holston also said that Troy's blood eradicated traces of that U Virus, and that the blood was the key to a..."

"He's not of this world," Oswald mutters in a faraway voice.

"No, he's not," I agree, and I sense Crystal's anger starting to rise.

"I mean, just look at him! He's such a beautiful specimen!" She sounds so much like Holston, like how he sounded whenever he spoke of the Altered. He would get smiley, and giggly, like an excited schoolboy. Oswald's demeanor is freakishly similar. Her eyes light up at the mere thought of solving a medical riddle. "He probably shouldn't exist on this Earth. Human, Infected, and Altered all in utero. He's undefined. *Un*human," she continues. "A new species. If only I had the tools and time to study him, I would track his entire body makeup, and..."

"He's not a lab rat!" Crystal screams. "He's just a little boy! And I'm not gonna let you cut him up to look at under some microscope!"

Oswald stiffens.

I put my arm around Crystal's shoulders. "Whoa, whoa!" I say in a soothing voice. "Calm down. No one's going to do anything to Troy.

Dr. Oswald is going to help us. She's going to look after him. The only thing that is going to go under a microscope is samples of his hair and blood. Isn't that right, Doctor?"

Oswald nods her head. "Absolutely," she says in a reassuring tone. "Your son is special. He's going to help billions of people stay safe. I promise you, I will do everything to continue Dr. Holston's work. I will make sure that there is never another outbreak of the Zorna flu virus. And above all, this will happen with Troy's health and safety in mind."

Crystal relaxes, and I let go of her. "Can Troy fix Marco and Amber?"

Oswald's face twists.

"Zombaxin," I say. "Friends of ours. They've taken it, and so far, they haven't come out of it."

"What do you mean, they haven't come out of it?"

"They took more than one pill, and they haven't gotten back to normal. It's like they're still infected."

"How much did they take?"

"Six pills," Crystal interjects.

"Hmm," Oswald says thoughtfully. "How long has it been?"

"A few days. They're barricaded in a room and there are people watching over them, so they don't hurt anyone."

"Hmm," she says again and rubs her cheeks. "Have either of you two ever tried the drug?"

Crystal wildly shakes her head like a child being accused of stealing the last cookie from the cookie jar. "No ma'am."

I remain still.

Don't answer. Never admit guilt.

"Griffin..." Oswald sings in a motherly tone. In a Holston-ish tone. In a tone that is so ingrained in my head as one of superior authority that it takes me back to being ten years old and getting caught red handed for a minor offense.

I cave and hold up one finger. "Just once."

She narrows her eyes in disapproval. "Do you have any pills in the apartment?"

I hesitantly get up from the couch and go to the bedroom. Troy is snuggled up under the covers and gives me a 'thumbs up' sign when I enter the room. I smile at him and go to Amber's nightstand on her side of the bed. She keeps a lot of her junk in there, Zombaxin included.

I trot back into the living room and hand Oswald the orange container.

"This isn't my field, ya know," she says. "I might need help with..."

"Anyone but Trager," I cut her off. "Your uncle mentions a few people that he trusted. Trager was off limits."

She nods her head and stands up. "A vaccine would be just the thing to make people like the AAC go away. There are a lot of people who are not very happy with the Altered."

"Oh, believe me, we know," I say looking back at Crystal.

"But this," Oswald holds up the bottle in one hand, "and this," she holds up the package of Holston's things in the other, "could very well be what we need to see some peace for you guys. If anything, Crystal here could be viewed as a hero. The full culmination of my uncle's journey."

"I hope so," I say quietly.

Oswald makes her way to the door. "I'll be in touch soon," she says as I open it for her and see her out.

●

Hope is something that the human mind creates for itself in the never-ending quest for self-preservation. It's a want. A desire. A wish for things to come. Optimistic anticipation, if you will. Little children hope Santa Claus is real. Teenagers hope they'll one day get a good paying job and live a comfortable life. Adults hope they'll be able to support their growing families and be able to happily retire. "Hope for the best." But hope isn't tangible. It isn't visual. It isn't audible. And most of all, it isn't real. It's a myth, a lie. Because just when you start to get a tiny taste of it (oh, I hope everything will work out in the end)—its comfort level, and the expectation that comes with it—reality slams its prickled wooden door right against your forehead. Reality jams its serum-filled needle right smack into your vein. And when you wake up in a white room with a two-way mirror hanging on the walls, you realize that there is no more hope. *All hope is lost...*

To say that Crystal, Troy, and I were getting comfortable would be an understatement. It was downright scary how quickly Troy got attached to me. He would look to me for approval, asked me to help him take care of himself, and would have rather slept in the room with me over his mother. It was a bizarre conglomeration, a picture-perfect portrait of an inhuman family, and for a split second, it kinda felt like it might have lasted.

I could only be so lucky.

We played family for all of two days—two days where I felt relaxed and not on edge. I hate to admit it, but I barely thought of Amber or Eugene or Zombaxin or Dr. Graves, or anything else. Troy was a calming ray of sunshine and taking care of him consumed me. The TV was the only source of outside entertainment, so we ended up playing a lot of hide and seek in the apartment, or he would make up his own games to play using a deck of cards and some paper. He was very smart—very clever—and learned new things rather quickly.

The three of us were lying in my bed watching TV. Troy was snacking on some chocolate chip cookies, and Crystal and I were pretending to share them with him. She and I, Altered as we were, were not hungry in the least. But Troy? That kid had some appetite, let me tell ya! Crystal had warmed up to me by this point, as well. I think she liked the calmness and stability that I could offer, as opposed to the chaotic, secretive (and don't forget dirty) lifestyle that she had with Eugene and the gang. I know she missed him, but I think she was starting to see that the grass was definitely greener on my side.

Anyway, we were watching some cartoon on TV that Troy really got a kick out of. He had memorized the entire opening theme song and laughed like a maniac when the characters would get into some crazy situation. "Giffin! Giffin, watch!" he squealed. I paid very close attention to the screen as he rolled over with laughter.

"That was too funny, Buddy!" I said in mock amazement. "I can't believe he dropped that piano on that guy's *head*!"

And he roared again. Crystal smiled. It was rare when she did, but she took such pride in Troy, anything he did seemed to warm her heart.

"What if I dropped a piano on *your* head!" I said as I pounded one fist on the bed and shook the top of his curly hair with my other hand.

"No Giffin! No! That would *huwt*!" he yelped.

The three of us were laughing hysterically when we heard the first pounds on the door. We all gave each other a 'did-you-just-hear-that?' look, and I hit the mute button on the remote as the second wave of ominous pounding echoed in the apartment. Crystal let out a small squeak and I put a finger up to my mouth to silence the both of them.

"Griffin King, 024, this is the Tampa Sheriff's Department! Open up!"

Troy flung himself into Crystal's lap and burrowed his head against her chest. I shook my head slowly and pointed to the closet, silently instructing her and Troy to get inside. She eased herself off the bed, scooped Troy in her arms, and made her way to the closet. I followed her, and shut the door, concealing them inside.

The banging on the front door continued. When I finally opened it, two police officers barged through, with a woman dressed in a business suit following behind them.

"Hey! What's going on?" I yelled.

The male officer held up his badge. "Griffin King?" he said. "I'm Detective Davis, this is my partner, Detective Galloway," he pointed to the female officer. "And this is Dr. Rennard," and he motioned to the middle-aged woman behind him. "This is the last known residence of Amber Fields, 025. Is she home? We need to ask her some questions."

I panicked. "W...w...what is this about? Amber? She doesn't live here."

Davis raised his eyebrow at Detective Galloway, and she started looking around the living room. "What do you mean?" Davis asked.

"We broke up," I lied, "and I haven't seen her in almost a month. I don't where she is."

"Mr. King, are you aware that there have recently been a string of attacks in this area?" Galloway asked.

"Ma'am, I don't know what you're talking about."

"Don't '*ma'am*' me!" she snapped. "Just tell us where Miss Fields is."

"I told you! I have no idea!"

Detective Davis walked around me in a circle, eyeballing me up and down. He was much taller and had to tilt his head to meet me eye to eye. "You doing the Black Death, boy?" he snarled.

I think I gulped. "The what?"

The doctor moved a step forward and I noticed something I hadn't before. She had a scar underneath her right eye. A bump raised up so slightly, like an old mosquito bite that someone picked at and picked at, and just never went away. *She was Altered!* "Black Death. Zombaxin," she said, her voice deep and smooth.

"No," I said, and breathed a sigh of relief knowing there was none left in the apartment.

CHAPTER 16

Galloway walked up behind me, put her hands on my shoulder, and began ushering me to the door. "We're gonna need you to come to the station with us for some questioning."

"Like hell I will!" I screamed and shrugged from her touch. "I'm not going anywhere with you! I told you, I don't know anything! If I'm not under arrest, please leave."

Davis made a motion to his hip like he was going for his gun. Dr. Rennard outstretched her arm in his direction and walked closer to me. "No need for that, Detective," she said. "King is going to co-operate one way or another."

Co-operate?

I was still trying to wrap my head around what was happening. Did they have evidence against Amber to link her to the murder in the park? Did they know we had used Zombaxin? Were they trying to frame me for something? Were they after *Troy*?

I knew I needed to get them out of the apartment as quickly as possible. It was only so long before Troy would get antsy in that closet.

"Just call my doctor," I said, yelling, hoping that Crystal would hear me and understand. "Just call my doctor, Doctor Dorothy Oswald. She can help you with anything you need to know."

"No. That won't be necessary," Galloway said in her no-nonsense tone. "You're gonna come with..."

"Doctor Dorothy Oswald!" I yelled. "She knows everything, and she'll help you!"

Detective Davis reached out, grabbed me by my arms, and held me in place. I went wild and bucked back and forth against his strong hold.

Galloway came behind me clicking open her handcuffs. "Hold him still!" she shouted at Davis.

I swiveled my head around and hissed at her.

Frightened, she hopped back a few steps.

"He can't hurt you any more than I can," Rennard said. "Griffin, we just have some questions for you. You can either come with us peacefully, or not. That's your choice."

I struggled again under Davis's grip. Like an animal trapped in a snare. I hissed at Rennard, but she was unfazed by my actions. Her eyes were icy blue, like there was a faint trace of infection left in her system. I wanted to scream, "What is this all about? Why are you doing this to me?" because she's *like* me. She's Altered! Shouldn't she have some sort of allegiance to her own kind?

She blinked a few times before breaking her gaze. Then she took another step closer to me, her gait seemingly in slow motion—cool and calculated, almost ghost-like and almost sexy in a way. Her slender body glided, not walked, and her shoulder-length blonde hair caught the bounce of her stride like one of those models in a shampoo commercial. "Okay," she sighed, and opened up her shoulder strap purse. She reached in and pulled out a hypodermic needle.

My heart raced. "What is this? What are you doing? What is that for?"

She flicked the needle's edge like some mad scientist from a horror movie and snickered. "I guess you made your choice," she said as she jabbed the needle into the back of my thigh.

I felt fuzzy and hazy almost immediately. The last thing I remember yelling before I collapsed was, "Doctor Oswald!"

17

I HAVE A POUNDING HEADACHE RIGHT ABOVE MY LEFT temple. Every time I turn my head, or move my body, the throbbing sensation increases to maximum level nearly blinding me. The fluorescent lighting in the room doesn't help much, either. I remember my mother telling me long ago that headaches like those were caused by dehydration. As I move my tongue over the roof of my mouth, a metallic taste dances on its surface, and I imagine a nice cold glass of lemonade in my hands. Yes! An icy drink would surely cure my dehydration, take away that God-awful thrashing pain in my head, and relieve me of the disgusting taste in my mouth.

Flashes of images come back to me as I survey the observation room. This scene is all too familiar, and memories of the Re-Assimilation Center competes for space in my conscious mind. *I woke up on a similar hospital gurney, not too long ago.* Now, I'm in a rectangular white room. The bed I'm on is placed horizontally against one of the short walls with a padded door on the opposite side. On the longer walls, to the right and left of me, are two long mirrors—those two-way types like they had in the Re-Assimilation Center. In the corner of the room, next to the bed is a yellow lab shower with a triangle lever hanging from the shower head. It's the kind they had in the high school science classrooms in case anyone got hurt during a lab experiment. Those showers never worked, though, because the one time that ditzy chick in chemistry spilled some chemical up her arm and ran to the shower in a panic, water never came out of the damn thing. I bet it's safe to say that mine doesn't work either, although I'd really like to rinse out my mouth right about now.

So, I remember the Altered doctor and the cops at my house. They were snooping around looking for Amber. Yeah, right. That was just a ruse—a way to get me to open up before they say, "Oh, yeah, come with us for some more questions." They knew damn well that Amber wasn't there. The purpose of that visit was to get to me. The lady cop was looking around the apartment like she was interested, but she wasn't. They had their mission, and they got me, because if they were there for anything else, they would have ransacked the entire apartment.

But I don't necessarily know for sure if they did or not. That Rennard lady stuck me in the leg with a needle and I went black and fuzzy. A tranquilizer, I assume, because it hit me like a ton of bricks—and fast! I have no idea if they raided the place after I was out cold. For some reason, I don't think they did. *I* was their objective. I have to believe this if I'm to believe Crystal and Troy are safe. I remember screaming Oswald's name, and I hope that Crystal had the sense enough to understand.

I stretch my arms up over my head and a deep yawn subtly rises from my chest. It comes up from my throat and out of my mouth, clogging my head and ears with its filling sound. Once it releases, though, my ears pop with a *whoosh,* and suddenly, the silence in the room becomes clearer. It reminds me of traveling on planes with my family. We had moved from New York to Florida when I was a kid, and we had visited our relatives about once a year. I remember always having terrible earaches on the plane rides. The pressure in my ears would be unbearable. I chewed gum, listened to my headphones, drank a lot of water—nothing worked. I would sometimes pinch my nose shut and blow air out to try to relieve the pressure in my ear canals. That would work for a hot second, and then right away they would clog back up. Finally, as I got older, I found taking a decongestant pill right before take-off would work. It knocked me out for the entire flight, but I wouldn't be in pain.

I was just on a plane.

I remember hearing a loud rumbling noise (which was probably the plane's engine) and my eyes fluttering open. My seat was reclined all the way back into a laying position. I turned my head to the side and saw the two detectives and Dr. Rennard sitting in the aisle next to me. I think I tried to say something, but when Rennard saw that I was coming out of it, she got up from her seat, and stuck me on my arm with another needle. I passed out again, and the last thing I know, I woke up here.

But where is here?

The air in the room feels different. It smells different, too. It's not as *wet* as I'm used to, if that makes any sense. It even tastes different, or that could just be the remnants of the metallic flavor coating my taste buds. I don't know. I can't explain it. I could just be disoriented from the drugs, the plane ride, the pressure change, or something, but there's one thing I'm certain of: *I've a feeling I'm not in Kansas anymore.*

Regardless of where I am or how I got here, I was kidnapped, plain and simple. For what reason, I have no clue. Am I too connected? Do I know too much? Have I seen too much? There are only a few possibilities that really stick out—either Graves turned me in, or Oswald turned me in, or Eugene or someone in his crew turned me in. That pretty much narrows it down. I have to think that I can automatically eliminate Eugene or any of those guys as the culprit. They had much more to lose than I did, and let's be honest, they were in some deeper and darker shit I could ever dream about. Unless they turned me in for full immunity, there would be no other reason to give me up. Ain't nobody these days who would be willing to give any privileges to our kind, so I seriously doubt it was any of them.

Wait! What am I talking about? Turn me in? Give me up? What did I do wrong?

Okay, okay, so I took an illegal drug that potentially put people in danger, and I kinda helped cover up a murder, and I did break into the lab at the medical center to steal some important documents. Fine. You got me. Guilty as charged. But most people who are caught for crimes they commit aren't drugged, kidnapped, put on a plane to an undisclosed location, and left in some medical observation room either. So, I have to think there's definitely something larger at work here. Something larger than Eugene or Jimmy or the others in the gang could fathom.

That leaves Graves and Oswald. I wouldn't put it past Graves to rat me out, but the more I think about my last encounter with him, the more I think about how I *didn't* tell him anything about Amber or the gang. Those were details I told Oswald. Is it possible that she tricked me into trusting her only to turn me over to the authorities?

Could I have been wrong about her all along? Could she have been the one to stab me in the back? Did I just put Troy in grave danger?

I need to subtract all the unknowns from the equation and focus on what I *do* know—Dr. Rennard is an Altered. But she's a doctor. But she's an Altered, and that's the perplexing part. She doesn't give off the 'Feral vibe,' so for now I'll assume that she's a RAT (as Jimmy so affectionately refers to those of us originally treated at the Re-Assimilation Centers). What authority does she have, though? She was accompanied by two detectives—Galloway and Davis—so she's got the backing of the law, but to what end? Is this her facility? Has she brought me here not so much for questioning, but for *probing?* As in—*exploratory* stuff? As in—*experimentation* stuff?

Also, Eugene and Jimmy told me about an Altered woman who was snooping around and asking questions about Troy. I bet it was Rennard.

Why does her name ring a loud bell in my head?

I also know I'm nowhere near home. You don't get drugged and put on a plane to go for a little joyride, ya know? I'm definitely in some medical place, and I'm definitely not in Florida.

I hate two-way mirrors. Whenever I've been subjected to them, it's like I can actually feel hundreds of eyes staring at me. It's creepy and weird, and I've done this scene before. I've already had my *Terminator* moment back at the Re-Assimilation Center, and I don't wish to go through that again. I get up from the gurney, rub the side of my head hoping to prevent an onslaught of throbbing, and approach the mirror to the left of me. The glass is thick, and in my mind's eye I can see people on the other side. I look beyond my own reflection, smile and wave. "Hi," I say. "How's it going over there? Got anything to drink? The tranqs left an awful taste in my mouth and I'm kinda thirsty."

Of course, there's no response. I don't expect to get one.

I tap on the glass. "Hey!" I say a little louder. "What's a guy gotta do to get glass of water around here?"

I watch my face in the mirror and contort all my muscles in different ways. I furrow my brow and tighten up my lips. I open my eyes wide then scrunch my face up real tight. I shift my face at all angles until I find an expression that looks cartoonishly frightening, and I tap on the glass again, this time slower and harder. "Hell-ooo!" I sing. "Can anybody hear me?"

CHAPTER 17

I close my fist tightly and beat on the glass like a drum. Harder. Harder. Louder. Louder. The pounding echoes in the room. Fills my unclogged ears. Puts me in some weirdo trance. *Thump. Thump. Thump. Boom. Boom. Boom.* I become dazed, hypnotized by the sound and the rhythm. "Hell-ooo! I need help in here!" I scream wildly, but it's not my voice, it's like I don't even exist. Like the voice is coming in over a radio wave. Like I'm a caged animal trying to escape some holed up world in the *Twilight Zone*. Frantic. Panicked. "Help meeee!"

I need to get out. I need to get out. I need to...

I realize that I'm growling and hissing when I hear a tapping noise coming from the hospital gurney.

I hobble back to the bed to locate the noise.

Tap. Tap. Tap.

Underneath the bed, on the lower portion of the wall just above the baseboard, there is an air vent. I put my ear up to it to see if that's where the tapping is coming from.

Tap. Tap. Tap. Tap.

A metallic sounding echo coming from the other side of the wall.

I hit the steel slats of the vent a few times. Maybe whoever is on the other side will hear me, too. One. Two. Three. Four. I wait a moment, and there it is again! Four taps back in response. I hit it again, three times this time, and I'm met with three taps. I do two, and two come back. "Hey!" I say into the vent. "Hey! Who's there? What's going on?"

As if on cue, the fluorescent light in my room shuts off, and the mirror on the right-hand wall illuminates. I stand up to get a better view. "Hey! Hey!" I scream, pounding furiously on the glass.

It's another room, much like the one I'm in, and there are four people inside—two girls and two guys. The two girls are huddled on the bed together, holding each other for comfort. One of the guys is fussing with the lab shower, and the other dude is crouched low by their vent.

By a vent! That's the person who's tapping to me!

The guy by the lab shower dashes up to their side of the mirror and starts hitting at it with his palm. "Hey man! You still in there? Where did ya go?"

I jump up and down in the darkness, waving my arms in the air. "I'm right here! I'm right here!" I yell.

The guy hits on the glass some more. He's tall with black hair and dark eyes. His skin is a horrid shade of tan and dirt. Dried blood is caked on one side of his face from his temple, right under his hair line, to his neck. He's human. Not Altered. He doesn't have a scar. Bloodface turns his head to the other guy in the room and says, "Try the vent again! Try the vent!"

I get on the floor and fuddle my way in the darkness back to my vent and scream into it, "Hello! Hello! I can see you! I see you guys! Hello!"

The light in my room turns back on and I stand up. The mirror's image is just my reflection again. I can no longer see the people behind it. I kneel back down to the vent and start hitting hard at the metal. "Are you there? Are you there? Hello! Hello!"

I wait for a response, hoping the guy will start tapping back. Maybe we can form some kind of Morse code system? But there's nothing. No answer, but I hear some rumblings from the other side, so I press my ear up to the grate. I hear their voices—low, muffled, but hysterical. When the light in my room went out, there's must have gone on. Now my light is on, and they must be back in darkness. I can't make out what they're saying, but from what I can glean, one of them might be having a panic attack and the others are trying to calm that person down.

Suddenly, one of them starts screaming. I can clearly make that out. Screaming, screaming, screaming. The others are yelling, as well. There's a huge commotion, and a door slams. Heavy. A strong metal that clatters and clangs even through the air ducts. Maybe wrapped in chains.

There's continued sobbing and frantic voices. I think I hear someone say, "Oh God, no!" but I can't be sure because the air conditioner kicks on, and a gust of cool air blasts into my face and drowns out any other sound that had been traveling through.

18

THERE IS NO CONCEPT OF TIME, AND I ABSOLUTELY HATE feeling like this. No concept of night or day. I can only get a sense of the rising and descending sun whenever my lights go on and off. There doesn't seem to be a rhyme or reason to that, either. It's kind of random how they turn on for a little while, then shut down for a few minutes, then turn back on. It's almost as if a little child is flicking the light switch on and off at will.

When the light in my room is on, my horrid reflection stares at me in the two mirrors on the walls. However, when my light turns off, the two mirrors turn into windows, and I have a full view of what's happening on the other sides of me. The mirror on the left side shows nothing. There's a dim light within, but I can't really make out what's inside the room. I know for a fact there aren't any people in there. The mirror on the right side shows a different story. They started out as four people in there, but now only one dude and one girl remain. I watch them every once in a while, mostly in part because I hope they can hear me banging on the mirror, but I know that won't happen. Bottom line is this—when my lights go off, I can see them. When their lights go off, they can see me. I figured this out rather quickly. Once, while my room was lit, I pressed my body up against the mirror and was screaming and banging on it, horrified at my reflection in such close proximity. As soon as my lights went off, my reflection disappeared and I saw the image of the guy in the other room, his body up against the glass in the same pose as me. It was eerie and comical at the same time. They've tried to contact me as much as I've tried to contact them.

Speaking of contacting, I haven't had any more luck with the air vent. I'll bang on it every once in a while, and scream some stuff into it, but they can't hear me. There must be multiple air conditioning units cooling off this place, because I think air blows into the separate vents at different times. It was probably just a fluke that there was no air filtering through our individual vents when we were able to bang our simple tune out to each other. I know they're still trying to, though, 'cause I see the guy kneeling at the side of the bed and pounding his fist onto the metal grating.

I'm not hungry, but I feel like I'm going to die of thirst at any moment. And yeah, I did try the laboratory shower, and just as I thought, it didn't work. I'm okay for now, but if I don't get some water or something soon, I seriously might go insane.

Currently, the lights are on. I walk over to the right-side mirror and examine myself again. My face is a field of brown stubble that itches my cheeks. The new hair line on my cheekbone is right underneath my eye scar. Not even a full beard could cover that thing up! My hair is also coming in—a little longer on the top because of the recent faded haircut I gave myself. My skin is a muted shade of gray. I'm not sure if that's the way it always looks, or if it's just the wicked enhancement from the fluorescent light. I remember Amber always saying how much she hated fluorescent lighting in public bathrooms because it always seemed to bring out every little imperfection on her face. It especially accentuated her eye scar and that bothered her something awful. Now I understand what she meant, because here I am, under fluorescent lighting, looking like a mess.

Yep! It's just crazy, Altered Griffin in the house. The crowd goes wild!

I wonder what Amber is doing right now. Is she back to her Altered self, or is she still trapped in her chemically induced infected state? When I saw her at Eugene's, my first instinct was to help her, to save her from that insanity, but the more I think about it—the way her eyes were glazed over, the way she kinda smirked at me—the more I'm left believing that she is exactly where she wants to be. It hurts to think that I could have been so wrong about her. She *wanted* to be infected. She *wanted* to tap into her primal instincts. She *liked* it.

I'll be the first to admit that I've had urges and cravings, but for Amber, it was much stronger. She buried her urges and cravings for far too long, and when the prospect of returning to that state was in the palm of her hand in the form of a little black pill, she couldn't resist. She gave into it. That's probably why she was able to easily kill the homeless man at the park.

I wonder what type of person Amber was Before. Did she always have the instinct of a ruthless killer? Was there always a darkness in her soul? Does she even *have* a soul?

Even though I look in the mirror, I'm not really looking at myself. I'm looking through myself, if that's possible. I'm trying to find my essence, like going through some kind of wormhole to locate my soul. 'Cause if Amber is soulless, does that mean I am, too? My own eyes hypnotize me, and memories flash in my mind. Memories of Before, and Now. Memories of Griffin—pre, during, post. I see a young man, clueless, unsure of himself. This young man needs to make something happen in the face of impending doom. He needs to assert himself in some alpha-male way. I had so much promise for a good life, and it all got bitten away. I start to fade out and fade in. I can no longer see myself in the mirror. The images of my memories have overtaken my vision in a transcending trance. Darkness surrounds me. My vision, my being, my soul. I think about my dad, my mom, Josh, Graves, Sydney, Toby, Holston, Amber—images swirling around and around.

I remember lying side by side with Toby and how she wrapped her legs around my waist and kissed me passionately. I remember how I couldn't resist her, and how that was probably the last moment of happiness I had before I was turned. I remember her soft touch and her kitten-like voice whispering seductively in my ear. It's as if I can actually see that memory before me in the darkness. I can actually see me embracing my blonde headed mistress out of fear and comfort and hatred and desire and...

A crackling noise from a speaker makes me snap out of my daydream. I must be more dehydrated than I thought, because my room is dark, and I can see what's happening in the other room. The guy and the girl next door to me are in a passionate position, and I quickly look away when I realize what's going on. It doesn't shock me they would resort to that. People act oddly when thrown in extreme circumstances.

Let them have their moment.

I turn around and face the opposite mirror, which is now a window revealing to me a chamber-like room. I look above the two-way mirror and notice something I hadn't before—two speakers on top.

I move closer and press my face to the glass. My stomach knots up at the scene within the room. Bound in chains suspended from the wall is the other couple. The speaker crackles again, and their voices come through.

"What the hell are we gonna do, Blake?" the girl cries.

The guy, Blake, tugs at his shackles. "I don't know, Margo!"

"It's all Kate's fault! We should have never..."

"Shut up! It's not anyone's fault! We all screwed up! We can't start saying someone shouldn't have done something, because we *all* shouldn't have done *any* of it!"

Margo cries some more and jerks her torso back and forth.

"Stop doing that!" Blake screams at her.

"Why?" Margo yells frantically. "They're just gonna kill us, I know it! I know it!"

"Don't talk like that! We'll find a way out of here."

I can't help but laugh to myself. This whole scene is unfolding like some cheesy torture-horror movie where the kids are on vacation and get involved with the wrong people. I loved that movie *Hostel* where those stupid kids get kidnapped and tortured. I remember after we watched that movie, Josh said, "Guess we're not backpacking in Europe after graduation, man."

For some reason, I feel like I'm being punked. Is someone gonna come walking through the door at any minute and say, "Ha! Ha! Gotcha! Funny joke, right?" 'Cause that's how this feels. That's how this whole situation feels. Like one, big elaborate gag that's probably gonna be broadcast on some dopey reality show.

Now we present to you "Fear School" —starring Griffin King and company.

Two white suits enter the torture room, but I don't think they're there to point at a hidden camera and smile. White bio-hazmat suits with full on face masks. One carries a tranquilizer gun and has a black riot gear shield thrown over his shoulder. The other holds a syringe. A circular emblem is on the lapels of their suits. I can't make out the image, but I see the letters *PIADC* in bold blue. Blake and Margo scream and thrash against their chains when the suits enter.

The suit with the tranq gun and shield moves to the corner of the room, barely in my line of sight. The other suit walks over to Margo and grabs her chin with a free gloved hand. The hand moves Margo's face from side to side, and I notice something I hadn't before—Margo has a scar! She's an Altered!

Margo kicks and screams and spits at the suit. "Let me go! Let me go!" in addition to a barrage of expletives.

The suit goes over to Blake and does the same inspection. He's human. He doesn't have a scar.

Blake freaks out, too. He thrashes and yells and curses on the top of his lungs. In a movement that happens so quickly that I almost don't see it, the suit jabs the syringe into Blake's arm, and he howls from the sting. The suit unchains him and quickly leaves the room.

"She let you go? She let you go?" Margo screams. "Why did she do that? Why did she..."

"She stuck me with something," Blake says, rubbing at the injection site on his arm. "Bitch injected me..." He tries to move toward Margo, but stumbles.

"Blake? Blake? Are you okay? Get up and get me out of here!"

"I... I don't feel good," he says. He slurs his words like he's drunk. He's groggy. Falls to the floor.

"Blake! Blake, get up! Blake..."

Blake curls his legs into the fetal position on the floor and moans.

Margo's eyes go wild. "What's wrong? What's wrong? Talk to me!"

Blake rolls onto his back and lets out a frightening scream. "Make it stop! Make it stop! What did she do to me? Oh God! Someone help me!" His eyes roll into the back of his head as he convulses in agony. His whole body twitches with rigid jerky movements for about a minute, while Margo screams her head off.

When he finally stops, sits up, and opens his eyes wide, I know exactly what he was injected with. The white haze is a tell-tale sign of only one thing.

Infection.

Blake rises and turns to Margo, smelling the air around her, hissing through his gritted teeth.

"Oh no, Blake! Oh no! Oh no!"

Blake grabs Margo's arm and bites hard, but his nose scrunches up when he tastes her, and he backs away, sniffing the air again. Margo quickly clamps her hand down on the bite and continues with her sobs and screams. Blake picks up a scent in the room like a wild dog and turns his attention to the suit in the corner. With teeth bared, he screeches his infected vocal cord screech and lunges at the suit. The suit lifts the tranquilizer gun and shoots Blake in the neck, rendering him immediately unconscious. In seconds, the other suit comes back in and the two of them drag Blake's body back to his shackles where they put him back in chains.

"What did you do to him?" Margo screams, and kicks, and spits.

Syringe suit leaves, and soon returns with a naked girl with a bag over her head and hands bound with rope. Riot Gear helps Syringe drag the naked girl to the spot next to Blake and chains her up. Syringe takes the bag off the naked girl's head. It's the girl from the other room. They must have dragged her away while in the throes of passion.

"Kate? Kate?" Margo screams. "Are you okay? What's going on? Where's Jarrod?"

The naked girl, Kate, hangs her head down low. Her dark hair partially shields her naked body. She sobs uncontrollably and her words are inaudible. "They… they… they took me!" is pretty much all I can make out.

Margo screams again and takes my attention from naked Kate. Syringe suit has injected Margo and releases her from her chains. Again, Syringe leaves the room, and Riot Gear assumes his previous position.

"Oh God, Kate!" Margo says, her words starting to slur much like Blake's had. "She infected me. She gave me the stu…" A gurgling sound makes its way out of her throat. She bends her body forward and spews out a black bile vomit. Her transformation is much quicker, because after she throws up, she stands up straight and stretches her arms over her head, like she's just been awakened from a deep sleep.

She's not wild like how Blake was. In fact, she moves gracefully, methodically. Her movements stir something in me—I understand the calculated precision of her actions.

Her brain and body are fighting the infection, like there's an inkling of internal struggle. She's done this before. Felt this before, and she's conflicted on whether or not to fight against the fever or go with it. Her Altered self reverts almost immediately to the memory of her previously Infected self.

She eyes Blake's hanging body and smells the air around him, but she ignores him not because he's passed out cold, but because he's not what she wants. He's still infected, and no use to her. She hisses and screeches, and she thrashes her head back and forth like a mental patient in an insane asylum. She's losing control. Losing her grip on her consciousness. From her side profile, I see her eyes are completely white. She is gone.

With one last screech, Margo descends upon her friend hanging there like a hunk of naked meat. She tears a hole into Kate's side. Kate lets out a yelp and passes out from the pain. Margo turns to the corner of the room, a chunk of flesh hanging from her mouth, but Riot Gear is one step ahead. He tranqs her in the arm, and as Blake did, she too falls unconscious. Immediately, Syringe suit is in the room again, and they both chain Margo back up.

What is this game? What is this torture experiment?

Syringe suit takes off the helmet and it's none other than Dr. Rennard. I should have known.

"Is it safe to..." Riot Gear begins. Rennard makes a hand gesture, and Riot Gear pulls off the helmet with a hiss. It's Detective Davis. I'm gonna go out on a limb and say he might not really be a detective after all...

Davis points to the bloody gash on naked Kate's side. "Will she..." he stutters.

Rennard shrugs her shoulders. "You didn't tranq her, right?"

"No! No! She must have passed out from shock. Or pain. Or both."

Rennard nods and keeps her eyes trained on Kate, like she is waiting for something. She smiles wide when Kate stirs. She moans faintly and her chains rattle a little.

"She's movin' over here, Doc!" Davis says in a heightened tone.

"It's okay. Let her go. Let her come to."

Now I'm on the edge of my proverbial seat. What are they gonna do when she wakes up? Is Rennard gonna inject her with the virus, too?

I get my answer when Kate opens her whitened eyes, and her slack-jawed mouth emits a deep, infected moan.

Rennard snaps her fingers. "Excellent!" She unclips a walkie-talkie from her utility belt and presses a button. "We a have a positive on transference," she says into the black device. "I repeat—we have confirmed transference."

She releases the button to a hiss of static. A voice crackles through on the other end saying, "Meet me in my office."

All of a sudden, the light turns back on in my room and I'm left staring at my open mouth reflection.

I close my mouth and make my way back to the gurney. There are two pressing questions that I have right now, on top of the initial 'where am I?' and 'what the hell is going on?'

Why did they let me watch all that? And when's it gonna be my turn?

19

SOMETIME AFTER I WITNESS THE EXPERIMENT IN THE room next door, the lights go out again, and I am able to see the guy in the room on the other side of the wall. Jarrod, I believe the girl called him. He sits on the bed with his head in his hands, and I can't tell if he's crying or not. He looks up sharply when the door to his room opens and someone shoves the Altered girl, Margo, inside. She's normal now. Apparently whatever drugs Rennard gave her have worn off. I look up above the mirror on my side and see there are speakers there, but they're not turned on because I can't hear a thing.

However, Margo and Jarrod's actions speak volumes. When she stumbles and falls into the room, he immediately jumps up to comfort her and ushers her to the hospital bed. It's obvious he cares for her, not in a lover- type way, because, well, he kinda had that thing with the other girl, Kate.

Margo is crying, sobbing. She holds up her arm and shows him where she was bitten by Blake. Blood no longer flows from the wound, but it's still fresh, gaping, and oozing with body fluids that will soon turn into an infection if not treated. Jarrod puts an arm around Margo's shoulder and smooths her hair away from her face. He must be speaking gently to her, because her shoulders are more relaxed, and her breathing is becoming steadier. He takes his thumb and runs it across her face, as if to massage her scar. She, in turn, uses her opposite hand to do the same to him. And that's when I realize, he's Altered, too.

Jarrod, Kate, Margo, Blake—two Altereds, two humans, and one completely messed up experiment. One that I was privy to see, no less. I'm definitely not in a good position right now, and the thought of me ever getting out of here is quickly becoming more and more of a fantasy. I have a sickening feeling that my days are truly numbered here.

The light comes back on, and I can't help but sigh loudly. All this on off, on off, on off, is irritating. At first, I thought whoever was in charge was trying to simulate a sense of night and day, but now this is just ridiculous!

My heart almost stops when Dr. Rennard opens the door and walks into the room. Her hair is pulled back into a tight bun, and she's wearing a white lab coat over a business suit. Detective Davis comes into the room behind her. He's wearing a bio-hazmat suit, minus the helmet, and rolling in a metal cart with food. One thing I do discern between the two of them—Davis is normal, and Rennard is Altered, which is probably why Davis is in full protective gear, and Rennard is nonchalant and casual about being in the room with me. I straighten up my back so I look taller and stare her down.

She motions to the cart behind her. "Hungry?" she asks.

I continue my stare.

She smiles and her eye scar wrinkles up a little. "Sure, you are," she says as she takes a step closer to me.

"Are you for real?" I ask in disbelief.

She chuckles. The sound is near diabolical as it passes through her closed lips like some kind of fairy tale evil stepmother. "Have some water at least."

"Like I would ever trust..."

She nods to Davis who tosses me a sealed bottle of water.

I catch and examine it. It's sealed tight, alright. Couldn't have been tampered with. Fresh out of a package of some no-name dollar store brand of bottled water. It should be okay. I don't see how they could have put anything in it. And I'm so terribly thirsty!

Just looking at the liquid inside the clear plastic makes my throat feel grittier, scratchier. I unscrew the top, remove the protective plastic ring at the perforation, take a long drink, then close the bottle up.

I lift my shoulders up and outstretch my arms. I know I have to get straight to the point and ask as many questions as I can if I'm to figure out where I am, and most importantly, how I'm getting out of here. I need to feel Rennard out. Maybe I can tap into out Altered kinship, ya know, work the 'we're on the same side' angle?

"So, what is all this? What is this all about?"

She nods her head forward in a slight bow and closes her eyes. It's a 'knowing' gesture, like she's going to grant me some kind of deserved knowledge. "Welcome to the Plum Island Animal Disease Center."

PIADC on their suits. Plum Island. Trager.

"Excuse me?" I ask, stalling, trying to process.

"You'll see that this is a fabulous facility located off the eastern end of the North fork coast of Long Island, New York." She speaks in a tone that is operational—a flight attendant giving instructions before takeoff, or a tour guide spouting out useless information about a particular location. "Used as an animal research center to study foot-and-mouth disease in cattle, Plum Island quickly became a place where many animal diseases where harbored, researched, and mostly eradicated. Government run and own, a division of Homeland Security, Dr. Trager, who had been head scientist for years here, was given the opportunity to purchase the facility from the state of New York when it went up for sale. Trager had many projects in development and was working on a vaccine for hog cholera at the time the site was put on the market. The officials were nice enough to let him be the first to make an offer on the island, which they accepted. And, well, here we are today." She claps her hands together.

"But why are you telling me all this? Why should I care about that?"

"Well, it's always been my belief that people should have some type of knowledge where they call home, and..."

A lump forms in my throat. *Home?*

"... sticking around for a little bit and helping us with..."

"Wait! Wait! Wait!" I yell at her. She takes a step back, and Davis pushes the cart to the side, readying himself to intervene if necessary. "What the hell are you talking about? What the hell am I doing here? Why did you make me watch that little torture display?"

She snickers again, closed mouth, dry, borderline maniacal. "Nobody made you watch anything! You did that on your own."

Heat rises up behind my eyes. My vision is cloudy with rage, and my hands tremble. I'm fighting the urge to tear her throat out, so I take a deep breath. "Okay, okay," I say trying to calm myself down.

"You gave me your little Plum Island history lesson, now explain to me what the hell is going on."

"The Zorna flu has mutated." Her eyes shift slightly, and bells in my Altered brain immediately start *ding, ding, dinging*.

"Mutated? Or manipulated?" I say.

She ignores me. "What you witnessed earlier was proof that transference can occur. People like me and you," she grabs my wrists and tugs my arms down firmly, "people who have been Altered, can't be re-infected. We're safe for the most part. We're not sure why, but a bite has no effect on us."

"Black Death? Zombaxin?" I say, reminding her of the recreational drug so many Altereds have been recently using.

She nods her head. "Whoever is distributing it has developed a new compound to match the mutation of the Zorna virus. It's an improperly inactivated strain of the Zorna flu, which is why any Altered who takes this new form of Zombaxin will temporarily exhibit infected-like symptoms, but if they are to bite a human, they can transfer the virus through blood and saliva."

"Do the Infected humans turn back to normal? Is it temporary like it is for the Altered?"

She shakes her head.

And that's exactly what I saw before. The cycle rings clear: Rennard injected the Altered girl, Margo, making her temporarily infected. Margo bit the human girl, Kate. Kate became infected.

Which must mean that Kate is still infected and chained up in the torture room.

"But the serum. The antidote that cured me. That cured *you*," I say, stressing the 'you,' acknowledging our common lineage.

"Dr. Trager is fairly certain that it would turn an infected human back to normal. Make them Altered like us."

I blink my eyes to keep them open. They feel heavy all of a sudden, so I take another sip of the water in my hand. "What about the guy? Blake? He's human. I saw you inject him, and..."

"Yes. I did. I gave him a dose of the mutated virus to see if his bite would have an effect on the Altered girl. Which it obviously didn't."

Infected Blake bit Altered Margo. No effect.

"Is he still... ya know, infected?"

She nods.

"And the girl? The naked girl? Is she still infected from the bite?"

She nods again.

"So, give them the cure!" I scream. My skin crawls with anxiety. I run my hands up and down my arms to try and scratch the feeling away.

"It's not that simple, Griffin. This is where you come in. It's no secret that Dr. Holston thought you were special. Dr. Holston knew it the minute he laid eyes on you. You were his Altered progeny. Dr. Trager only wishes to finish what Holston started, and you're a big part of that plan."

My head spins and I don't feel like I am in control of my body. I think the dehydration is still getting to me because I slump down to the floor, place the bottle next to me, and rest my elbows on top of my knees. "I don't get it," I mumble, defeated.

"You have a sense about you," she starts. "You're different. You have a kind of instinct inside of you that sets you apart from the others," she lowers her voice, "even me." She kneels down in front of me, so we are face to face. "Dr. Trager thinks that you have a natural ability to control yourself when you're infected. There's something at your very core that gives you certain abilities, and this is something we are interested in, Griffin. We let you watch our demonstration, and I'm telling you about our work because we believe the memories that you store and the images that you reflect upon have a tremendous impact on your infected condition. Your psyche. Your essence. Your *soul* is comprised of the internalization of your experiences."

She's talking too fast, saying too much at once, I can't truly comprehend what she's talking about. It all sounds like forest noises of animals scurrying and birds cawing. I can't discern the words or their meanings. When I look up at her, our eyes lock. For once I can't get a grip on her facial expression. Is she somber? Angry? Anxious? Happy? All of the above?

I nod my head in her direction and graze my eyes over her scar. "How did it happen?" I ask. "How were you able to..."

She lifts her hand to the side of her face and rubs the skin under her right eye lovingly. "Dr. Trager saved me. He saved me more than once. Before the Outbreak, I was in a dead-end job with a dead-end life in New Mexico, and he offered me a way out. And then, of course, the world changed," she pauses, "and I changed, and..." her voice trails off a little bit as she drifts temporarily into a memory. "Dr. Trager is a genius, and I owe him my life," she continues, gushing.

Gushing like a lovesick teenager and not like a professional. "You'll see. He's going to revolutionize everything. He's going to make the world a better, safer place."

"Better? Safer?" I repeat.

Trager is crazy. He's going to take everything that Holston worked so hard for and bastardize it. He's going to cause chaos around the globe, and swoop on in as the almighty savior—to get the recognition that Holston deserved. A thought invades my mind—*did Trager orchestrate the first Outbreak?* But I don't say that thought out loud. Something inside me knows better. Something inside me knows that I'm not alright. I'm not fine. I'm shifting...

"He's going to experiment on me, isn't he?" My voice is thin, tired.

The lights flicker in the room. Davis reaches for the handle of the cart, swivels it back toward the door and leaves.

"He's wearing gloves," I mutter. "Why is he wearing gloves?"

My focus shifts, becomes grainy and fuzzy. My body tilts to the side and I lie on the cold floor with my knees to my chest. I knock the bottle of water over and it spills into a small pool by my head.

"You can't hurt me," Rennard says. She sounds like she's a million miles away, but I know she's standing directly over me. "Detective Davis is just taking an extra precaution. Just in case."

"Just in case," I repeat, but I'm not sure if I said it out loud or in my head.

20

ONE WOULD THINK I WOULD HAVE LEARNED MY LESSON by now. I accepted a sealed bottle from a crazed scientist, thinking that everything was on the level. I should have read the fine print. I guess I was more dehydrated than I thought because I probably would have thought the whole 'water-bottle' situation out a little better. Bottom line is this—Rennard drugged me—*again!* I really need to stop putting myself in these situations. I fear though, that when my eyes finally come into focus, this quite possibly may be the last situation I ever get myself into.

I'm chained to the wall in the experimentation room. It was bound to happen. I knew it would. Thick metal cuffs are clamped around my wrists and ankles, held in place by heavy chains fastened to the stone wall. I have a limited range of mobility—I can walk in a small area around me and can move my arms and legs to a certain degree. The room is cold, and relatively clean, but the metallic scent of old blood hangs heavy in the air, telling me this room has seen many horrors.

I'm not alone. All four of the people from my neighboring room are chained in the same fashion. The Altered girl, Margo, hangs next to me. The Altered guy, Jarrod, is next to her. Then there's Blake next to Jarrod, and Naked Kate (who is now fully clothed) next to Blake. Everyone is drugged up or passed out and just hanging limply on their shackles. Blake's stomach protrudes like a basketball as he dangles unconscious. Kate's head hangs to one side, her hair nearly sweeping the floor. I straighten myself up and survey the room. Always have to keep my eyes open and aware. I got myself into this stupid mess, I gotta figure out how to get myself out of it.

Margo moans and shifts against the chains. She mumbles something. I can't understand her at first, but slowly, her words are recognizable. "Change them back. Just change them back. What's going on?" She rubs her forehead right above her eyebrows, and her restraints clang and clash, startling her into awareness.

"Hey! Psst! Hey!" I half whisper, trying to get her attention.

She's groggy and shakes her head quickly as she looks around. When she understands that she's back in the experimentation room, she freaks out. "No! No! No! Not again! No more! Please!"

"Hey! Hey! Hey! Look at me! Calm down. It's okay," I say in a soothing voice.

She tilts her head and looks at me puzzled. "It's... it's... *you*!" she says loudly, unaware of the volume of her voice.

I put a finger to my closed mouth. "Shhh!"

"They had you in the room right next to me! Jarrod and Blake tried to..."

"I know, I know. I tried, too. Listen, they're probably listening to us right now, so just lower your voice a little and maybe we can figure something out. I'm Griffin."

"Griffin," she mindlessly repeats, still trying to free her mind from the cobwebs of a tranquilizer fog. "I'm Margo."

"I know."

"Huh? How do you kno..."

"It's a long story. I watched what happened here. They let me watch. I pretty much got the gist of what happened to all of you."

"Oh my God, Griffin!" she cries. "What the hell are they doing to us? What's going on? Are they gonna kill us?"

I raise my hand and try to reach out to her. "Slow down, slow down. If they were gonna kill us, I think they would have done that by now. I think they need us for some kind of testing."

"Because we're Altered?" she asks.

"Yeah, I'm pretty sure. I think they want to test a new type of Zombaxin on us to see what happens."

She shuts her eyes tightly and her face crinkles up into a ball. "Zombaxin!" she breathes heavily. "God damnit! I told him not to mess with that stuff!"

"What are you talking about?"

"My stupid brother. Jarrod." She motions to the guy next to her. "I told him it was bad news. Not to get involved with it. But he didn't listen to me. And look where we are now!"

"What happened? Do you know how you guys got here?"

She nods. "Yeah. We pretty much figured it out. It was seriously just one bad choice after the next."

"So, if Jarrod's your brother, then what about the other two?"

"Blake and Kate? They're our friends, I guess. I guess we're like couples or something. Me and Blake, Jarrod and Kate. It's a long story."

"Go for it. Enlighten me."

She's aware of her surroundings, aware of our predicament, now. "Blake and Kate are from California. Jarrod and I met them through an Altered fetish website," she whispers.

"A what?"

"Ya know, for like, people who have an interest in the Altered. They're curious about us or find us sexy. That kind of stuff."

I remember Eugene telling me about the Altered fetish parties that he went to. It boggles my mind that there are people who are so interested in what we went through, and not in a sympathetic kind of way. They really believe that being infected is a social status, or something that's cool and sexy. A turn-on.

If they only knew.

"At first it was kinda fun and all. It was like we were all boyfriend and girlfriend, well, minus me and Jarrod 'cause that would just be weird with my twin brother and all. Blake and Kate would come visit us in New York and we went out to visit them in California a few times. They were cool enough, ya know? Jarrod and I thought Blake and Kate were fun. Like, they treated us like rock stars. Like royalty. I didn't mind answering their questions, or watching zombie movies with them, 'cause they always gave us the star-treatment. Hotels. Dinners. Limo rides. It was cool. That's why I didn't mind so much when Blake first asked if he could lick my scar."

I shudder. "He actually did that?"

She chuckles softly, and it lightens the mood a little. "Yeah. Weird, right? I hate the damn thing, and here he was wishing he had one of his own."

"I guess people want what they can't have," I say.

"Must be. I'd cut it off my face and give it to him if he really wanted me to!"

I laugh right along. "So how did you get from there to here," I ask, swiveling my head in a semi-circle.

"Blake and Kate were visiting from Cali, and we had a plan to spend the week out in Montauk at some hotel on the beach. Well, Blake said he got hooked up with a guy out there who could give us the ultimate high."

"Black Death."

"Yep. Good ole' freakin' Zombaxin. Blake had heard stuff about it through people on the website, and thought that if me and Jarrod did it, then we could, like bite Blake and Kate, and do some weird role-playing shit. I don't know. I didn't really wanna do it, because what I remember from being infected was not fun, and I didn't want to revisit all that again, ya know?"

"What about your brother?"

"Jarrod was all about it. He couldn't wait to be infected again. Said he wanted to mess people up really bad and stuff. He said he wanted to OD on it so he would be permanently infected again. He said he didn't care if it came down to killing Blake and Kate, 'cause he was starting to hate them anyway, to be honest. Hated all people. Looked at them as cows. He was filled with so much rage and hate against everyone—humans, Black Bloods..."

"Black Bloods?"

"Yeah, ya know? Black Bloods, RATs, whatever you call those Altered who got preferential treatment."

Oh! Margo and Jarrod are Ferals.

She points to her scar. It's not raised up high, but the skin is a shiny pink color and there's a small remnant of the hole where they injected her with the serum. "When you're on your own like we were, it's hard not to have a chip on your shoulder. Anyways, we meet up with Blake's connection at our hotel and he tells us all about how to do the drug, what's the perfect environment, blah blah blah. We were right in the middle of making the transaction when there was a knock on the door. Kate, like a dumb blonde, opens it. The next thing I know there were two people shoving their way in the room and lights out. Somebody came up from behind me and knocked me out, and then the four of us woke up here."

"You were set up, you know that, right?"

She looks at me like I've insulted her intelligence. "Yes, Captain Obvious. Doesn't take a brain surgeon to get that one."

"Do you think it was Blake and Kate who set you up?"

She thinks for a second. "At first Jarrod did, but after talking it through, it didn't make sense. Why would those people take Blake and Kate, too?"

"How well did Blake know his connection man?"

She shrugs her shoulders. "I dunno. He was some shady guy he found off some sex website. He could have been anyone."

My lips tighten in thought. I'm fishing for an angle, any way to freedom. "How long do you think you've been here?"

"Longer than you, that much I know. It was a while before we saw you in our mirror. If I had to guess, I'd say two weeks."

I snap my fingers. "So there has to be someone looking for you, right? Somebody has probably reported you all missing by now!"

She shakes her head. "It's just me and my brother. Ya know. After the Outbreak happened."

I nod my head empathetically. I know what it means to lose your entire family. "And the human couple. Blake and Kate? Anyone looking for them?"

She shakes her head again. "Nope. Everyone who they loved or who loved them is dead."

I sigh. The prospect of a search party is out the window. "So, what happened to you and your brother?" I ask. "Ya know, from before. Becoming Altered..."

She breathes in. "Everything is such a blur from that time, but I remember the people in the white suits coming in and injecting our faces. And then they just... *left*." She shrugs her shoulders. "I was screaming, 'Come back! Come back!', but I wasn't really screaming. I was too new to have my voice work, ya know what I mean? I started moving before Jarrod did, but by that time, the people were gone, and it was too late, and we were left standing in a pool of dead bodies, forced to be on our own. Of course, we had no idea what was going on at first and took shelter in a strip mall. We were chased by infected on a daily basis, but learned real fast that when they bit us, we didn't get infected again. And really, after they bit us, they wanted nothing to do with us and would run away."

The Infected don't eat the Altered.

She continues, "So, we just kinda winged it until everything died down. What about you?"

I pause and debate whether or not to tell her my story—to reveal to her that I'm a 'Black Blood.' That might not sit well with her, and especially not with her brother. Just when I'm about to open my mouth to tell her some jagged version of my truth, Jarrod wakes up and Margo turns her attention to him.

"Jaah? Jaah? You okay? You okay?" she says stretching out her arms to touch him, but unable to reach.

He moans a little and comes out of the drugs rather quickly. "Yeah. You?"

"I'm fine. I'm fine," she lies.

Jarrod turns his head to his side and looks at Blake and Kate still hanging and unconscious. "What happened? Are they dead?"

"No," I answer. "But I think they're still infected."

Jarrod turns his head to look at me. "Hey man! You're the guy!"

"Shhhh!" Margo prompts and swats her hands at him. "He's Griffin. He thinks he knows what's happening to us. We're gonna try to figure out how to get out of here."

Jarrod jerks on his chains. "No! We're not gonna figure out nothing!" he screams. "These people are gonna let us out!" He bucks and thrashes in the restraints, raises his head and starts growling and hissing. "Let us out! Let us go!" He screams at the top of his lungs.

Margo looks at me worried. I know she is scared that someone will come in and drug him up again. Suddenly, I feel the essence of Eugene come over me. Eugene, the peacekeeper, the tribe-mender... "Hey, dude!" I call over to Jarrod. "Yelling like that is not gonna help our situation."

"Fuck the situation," he growls at me. "We need to get the hell outta here!"

"Please, stop, Jarrod! Please!" Margo cries.

I hold up my chained arms in demonstration. "Dude, how? We're all chained up pretty tight. Unless you're Harry-fucking-Houdini, it doesn't look like we're going anywhere!" My voice is loud. Steady. Firm. It echoes in the chamber, rattles inside Jarrod's head, making him explode with rage. Margo winces every time he howls and growls. His anger is completely out of control, and he goes wild whipping his body around in inhuman ways. His voice and the sound of the metal chains fill the room with a cacophony of wicked clanging and clashing. Now I'm really glad I didn't get a chance to tell Margo that I'm a RAT!

Blake and Kate's bodies stiffen up and straighten out almost simultaneously. Margo looks at me and points to them. I nod my head. I'm one step ahead of her. Jarrod continues his crazy, but I can hear Blake and Kate moaning above his screams. I lean my body forward to get a better view of them, and I'm met with the white haze of their infected eyes. Margo curls her body up as best as she can against her restraints. "They're still..." she says.

"Yeah," I say, "but the good thing is, they can't hurt us. They can't re-infect us."

She lifts up her arm, showing me a bite from Blake. "I know that," she answers. "They infected Blake and he bit me. I was fine."

"I know."

"But they can kill us, can't they?"

Here I was, worried about being re-infected, and the idea of imminent death had never occurred to me. "Yes," I answer. "They can kill us. But they won't. The Infected don't eat the Altered."

"Griffin? But what if that's all part of the experiment?"

I freeze. Everything stops. The sounds of Jarrod's freak-out and the ever-growing moans from the infected wash over me, fill my ears, fill my head. What if Margo is right? They figured out that re-infected Altereds can infect humans, but what if they're trying to see if infected humans can re-infect the Altered?

I look over at Blake and Kate again. Their arms jerk up and down frantically. Blake smells the air around him, and a low, vicious growl rises from Kate's throat. Jarrod's insane tirade upsets them. Hell, it upsets me, too. Not only is Jarrod an Altered, but he's a disgruntled Feral—filled with hate and anger and resentment since the day he changed. He's just like Jimmy, and the big black guy at Eugene's, and the thousands of others who were left behind. Nameless, faceless, not on any of Holston's 'follow-up' lists. Jarrod's face twists ferociously, animal-like. His voice screams out, mirroring his once infected state, with no regard for his sister's pleas to stop. And suddenly, it all becomes clear—Jarrod's mindset is the tool, the perfect killing machine.

Dr. Trager is going to use the Ferals to spread the virus.

It makes sense. Take a whole bunch of hateful, discontented Altereds, get them high on Black Death, set them loose on the humans, and one by one the dominos fall. Sure, the Ferals would go back to being their normal, Altered selves, but the disaster left in their wake would be catastrophic. A second Outbreak. A world filled with nothing but Infected and Altereds. The human race decimated.

My heart beats so fast, I'm afraid it's going to burst out of my chest. "Please, try to get him to stop!" I bark at Margo. But she's no use. She's bunched her body up again with her face in her hands. My anxiety rises to peak capacity, and I, too, start tugging at my chains.

Suddenly, a loud buzzing noise goes on inside the chamber and everyone stops. Jarrod stops thrashing and yelling, the Infected cock their heads sideways, Margo looks up from her palms. The door opens, and in walks Rennard followed by Davis and Galloway dressed in biohazard suits and bio-helmets. *Galloway and Davis, the famed detectives.* Galloway carries a white metal box with the biohazard symbol on the front, and Davis pushes a wooden hutch. I smell rabbits. We prisoners watch as they nonchalantly saunter into our domain. Kate moans at the fresh meat before her.

Galloway hands her white kit to Rennard. Rennard smiles and lifts it in the air, giving it a loving pat on the front side. "Are we ready to begin?" she asks.

"Ready to begin what, you bitch!" Jarrod yells.

God only knows.

Jarrod screams. Margo cries. Blake and Kate growl and moan. And I stare, emotionless, at the box.

Guess I'll find out soon enough.

21

RENNARD PUTS THE KIT BACK IN GALLOWAY'S HANDS and opens it up. "Here we go," she says as she pulls out two syringes. "You see what I have here?" She holds one needle up high. "These are two different compounds of the Zorna virus. One is what you all know as Zombaxin—a diluted Hz7RNA strain merged with other chemicals. It's the one that offers an Altered temporary relief from their human shell. The Black Death. What you probably *don't* know is that Zombaxin is highly addictive, partly because there are traces of morphine in the black pills. A Zombaxin user not only gets the adrenaline rush of temporarily being infected, but the morphine is what makes an Altered crave more."

"The hell it does!" I yell at her.

She chuckles. "So, you *have* indulged in a little bit of Black Death, Mr. King."

I spit on the floor. I don't know why, it just seemed like the appropriate response. And besides, if she were any closer to me, I would have spit on her—lady or no lady, doctor or no doctor. Jarrod leans forward and stares at me. "You did it?" he mouths to me, and I hold up one finger to indicate, "just once."

Rennard holds the other needle up and continues, ignoring our silent exchange. "The other is a more concentrated formula. Let's say it's Zombaxin on steroids!" Her eyes widen and her mouth pulls up on one side in a devilish grin. "The purified form—Zombaxin Plus—is one that would make an Altered overdose within minutes. And by overdose, I mean 'turn back,' as in become re-infected. The re-infection would be instantaneous."

Margo squeals like a frightened child.

Rennard looks back and forth at each of the needles and childishly pouts her pink lips in mock concern. "But which one is which? Is the Black Death in here?" She wags the needle in her left hand. "Or is this one Zombaxin Plus? Who knows?" She shrugs her shoulders in a sarcastic, condescending way. "Guess there's only one way to find out."

I spit again, this time not on the floor, but in her direction and she shakes her head in disappointment. She places the needles back in the kit but doesn't close it up.

"When I get out of here, I'm going to kill you, you know that?" Jarrod snarls through gritted teeth.

Rennard ignores him, turns her head, and nods at Davis. Davis opens the top screen of the wooden hutch, reaches in and pulls out two black, medium-sized rabbits. One has an orange tag on one of its paws, the other has a pink tag. Rennard walks to the hutch and pulls out a third one with a blue tag. Blake and Kate moan and hiss more fervently at the sight of the animals.

"My assistant, Mr. Davis, and I have a few of our furry friends. They look the same because they are brother and sisters, but each one is special in their own way. One is completely healthy, a perfect little cottontail, my perfect pinky-pie. The blue one has been infected with Rabbit hemorrhagic disease, also known as RHD. See, you all wouldn't know this, but RHD was once a major problem in the domestic rabbit population. The poor things get a high fever, blood clots, organ failure. It's a painful, tortured death." She brings the face of the rabbit she's holding up to her nose and makes an obnoxious twitchy clicking sound that's supposed to resemble rabbit affection. "After the last outbreak of RHD, Dr. Trager's team, myself included, were able to officially eradicate RHD from US soil." She grips the animal by the collar and dangles it in front of her face. "But they couldn't have known that, could they?" she sings to it in a maniacal, baby tone before cradling the animal back into her arms. "The orange one is infected with the Zorna virus, just for giggles. To see what will happen."

"You're sick," Margo mumbles.

Margo's right. This whole act, this whole display, sickens me. What is Rennard trying to prove? What result is she hoping to gain from this experiment? I feel like I'm on the set of the torture movie again. "Ya know, Rennard," I say, confidently, "how near the end of an action movie when the villain has the hero captured and he starts spilling his guts about the overall master plan?"

Rennard stares at me blankly, her icy eyes shooting daggers at me. I should just shut my mouth right now, but something inside of me forces me to continue. Margo and Jarrod's heads turn, and they stare at me, too.

"Ya see," I continue, "it's kinda funny, 'cause the hero always seems to find a way to pull through and win in the end. Foil the evil plan. Escape to victory. Right now, you're looking like the big-mouth villain who just can't seem to shut the fuck up!"

Margo and Jarrod laugh like two stoned teenagers. Galloway and Davis shake their heads in disgust.

Rennard smirks. "Oh, I assure you, Mr. King, this is surely no movie. And unfortunately for you, I don't see any heroes hanging in front of me." She places the rabbit on the floor and walks over to Kate, grabbing at her chains. "The only way your friends will get out of their infected state is if I alter them with the serum." Rennard tugs the chains, making Kate howl. "But let's just see. Kate was bitten by an infected Altered whereas her boyfriend, Blake, was injected directly. I want to see how she responds to food. Let's do a little experiment, shall we?" Davis lets his two rabbits go and readies his tranquilizer gun. The animals hop in unison over to their brother, unaware of the fate they will soon meet. "Let's see which little bunny your friend wants to play with." She reaches her arm up and unlatches Kate's restraints. Kate bites at her, but Rennard doesn't flinch. She takes a step back.

Once freed, Kate leaps forward onto the floor, screaming the song of the Infected. It's a high-pitched wail, as if multiple voices were being emitted from one throat. The dirge is familiar, and I close my eyes with a dark memory. Margo covers her ears with her hands, but I welcome the music. *It reminds me of a time when...*

There's no hesitation in Kate's actions. Her immediate attention is placed on the pink-tagged rabbit. The healthy one. She's ignored the others. Her hand reaches out, snatches the animal by its neck and tears into its throat draining it of the substance she has been craving. As she raises her red-stained face, Davis shoots a tranquilizer into her, and she goes down like a ton of bricks. Rennard chases after the two other animals and returns them to the hutch. Davis chains Kate back into position on the wall then rolls the hutch out of the room.

I watch Rennard intently, hoping that she'll unhook my chains, hoping that she'll give me the opportunity to unleash all my rage onto her.

I could only be so lucky.

Galloway has been holding the white kit this entire time, and on Davis's departure, she takes center stage and offers the needles back over to Rennard. She's smiling, like she's proud of her role in this exhibition.

Rennard picks up both syringes and waves them around. "But the animal world is vastly different," she says, as if she were continuing a demonstration in front of a group of would-be scientists. "What of the human mind?"

The door slams. Davis has returned with a hostage—a man of medium stature with his hands handcuffed in front of him and a black bag over his head. Blake growls and hisses as Davis marches his prisoner across the room and stops next to the needle-wielding Rennard. Davis removes the black bag, and Margo gasps.

"You!" Jarrod screams.

The sandy haired man looks scared and confused.

Jarrod goes wild, not noticing that Rennard is approaching him and Margo with the needles. "What the hell did you do to us, you son of a bitch?"

I turn and catch Margo's attention. I narrow my eyes to silently ask her what's going on, and she mouths "Blake's guy."

Blake's hookup. The guy who was going to supply them with the Black Death. The guy who orchestrated the ambush on the two couples.

"Jarrod!" I call out, hoping to get his attention. It's useless. He's cursing and screaming and threatening Rennard with a horrible death. Rennard is going to inject him, and he doesn't even know it. I look at Margo. "Stay focused," I say quietly. "Don't give into it. It feels like puppet strings in your head—don't let them pull you in directions you don't want to go."

"Okay, okay," she mutters through her sobs, but I'm not sure how strong she'll be once she's injected.

Rennard gets in between Jarrod and Margo, injects them simultaneously, drops the needles to the floor, unlatches their chains, and quickly steps back. Their change is almost immediate. Black bile pours from Margo's nose. Jarrod staggers a bit, his upper body jolts violently from the change. He screams for a moment but stops when the change is complete. He walks forward with familiar hesitation and inspects his unchained anatomy.

There's no hesitation in Margo whatsoever. In a flash, she's upon the man in the room, pinning him down with her infected weight, bobbing her head up and down like an ocean buoy turning white to pink to red to brown with each motion of up and down. When the final evisceration takes place, Jarrod languidly kneels down to partake in the spoils.

Once it is obvious the man is dead, Galloway and Davis tranquilize Margo and Jarrod and return them to their restraints. By watching this unfold, I think I've learned a few things: whatever drugs they were given acted quickly, and less violently than the actual virus transformation. When I was infected with the virus two years ago, it seemed like forever for me to turn. It's apparent that Margo got the Zombaxin Plus, as I was able to see in Jarrod's movements and gestures that he was trying not to give in to the virus. He obviously didn't have much luck with it because it didn't take him long to dive into the stomach cavity of the prisoner. I suspect they'll leave Margo hanging here, with infection running through her veins, and eventually return Jarrod to the comfort of his room to wait in anticipation for another round of Altered experimentation. If Jarrod got Zombaxin, he'll come out of it. If Margo got Zombaxin Plus, she won't.

I close my eyes. "You do whatcha gotta do," I say to Rennard when I sense her coming toward me.

When she doesn't answer, I open my eyes and watch her face twist. "For you, I have nothing," she says.

Nothing? You call this nothing? Witnessing this carnage and torture is nothing?

Now it's my turn to be unchained. Galloway jerks my hands, wrists and ankles back and forth to unloosen the shackles, and Davis has returned, ready to handcuff my hands behind my back.

Rennard leads me through a hallway in the facility, the first time I'm seeing more than just the three rooms. Long gray corridors with laminate flooring. I try my best to memorize the path she takes me down, in hopes that I will remember which way to go when I make my escape, because I will escape. Eventually. I've planted that idea in my heart, and I'll be damned if I let that seed die. Davis pushes me every now and then. I guess I'm taking too long memorizing the directions.

Left at the torture room. Right at the broken vending machine. Straight past the fire alarm on the flower wallpaper.

We come to another examination room. It closely resembles my original holding cell—lab shower in the corner, white walls and tile. Dr. Trager sits at a small table in the center of the room and smiles when I enter. Davis shoves me into a chair with wheels and rolls me closer to Trager.

"Good to see you again, Griffin," he says.

I don't respond.

He pushes a small device in front of me. It's a viewfinder, like for a vision test at the optometrist's office. "Thank you so much for being so cooperative," he smiles. "It makes everything flow so much better without complications. Now, I want you to do a simple little test for me. Look into the vision screener. There will be a set of images. Look at the images and answer my questions as honestly as you can."

I stare at him. His smile is huge, almost scary. It curls up sharply and makes the apples on his cheeks protrude underneath his eyes. How can he even see with his cheeks so high up?

"Okay, let's begin."

His smile deflates when he realizes I'm not playing along. Soon, Davis's strong hand is on the back of my neck, forcing my eyes onto the machine.

"What do you see?" Trager says, and an image of a young boy with brown hair flashes in the device. I try to blink to block it out, but I can't. I can't even move. I hear a 'click', and another image shows up: a longshot of a house and a bunch of people standing in front of it waving at the camera.

"What do you see?" Trager repeats.

Again, I don't answer. But this time, there's a shock on my thigh—a slight buzz that makes my leg twitch.

The picture changes to a corpse—a dead body covered in blood and gore. "What do you see?" Trager asks again. This time, my silence is met with a jolt on my leg—full blast electricity sears throughout my body. I scream instinctively from the pain.

It takes a good two minutes for the pulsating feeling to shake itself out of me.

The machine clicks, showing me a picture of a field of cows basking in the midday sun. "What do you see?" Trager says, raising his voice.

I know if I don't answer, I'll be shocked again, and I'm afraid of how high they'll turn up the voltage. Could it kill me? "Cows," I say without giving it another thought, and my heightened senses can hear Trager breathe a sigh of relief.

"Good," he says. "What do you hear?"

"I hear Davis breathing like a sick animal behind me!" I spit.

Another zap!

Blinding lights flash in my head, the image of the cows looks spotty with dark clouds. I think I may have had a seizure or something from that one. I just couldn't help it, though. The words came out of my mouth without any thought, and I'm sure Davis was just as quick to jolt me.

Trager keeps his composure, and the picture flips. It's the picture of the young boy with brown hair again. "What do you see?"

"A boy. A little boy with brown hair." I stare at the picture, at the little boy. He looks so familiar, like he could be anyone I know, or knew. As a matter of fact, as I stare into the kid's eyes, he kinda reminds me a little of Josh. My old best friend. The guy I watched get torn apart by an Infected. He looks like how Josh looked when we were kids. When we didn't have a care in the world. When things were normal and fun and...

"What do you hear?"

"He's laughing," I say mindlessly. "He's laughing 'cause he's happy."

The picture changes. "What do you see?" Trager's voice is cold and almost mechanical.

"It's a house with a group of people outside." Like at the barbeques my parents would host. Dad would grill food, Mom would make her famous lemonade, all the neighbors would come by with their kids and we'd go swimming and play games and take goofy pictures.

"What do you hear?"

"They're saying 'Goodbye,'" I answer.

A sharp pin prick catches my right triceps and in an instant, radiating heat spreads down my arm.

"What do you see?"

It's the dead body picture with the blood and guts all over. Just as I say, "A dead body," the image starts to shift, move. The blood on the body dances in swirls like little tornados above torn out entrails. I try to blink, but my face is so hard pressed against the viewfinder, I can't. My ears start to fill with a hissing sound, like white noise from a TV.

"What do you hear?"

"The ocean," I say. My head feels bogged down, and my stomach starts to growl.

I hear a click and see the picture of the cows. They're walking in the field and moo-ing at a dragonfly. The dragonfly buzzes by their ears and annoys them.

"What do you see?"

"Pretty cows," I answer in a daze. A thin veil trickles over my vision. A haze that I know all too well...

"What do you hear?"

"The dragonfly's wings against their skin."

My stomach roars, and my internal temperature rises. I've been infected. It's a low dose. I can tell because the changes in me are subtle, and I feel the slight effects like a haunting dream after you've woken up. But there's no denying the feelings are there and they're real. I don't have the feeling of being completely consumed with infection—I'm still cognizant enough to have more than enough control.

The picture screen shows the smiling boy. I didn't even hear the machine click over. He smiles and waves to me. He gives me a wink and points at me. *Like Josh.* It has to be Josh. I smile and breathe in, and I swear I can smell him.

I smell his innocence like an orange grove in the summer.

"What do you see?"

I smell his anger like burnt garlic in a vat of olive oil.

"I see the little boy. Hi, little boy!"

I smell his naivety like the peppermint of a candy cane.

"What do you hear?"

I smell his anxiety like roasted chicken with rosemary and a side of applesauce.

"Nothing. He's not saying anything to me."

I smell his fear like barbecued hot dogs with sauerkraut.

"And how does that make you feel?"

I smell his insides like fresh blood passing over my lips...

"Hungry."

22

NEW YORK IS NICE IN THE FALL. THE WEATHER DROPS a few degrees and there's a crispness in the air. At least, that's what I remember from when I was a kid. Even though I spent the majority of my life in Florida, I had a sense of New York identity instilled within me. Maybe it was because my parents never truly considered themselves Floridians and that notion was passed down to me. My sister was a true Florida child—her only memories of New York were when we took our yearly trips to visit. Sydney never had the sense of what it was like to be a New Yorker. People looked at my parents differently as soon as they opened their mouths and their accents peppered whatever they were saying. It was like a stigma, a mark of standoffish prestige. "Oh," people would sing, "You're a New Yorker." My mother had always said, though, that the one thing she missed about living in the North was the change of the seasons and the water. I understood the seasons part, because in Florida, the temperature usually went from hot to hotter. But in New York there was an actual change, a physical turn of the cycle of life. I never understood what she meant by the latter.

Trager has a window in his office that I often find myself staring out of. I like to observe the flora and fauna of the area—get to see a little bit of the natural world before my battery of tests and experiments. Lord knows it's been forever and a day since I've actually breathed in fresh air. Anyway, I like to watch the various birds—ospreys and bluebirds—flitter about in their environment. I like to observe their patterns and their daily routines, like how I watched the Infected from the second story window in my parents' house. The flora has changed outside. The small white flowers on the bushes in front of Trager's window have shriveled back to the green of the leaves. I also noticed that the air conditioning hasn't kicked on as frequently. I gauge it to be early October, which would mean my time here at the PIADC would be close to two months.

Plum Island Animal Disease Center. Should be renamed Plum Island Altered Disease Center.

I'm tested daily. Every day, there's something new—an eye exam, a Rorschach test, a therapy session, an allergy test, a new drug administered to me. You name it, it's been done to me. For the big ones, they have to physically debilitate me—drug me up so I'm nice and sedated. They once injected me with a pig-blood compound, but I was too woozy to even fight back or protest. Holston must be rolling over in his grave right about now.

The one thing that is constant is my medication. Every morning, Rennard injects me with a small dosage of the virus. It's not enough to make me turn, but it's enough to give me a morning head change. She says she doesn't believe I can OD on Zombaxin or Zombaxin Plus because of my daily exposure. Is that supposed to make me feel better or something? I certainly don't feel like myself or any version of myself, for that matter. I'm not the Griffin from Before, or During, or After. I'm a new kind of monster now. Griffin 2.0. Neither human nor Altered. The infection courses through my veins, just burning enough to let me know it's in me, lying dormant twenty-four-seven, not knowing if it will break free at any given moment. It's a darkness eating at the remnants of my soul and replacing it with a permanent plague within. It's a gradual shift, a gradual change, much like that of the changing seasons in New York.

Once during a session, Dr. Trager told me of the differences between me and Jarrod, my experimentation partner. The basic gist is this: Jarrod is a pure war-machine, and Griffin is the cerebral one. He said we were the perfect pair, which led me to believe that he's crafting us into some kind of Altered soldiers. My experiments have been mostly psychological, but Jarrod is getting it much worse than I am. Sometimes, just to mess with me, they turn on the speakers between our rooms just so I can hear him sobbing or mumbling to himself. Sometimes he's still fresh with infection that he's tearing at the bed sheets on his gurney or smashing his head against the mirror.

They've broken him. Broken him to a point where I think he is completely at their mercy. Probably just the way Trager wants it.

I hate Trager. I hate him more than Graves. With Graves, the manipulation and sarcasm were at least heartfelt, if that makes any sense. Like, Graves had a grand ulterior motive for the games he played. He worked solely off his extreme emotions, and when it came to me or any of the Altered, Graves's one gut instinct was that of avenging the memory of the son he had to put down. I once had thought that Graves had soulless eyes, but that was before I was acquainted with Trager. Trager is a different kind of crazy. He's beyond Graves in terms of soullessness. I don't even think I have the words to define what Trager is. Power-hungry? Manipulative? Egomaniac? Psychotic? All of the above? I don't know. But what I do know is that his eyes tell a horrific and painful story, and his cold hands are indicative of a life of struggle. There's an air of confidence about him with a hint of shame and uncertainty. I sense that about him. He's cocksure with a touch of scared little boy. *Holston, Jr.* If Holston had a son, I bet he would have wanted one like Trager, and not like me. But maybe Holston got to Trager too late, didn't have enough time to properly mold and shape him. Maybe Trager was too far gone by the time he partnered up with Holston?

Whatever it is about Trager, I know Rennard is all about it. It's obvious that she's his right-hand man, and it's obvious that she's completely in love with him. No. Maybe not love. More like obsessed with, idolizes, worships the ground he walks on. She's younger than Trager, probably somewhere in her 40s, and she's attractive enough, if you're into the cold stare of ice blue eyes. I could see why Trager would be attracted to her—I mean she'll do practically anything he says, so that's got to be a plus for him. And I can see why she's attracted to him—he's a man in high position, she said he saved her life, and I guess for a balding dude in his 50s he's not so bad. But jeez, between the two of them, there's not much going on in the personality department. They definitely deserve each other—the Ice King and Queen themselves.

I like to call Rennard *Miss Lippy* because she's a talker. She doesn't get too personal or anything—lord knows I've tried asking her questions—she mainly sticks to telling me the history of Plum Island, or the latest compounds they're working on. Damn, I think I know more about this place than I do about my own hometown. But

I remember something my dad used to say: Loose lips sink ships. And a few times, I've caught her in a moment, caught her off guard, and she's let some things slip out. Things that I've been cognizant to pay close attention to. Things that I've been storing away in my back pocket to use later on.

There's an emergency exit in the north wing, but it leads to the beach and it's beautiful. Trager's office controls the facility.

Our staff of over forty highly qualified scientists, virologists, and businessmen and women works around the clock to ensure the safety of every test and experiment conducted here on the island.

There used to be a train system on the island when it was called Fort Terry.

Lyme disease started here on the island and accidentally escaped.

The lighthouse is one of the best in the state.

There's a dock in what's called Plum Gut Harbor with a few boats that transport the doctors back and forth to the mainland.

I thought her heart had stopped when she told me that last little nugget. She was infuriated with me, and the next day, dragged me to the experimentation room and had me chained to the wall again. Jarrod was there, too, but that was nothing new for him. He's their whipping boy. I've seen them inject him with Zombaxin, watch him turn, and then stab his face with serum, all in a ten-minute time frame. His poor body has been rearranged so many times, I can't even imagine what his insides must look like. Under his right eye, where his original Altered scar was, is nothing but a mass of red and raw flesh protruding from the side of his face. They jab him and stab him at will.

Anyway, the day Rennard threw me in the room with him is one I don't think I'll ever forget. Her dirty blonde hair was pinned back into a bun and her lips were a deep coral shade. I remembered that because I thought if I had escaped, I would have grabbed her by her bun and eaten her lips right off her face like fresh salmon straight from the Atlantic Ocean. Jarrod and I were given a full dose of Zombaxin Plus and both turned immediately. What was concerning to me, though, was the fact that the turn was seamless. It was quick. I didn't even notice the change. It was as if someone had turned on a light switch in my head.

Galloway and Davis brought in two humans and let me and Jarrod down from the wall. Even though the virus was full-blown raging in my body, Rennard later told me that it took me much longer to attack my victim than it did for Jarrod. I held out for as long as I could, but ultimately the virus was much too strong for me to deny, and I gave in. Rennard said she clocked me at five minutes, three seconds before I struck. Jarrod clocked in at thirty seconds. I don't remember anything about the person I killed, only that I knew I had to finish the act, make sure the person was really, most sincerely dead and not lingering in between this world and the next. I also know I didn't need serum to bring me back out of it. The Zombaxin Plus wore off during the day, and I was back to my Griffin-y 2.0 self in no time.

I think something inside Trager actually felt bad for Jarrod and me. Soon after, he started allowing us to have 'visits' between the rooms. They enabled the microphones on both sides of the mirror and let us to talk to each other. I learned a lot about Jarrod during our little chats. I found out that that he and his sister were 28 years old, twins, from Nassau County, Long Island. They had been at a friend's engagement party when the original Outbreak happened. He said one minute they were all drinking and dancing and having a good time, and the next they were all rushing outside to investigate a car accident that had caused a major explosion. Within moments, Infected had descended upon the partygoers and the rest was history for him and Margo. If I had met him under different circumstances, it's quite possible that Jarrod and I would have been friends. We both have a similar build, look, stature. His strong, New York accent was comforting to listen to. Something about it was familiar and safe, like how my parents sounded when they were riled up. The accent was like a shield, a protective coating around any situation. The words sounded harsher, meaner, more pronounced and grittier. When Jarrod wasn't hallucinating or having a breakdown moment, he made sense. *And he made plans...*

That's when I knew they were listening in on us, and really, it was kinda stupid of me to not realize that right off the bat. Jarrod would do most of the talking when they allowed us, and the second he would mention anything about busting out of here, the line would go dead. Actually, the second either one of us so much as pondered the whereabouts of his sister, Blake or Kate, transmission would cease. We haven't seen or heard about any of them since our time together in the experimentation room, and Jarrod speculates that they're dead. He could be right. I'm pretty sure he's right.

He and I soon figured out how to talk to each other without really talking to each other. One day, Jarrod had gotten back to his room after one of Rennard's tests, and he was sulking as usual. The speakers rattled on, and I got up to try to comfort him in whatever way I possibly could, 'cause honestly, listening to him moan and groan for hours is not fun. It's just as torturous as what they did to him in the experimentation room. Anyway, I'm talking to him in a calm voice and all that jazz, trying to talk him off the ledge, when he said, out of the blue, "I bet it's really nice outside." But it wasn't what he said that caught my attention, it was how he said it. I prayed to anyone who would silently hear me that Rennard wasn't listening in, 'cause if she was, she too would have tuned in to the change in tone of Jarrod's voice. Trager might have picked up on it, but I doubt it.

With my ears perked up, I said back, "Yeah, I remember going fishing with my dad on a lake in upstate New York when I was a kid." I've never been to upstate New York, mind you.

Jarrod played right along. "My sister and I loved the harbor in the summer. My grandfather had a boat and used to tell us he'd sail us to Africa one day. I asked him about all the waves and animals in the sea, and he told me we would just sail on through it all."

I sighed dramatically. "Hell, I think I'd feel just a little bit better with an ounce of fresh air."

He laughed. "Ain't that the truth, brotha. Ain't that the truth."

That's when I knew what Jarrod was going to do—get to the water no matter what and swim his way off this damn island.

Crazy, right? Well, maybe not so much. See, Trager knows that a happy patient is a good patient, and I think Jarrod and I have been quite ornery lately. Rennard said last night that they're going to give Jarrod and me a break. A little reprieve. The weather is apparently nice right now, and some fresh air will do us some good.

A little escape plan would do me even better.

There's a warning knock at my door before it flies open. Galloway stands in the doorway with one hand on her hip and the other twirling a set of handcuffs.

"Forty minutes!" she barks.

I nod and walk over to her. "Okay."

'Cause really? What else am I supposed to say to that?

She clamps the handcuffs tightly around my wrists and gives me a little shove on my back. "Come on. Through the north wing."

There's an emergency exit in the north wing, but it leads to the beach and it's beautiful.

23

EVERY NOW AND THEN GALLOWAY GIVES ME A QUICK shove to move me along, but I'm walking slowly through the corridors of the building, taking it all in, taking in the blueprint of the space one last time, committing it as best as I can to my Altered memory. I pretty much know the twists and turns of the inside of the building, but this is the first time I'm actually being led outside. This is something I am definitely going to want to memorize.

We pass by Trager's office, but the door is shut. We pass by the worker's rec-room and I see three people wearing lab coats sitting on a couch and watching TV. We pass a soda machine in the hallway. Make a right. Approach the door.

"Stop," Galloway commands as she walks in front of me. She reaches for the giant key ring attached to her utility belt and unlocks the gray steel door.

The moment the door opens, the warm sun hits my face, blinding me to a mere squint. The sounds of the world explode in my ears—the deafening hums of insects and birds, a glorious cacophony of nature I had been deprived of for far too long crashing into my eardrums like a wild symphony. It amazes me how much I have taken for granted in my life, for now even the simplest bird chirp sounds miraculous. I need to stay focused if I'm going to try to get off this island. This might be my one and only chance.

"Let's go!" she barks. "Watch your step." I look down and see there's a little incline—three metal steps leading down to sandy grass. My hand rises to shield my eyes and I gingerly ease my legs down the stairs.

I inhale deeply, letting the cool air fill my lungs with its crisp freshness. I exhale with an "Ahh," and I notice the sides of Galloway's mouth upturn in an involuntary smile. "October, right?" I ask.

She nods her head. I smile. I was right.

She comes up behind me and pushes me at my mid back. "Remember—forty minutes, so enjoy it while you can."

I stumble forward, tripping over my own feet. If I had fallen face down into the sand, I think I would have been okay with it. To feel anything other than cold ceramic tile would have been a welcomed gift. But we march on in silence. I soak up the colors of the trees and bushes—greens just starting their descent into fall-time yellows. Soon, this place will be overcome with death and renewal, the process by which every living thing on this planet goes through.

Even me.

Physically, technically, I didn't die. Graves and Holston and Trager and every other doctor who has taken me on since the Outbreak, has told me at least that much. I did *not* die. Not in the sense of a heart-stopping, brain- ceasing-to-function way.

But I did die.

Call it the soul, call it the spirit, call it what you will—I lost a part of mine when I became infected. And I lost another part of it when I was Altered. Those were like little deaths for me. Physically, it seemed like I became enhanced. A better kind of human! But the world became darker somehow. My vision, although more clear and acute, became just a little bit jagged and jaded. Like the trees in autumn, I gradually changed my colors, but what was left of me—what I became—is nothing but silvers and grays.

After walking for about a quarter mile, we come to a sign that reads "US Property—No Trespassing." Behind it is a brick façade lighthouse. The water from the Long Island Sound sprays upon rocks in the distance. The gentle lapping of the waves just beyond the structure is soothing to my ears. To the right of the lighthouse are two small sheds. They are both wooden and rundown. The one to the far right is missing a door, and I vaguely make out the shape of a white paddle boat hanging from the wall.

"Keep moving!" Galloway says. "Go around to the side of the lighthouse."

I follow her instructions and head to the dirt path to the back. The lighthouse is on a small cliff. The back end drops down about 15 feet onto sandy rock and water. There's a picnic table in the grassy area, and Jarrod is sitting on one of the benches. Davis stands like a stone sentry about three feet from the table keeping watch on his prisoner. Jarrod rises at attention when he sees me. A smile comes over his face as I get closer.

"Hey! Guess they let you out, too!" He comes over to me and slaps his hand on my shoulder. "What did we do to deserve this privilege?"

His hands aren't handcuffed, and I twist my body around to show him that I'm shackled and can't return a high-five gesture or back-pat motion. He rolls his eyes and shakes his head.

"What the hell is this?" Galloway yells as she trots over to us.

Davis's face twists. "Huh? What are you talking about?"

She grabs Jarrod's wrist and drags him forward. "This!" she screams. "Why isn't this one cuffed?"

Davis looks confused. His forehead crinkles into deep lines. "It's fine. Why are you stressing over it?"

"Fine? Fine? This is *not* fine, Fred!" She lets go of Jarrod and marches up to Davis. She gets right in his face and starts hollering at him something awful. He yells back at her, too, but she obviously has the upper hand.

I look at Jarrod and point to the west of us. "The harbor's that way," I say under my breath. He turns his head to look behind him, and I know he can see what I see. "There's a ferry docked out there. Well, it's more like a four-man speed-boat than a ferry, but you get the point."

"Guess you and I have the same thoughts, eh?" he mumbles.

"Not sure how we're gonna get over there, though. Might be a fifteen-minute jog, if not more. But that boat is pretty much the only way on and off this island. Rennard told me about how the workers get back and forth."

He swivels his head back to me. "Must be a straight run to Orient Point. The Northfork of Long Island. It's literally right *there.*" He points out into the distance of the Long Island Sound. "Probably a ten-minute ferry ride or so. Couple of hours if we had to paddle."

"There's a kayak or something in one of those sheds over there."

"We'd never be able to get it out from here. The bluff is too steep. We'd have to drag it to the beach, and that would slow us down."

I snort. "Guess you weren't kidding when you said you were familiar with this area?"

"Suffolk County boy through and through," he smiles as if I'm supposed to know what that means. I just smile back.

"Alright! Alright!" Davis yells, waving his hands around. "Emerson! Get your ass over here. Boss lady says you need some shiny bracelets."

Jarrod walks over to Davis and outstretches his arms, willing to don the silver handcuffs. He comes back over to me and speaks out of the corner of his mouth. "He doesn't have a gun."

I glance at Davis. "Yeah, but she does," I answer in the same manner.

"And now we're both locked up." I nod.

"Griffin, we gotta do something." He starts fidgeting. His whole body bounces up and down, and I know what a Jarrod-rage looks like. I'm afraid that being in the handcuffs is going to spark his fiery temper and make him do something crazy or stupid, or both.

"Just shut up and keep cool. Let me think this through," I command.

But the truth is—there's no plan. Nice ferry in the distance. Nice kayak in the shed. Beautiful day for a boat ride. Bringing that all together while my hands are cuffed in back of me and Jarrod's cuffed in front of him is a completely different story.

My focus drifts off to the water—the Long Island Sound to my right, possible passage to safety straight ahead. To think that I could be on my way to certain freedom in just ten minutes fills me with great anxiety. The need to get off this island mounts in me, and I try desperately to play every possible scenario out in my mind on just how to accomplish that goal.

"Well, if you think you can handle it!" Davis yells, his voice carrying over the splash of the water below. I look over at Jarrod who is also keyed in to their conversation.

"Of course I can handle it!" Galloway snaps back. "Go do whatcha gotta do and stop talking about it already!"

"What? You don't wanna know about how I gotta take a leak?" he laughs.

Galloway throws her hands in the air. "Too much information!"

Davis turns on his heel. "Be right back. Don't miss me too much."

"Yeah, yeah, yeah," she snorts.

Jarrod's eyes open wide. He stares at me hard and I can actually see the wheels turning in his head. His mind is working one step ahead of mine, and I feel like I can't catch up, I can't figure out his impromptu plan, I can't see the bigger picture. I shake my head "no," to try to stop him from whatever it is he's plotted. He shakes "no" back and brings his cuffed hands to his chest and pats at his heart three times, as if to say, "I got this."

"Hey, Galloway!" he calls to her. "You gonna let that piece of crap talk like that to you?"

"Quiet down over there, Emerson," she growls.

"Nah, it's just that he seems like such a big oaf of a man, and you're a strong, independent woman and all. Almost seems like he's your husband or something."

She glares at him. "I said to shut up, Emerson!"

"Oh, I see," he continues to goad her, "you're okay with domestic abuse. I get it. My dad used to beat my momma and she took it for..."

Galloway stomps over to Jarrod and gets up in his face. "I told you to shut your mouth!" she screams.

Jarrod smiles a joker smile—a crazed madman in a cage. "Or else what?" he says behind a toothy grin.

"I'll have to..." she starts, but never gets to finish. I hear the *crack* before I see Jarrod reel back his head and smash his face into hers.

She wobbles back, stunned, and her hands immediately rush up to cover her nose. Blood trickles between her fingers and down the fronts of her arms. In an instant he's on her again. He shoulder bumps her onto the ground, and once she's on her back, he straddles over her waist. She moans from her broken nose, in too much pain to defend herself. Jarrod hisses and growls like a predator, and before I get a chance to tell him to stop, he lunges his face forward and bites at the exposed flesh of the side of her forearm. His teeth sink deep into her skin, and he pulls back with such force that he tears a bloody chunk from her arm.

Galloway stops moving, passed out from pain. He turns his head to the side, spits out her flesh, and feels around her utility belt. There's a giant key ring attached to her belt, and with one hand he fiddles through the set of keys to find the smallest one for his cuffs.

He's free.

"Come here! Come here!" he calls to me, his white teeth stained with blood. "Turn around, I'll get you free."

Once the cuffs are off me, he reaches back down and takes her gun. Then, he stands up and wipes his mouth with the back of his hand. He kicks Galloway in the side and her body lifelessly moves with the motion of his foot. "She dead?" he asks.

"I don't think so. She's hurt, but not dead."

"We gotta move!" he says frantically. "Davis'll be back soon."

This is all happening too fast. My head tries to wrap itself around it. There's no going back, now, 'cause once Rennard and Trager catch wind of this, I think my time on this earth is super-limited.

He throws Galloway's key ring to me. "Take these," he says. "We're gonna split up."

"Wait! What?"

"Chances of the key to the ferry being on there is slim to none. You're gonna go back to the facility and find it. It's probably with the Doctor or something."

"And what are you gonna do?"

"I gotta look for Margo. If she's anywhere on this island it would be in the facility. I need to do a final sweep before we get the hell out of Dodge."

I shake my head wildly. "No way! You know what they said. Margo. Blake. Kate. They're gone, man. No way you're gonna find them!"

"Look, I don't care about anybody else but my sister. I have to try. Give me twenty minutes. Meet me over by that dock in twenty minutes. *Twenty minutes!* I swear you can leave my ass if I'm not there by then. Do you know how to drive a boat?"

"I don't think you *drive* a boat, Jarrod."

"You know what I mean, bro!"

"No. No. I've never driven a boat. You?"

"I think I'll be able to figure something out, and... oh no!" He stops in his tracks and turns toward Galloway on the ground. She moans and twitches. Stirs. She's *waking*.

"We gotta go," I say. "She's waking up and Davis is probably on his way."

"Look! Look!" he says, pointing at her.

Galloway's whole body convulses. Like she's vibrating in quick, short spurts. She turns her head to the side and black bile oozes slowly from the corner of her mouth. When she turns her head back to look back up at the sky, her eyes are whitened with the haze of infection.

I feel paralyzed, like I can't move, or talk.

Infected.

"Go! Go! Go!" he screams at me, pulling my shirt to follow him behind one of the wooden sheds. "Did you see her? Did you see her?" he pants.

I'm breathing hard, too, my body numb. Jarrod waves the gun around and I reach for his arm to steady him and slip the weapon from his fingers.

"That was me? I did that? I changed her?"

I put my finger to my lips when I see Davis walking back down the path and Jarrod immediately shuts up. Davis runs over to Galloway when he sees her lying on the ground. "What in the hell?" he yells and kneels down next to her. But she's on him in a second. Grabs the back of his neck and pulls him down onto her. She nuzzles her face and teeth into the center of his throat. He tries to scream, but the rush of blood in his vocal cords only sounds like violent gurgling.

I clutch the gun in one hand, the keys in the other, and look at Jarrod. He's pale white. "Back to the facility. Now."

We make it back to the facility and I use Galloway's keys to open the gray steel door. In the distance, she screeches and howls, and I wonder if Davis is dead, or if he too will be joining her. If a bite from Jarrod was able to infect her, I wonder if a bite from me could do the same thing. Jarrod takes off running the second he's inside.

"Twenty minutes," I whisper to his back, and he gives me a thumbs-up sign before he disappears.

I back-track my steps to Trager's office. His door is closed, but not locked. I turn the handle and gently push it open. His mouth hangs wide when he sees me, and it registers in his head that it is in fact *me*. I wrap my fingers around the handle of the gun and slide my forefinger into the loop by the trigger. I've never fired a gun before. Actually, this is the first time in my life that I've even held a gun, but I have no intention of letting that fact be known to Trager.

"Griffin?" he says in a soothing voice. "What are you doing, son?"

He's trying to calm me down, but it's very amateurish. Typical Psch-101 stuff. They do this in the movies all the time. Graves would have been so embarrassed for him.

"Get me on that ferry," I say as I jerk the gun forward in his direction.

He slowly rises from his desk. "What is this? What are you doing?"

"Jarrod and I are getting the hell off this island one way or another. So, you can either cooperate with me, or I can blow your brains out."

The words that come out of my mouth surprise me. I say these tough things, but if push came to shove, I don't know if I could actually do what I said. *Blow your brains out?* Could I do that? Would I even want to do that? *Wouldn't that seem like a waste of a perfectly good meal...*

He walks out in front of the desk and puts his hands up in a defensive stance. "Just put the gun down, son. Let's talk about this rationally." He takes a step toward me.

"There's nothing to talk about Trager. It's over. Rennard told me you basically control this whole place, so I know you have to have the keys to that boat. Give them to me and nobody has to get hurt." He moves closer and I jerk the gun at him again. "Don't move another muscle!"

"Rick?" a voice sings from behind me. I look over my shoulder and Rennard is in the doorway. "What's going on?" she says, her voice trembling.

"Anne, it's okay. Everything is okay." He speaks to her, but his eyes are locked on mine. "Griffin is going to put the gun down, and we're all going to have a nice, long talk. Isn't that right, Griffin?"

I don't budge. "Just get me the keys, Trager. Quit stalling on me."

His gaze stays cemented in place, but he extends his hands to reach for the gun. Without hesitating, I lower the weapon an inch, and when his fingers are just in reach, I waste no time. My mouth opens to perfect size, and my teeth clamp down on the tips of his fingers.

Rennard drops whatever it was she was holding. It crashes behind me, and she screams. Trager doubles over in agony. He's screaming, too. I see nothing but white spots in front of my eyes and spit out pieces of Trager's fingers onto the floor. He falls down in a heap, and Rennard swoops in to cradle him in her arms. "Rick! Rick! Are you okay?" she screams. He moans and curses and rocks back and forth.

I aim the gun at the two of them, back up toward Trager's desk and begin my hunt.

"What did you do?" she yells at me.

"Where are the keys, Rennard?" I say calmly, ignoring her hysterics. "I need the keys to that boat!"

"You're not ready for what's out there," she spits at me through gritted teeth.

I pause and take in the ugliness of her voice, then look back down to the desk drawers. She's trying to get a mental rise out of me, scaring me in some way, but I think I'm too desensitized for that, and she knows it. My fingers feel metal, and I hear a jangling as they brush up against what my heart so desires. I slip the set into my pocket with one hand while keeping my aim firmly on Rennard. I dance around the desk and move to the doorway. "I'll take my chances out there, thank you very much. Besides, I don't think you're ready for what's in *here.*"

"What are you talking about?"

"Trager is infected. Once he turns, you'll be of no use to him. You're Altered, Rennard. He won't need or want you anymore."

Her eyes go wild, and she pulls back a little to inspect Trager. He's starting to shake. Starting to convulse. Starting to turn.

"But... but... I'll just Alter him!" she stammers, panicked.

"Something tells me that's not going to work. I think it's different now. I mean, *I* did this to him, and do I look infected to you?"

Trager starts coughing.

"By the way," I continue, "Galloway is infected, too. She's running wild on the island. Davis is probably joining her soon."

I turn around and run down the hallway, not even giving her a chance to respond. I race out of the building and head straight for the dock. I hope no one is tailing me, but with Galloway and Davis, (and soon to be Trager) running around all infected-like, I don't think I'm a priority on the Center's list right now.

There's a long pier with a white speed boat bopping up and down in the water. It sways there, untethered and ready to rev up and go. *Plum Island Animal Disease Center* is written on the side in big purple letters. Jarrod is already here. He's waving me on.

I hop onto the boat and toss him the keys. "Make a miracle happen," I say, and sit down on one of the purple cushion benches.

He nods.

"Margo?" I ask.

He closes his eyes and shakes his head.

"I'm sorry, man."

He shrugs his shoulders and starts thumbing through the keys. "I got this, okay?"

I close my eyes and lean my head back. "Okay," I reply. "Ten minutes to Orient Point."

The boat's engine revs up, but I hear screaming above the roar of the machine. "Ten minutes tops!" Jarrod screams over the noise and pulls the boat out into the Sound.

CHAPTER 23

I'm jolted awake from a dreamless sleep. I think I heard Jarrod saying something about coming up to a pier, but I can't be sure. All I know is—we've stopped, *hard*.

I rub my eyes. The sun is at mid-point of the day and there's a glint on the water top. "Here?" I ask.

"This has got to be it," he says, turning off the engine.

We've pulled up next to a wooden pier, much like the one we came from. I look out and see hundreds of feet of sand in front of us, backed up by a giant black top parking lot.

"I guess let's do this," he says and hops out of the boat. He extends his hand to help hoist me up.

"Let's do this," I repeat. But exactly what we're doing is beyond me.

We make our trek up through the sandy beach and come to the parking lot. The lot is littered with cars parked at jagged angles, like they shouldn't have been there and there's an eerie silence blanketing the atmosphere that leaves me unsettled and on edge.

"So, what's next on the agenda?" he asks.

"Good question. I have to somehow get back home to Florida."

Troy.

I have to get to him. Make sure he's safe. If he's the key to all of this, I have to figure something out. Crystal. Dr. Oswald. Graves. Someone. Something. Who knows? Trager and Rennard did something to me that I can't explain. It's beyond serums and testing and experiments. I think I'm infected because I can obviously pass it on. So can Jarrod.

"Mind if I come with you?" he asks.

I shake my head, and we continue walking.

After about two miles, we come to an intersection. "Main Road," Jarrod reads the sign. "Hang a left here. There's a residential community down this way and some..."

A low rumble in the distance stops us in our tracks. We look at each other, puzzled. Then another explosion sets off, this time closer, shaking the ground beneath our tired feet. Main Road is lined with commercial businesses—a tackle and bait shop on the right, a gas station on the left, a souvenir store past the gas station. Dark black smoke billows on the horizon, a hill where a few houses are perched.

Another explosion. And another.

Like the world is shaking violently, jarring us from the great below, working its rattling sensations up into our essences.

"Listen! Listen!" Jarrod says, pulling at my sleeve.

I stop and cock my head to the side. Far away, so far away that I can barely hear, is the voice of a girl. A young girl. Five, maybe six, years old. And among the aftershocks of the explosions is the humming and mumming of a dirge. A low dirge. A rising song of moans and groans that carry off in the mid-day as howls and screeches and screams and...

I listen more closely, isolating the voice of the girl.

Another explosion.

Smoke is now closer to us, I smell it.

I still listen above the approaching chaos. The child's voice is scared. And hysterical. And desperate. And wild. She's babbling. Speaking so fast that I can't really make out the words.

Amidst the furor, I hear it. I hear her say it. And I know Jarrod hears it, too, because there's a glint of fear in his eyes. I listen again, and there it is—a second time, clearer, more distinct. It shakes my insides more than any physical element moving the ground beneath me.

"No! Please! Stop!"

Jarrod's body goes cold. His hand is like ice through the cotton sleeve of my shirt. We are both cemented in place, both trying to rationalize.

"It's happening again, isn't it?" he mumbles out of the corner of his mouth.

I pause. Take in his words. Try not to believe them. But I slowly nod my head when I hear the scream, louder, closer, like an explosion in my own head.

"No! Please! Stop!"

And we both take off running.

BOOK CLUB QUESTIONS

1. What do you think the title "Plague Within" signifies? How does it relate to the plot? How does it relate to Griffin's journey?

2. What motivates Griffin's actions throughout the novel? How do his motivations change over time?

3. Which parts of the book elicited the strongest emotional reactions from you? Why do you think these parts were so impactful?

4. Why do you think Amber felt the need to be infected again? What do you think that says about her moral compass? About Griffin's moral compass?

5. What do you think Troy's ultimate role will be?

6. If this book were to be adapted into a movie or series, what aspects would you be most excited to see on screen?

7. The characters in the story are all painted as "gray." Who do you perceive to be the villain? The hero? How can you justify their actions?

8. At the end of the novel, Griffin and Jarrod are clearly thrust back into a world that has been re-infected (the very thing Griffin said time and again *couldn't* happen). What do you think will

be different about this second Outbreak? How do you think the world is responding this time around?

9. How are The Altereds the new race of people? What are the societal implications of that?

10. What message or messages do you think the author is trying to convey through the novel?

AUTHOR BIO

MARIA DEVIVO WRITES HORROR AND DARK FANTASY for both a YA and an adult audience. Each of her series has been Amazon best-sellers and has won multiple awards since 2012. A lover of all things dark and demented, the worlds she creates are fantastical and immersive. Get swept away in the lands of elves, zombies, angels, demons, and witches (but not all in the same place). Maria takes great pleasure in warping the comfort factor in her readers' minds—just when you think you've reached a safe space in her stories, she snaps you back into her twisted reality.

www.ingramcontent.com/pod-product-compliance
Ingram Content Group UK Ltd.
Pitfield, Milton Keynes, MK11 3LW, UK
UKHW041852291224
453092UK00019B/313/J